# Even Birds Are Chained to the Sky and Other Tales.

## The Fine Line Short Story Collection

I0535061

The Fine Line Editorial Consultancy
65 Lorne Street
Edinburgh
EH6 8QG
UK

Published by The Fine Line

ISBN: 978-0-9567610-5-7

## Introduction

# Introduction

Even Birds Are Chained to the Sky and Other Tales is a collection of the winning stories from the Fine Line Short Story Prize. It brings together writers from countries as diverse as Yemen and Greece, India and Poland.

Aged from seventeen to seventy-eight, some are established writers whose names will be familiar; for others these stories are their first published works.

Reading the entries, we were struck by the diversity of the tales they told. Some were uplifting and comedic, while others were weighted with sorrow. Stories confronted us with the precarious balance between what we admit is acceptable in our lives and what we actually accept. We discovered startling strangeness in the lives of ordinary people and shocking ordinariness in the lives of strange people.

In a short story, capturing even an hour of a character's life is an accomplishment. To create a world into which the story lures the reader is a remarkable achievement. Each of the worlds in this collection is unique and captivating in its own way. These writers have used the tool of language with inventiveness and skill and have made it their own.

£1 of every entry fee was donated to the charities Irving House, Cricket for Change and Home-Start Worldwide as a thank-you for their remarkable work providing animals with a loving home, children with hope, and families with support and care.

Kate Gould

# The Stories

# Even Birds are Chained to the Sky
## by Mackenzie Marcotte

You can have peace. Or you can have freedom. Don't ever count on having both at once.
-Robert A. Heinlein

Rudy didn't know much about death until the day he released those spider monkeys. But he did know one thing, and that was how much he loved the sun, not because he understood just how entirely it controls all life, but because he had spent hours observing the way a stream of light bursts its way through the small glass containers and surrounded him with fragmented joy. His mother always complained of the smells, and yet she couldn't help but collect the small bottles, storing them in even rows along the vanity shelf. There they perched, trapped in their crystal enclosures, never to be tainted by a human touch.

"The odor's far too overwhelming for my taste, though the bottle is simply divine," he remembered her saying. "Rudy, dear, don't touch, that glass was blown in the hills of Hungary. It's really quite irreplaceable."

And so Rudy learned to touch with his eyes. He opened them wider each time, seeking only the satisfaction of those fragmented pieces of brightness. The beams appeared so alien to him, the way they were able to bend and break and color themselves with diluted shades of red, orange, and blue. He studied the curves of the bottles, the endless facets, the way ribbons choked the bottle necks, folding over their own endings in a garish display of femininity. For hours Rudy's eyes would watch the light change as day broke and instantly began its twelve hour retreat into night.

And then, almost as suddenly as the light's magical and mysterious behavior had caught him off guard a year earlier, it all came to a devastating end. It was the day Rudy forgot how to touch only with his eyes. There was a new bottle, adorned with a thick velvet ribbon boasting an intricate pattern of ivory spirals. The ends of the fat bow billowed down, cascading over the shelf and brushing the edge of his mother's vanity. The afternoon light caught the surface of the fabric and illuminated every velvety stalk. He began to wonder what his eyes could not feel, how the ribbon would weigh between his small fingers, and what sort of a texture the glass facets would provide. With little thought and much anticipation, the boy hoisted himself onto the vanity chair and took a closer look. He knew he was wrong to desire more than what his sight could provide, but now, at even closer proximity, the desire proved too great to resist. First, just a soft graze would do the job, he was sure. But as the tip of his finger brushed the velvet, the urge for more overwhelmed him. Up, and down, he stroked the ribbon until it was stained by the dirt on his finger tips, leaving evidence of his sin. He looked around at the rays bouncing off his parent's walls, painting dazzling shapes on the hardwood floors. He closed his eyes for a moment, overtaken by the sheer beauty of the simple afternoon sun, and as he began to sway he felt the cushion under his feet budge ever so slightly, just enough to displace his step and send him falling to the floor. In reflex, his grip on the bow tightened, the unopened bottle shattering beside him on the hardwood. And then, quickly following the first, the rest of his mother's prized perfume collection slipped from their positions and rushed to rest beside him, letting their contents flow freely as their restraints splintered into a million tiny shards.

And then, Rudy began to cry. Not because he understood the momentous destruction he had just engendered, but because the room around him had lost all joy and was now dark as the incoming night.

The glass had been swept, the floors mopped of their wetness, and all memory of the incident forgotten. Nobody reminded Rudy of his mistake, or of the fact that he had destroyed the greatest manifestation of his mother's memory. He had not known that the following day would bring fear, grief and sorrow beyond what any shattering glass could invoke. He had not known that as he extended his reach for the velvet ribbon his mother lay lifeless on a street corner, surrounded by stunned witnesses to Gifford County's greatest tragedy, all extending their own reaches towards his mother in a futile attempt to pull her back into their world.

***

Everyone said his mother was with Jesus now, and Rudy had overheard Mrs. O'Connell in the kitchen trying to console his weepy father so he knew that it was true. He couldn't understand why his mother would want to go with Jesus because the only one he knew worked at the local zoo and always smelled of crusted animal dung. However, Rudy did not ask. He only knew he would have to save her since nobody else seemed compelled to make a trip to Mr. Jesus' house. Gifford County Zoo was roughly sixteen hundred and twenty-nine steps from the McAllister home on Mulburry Street last time he had counted, so if Rudy left by noon and if the monkeys created a proper distraction then he could have mom back in time for Sunday night dinner.

The rescue would take place on a Sunday because everything in Gifford always closed by two and Rudy knew for a fact that nobody went to the zoo on Sundays. He tried to imagine what his mother might be doing in that run-down zoo hut, but he figured it was probably stinky in there and his nose twitched from the thought, so he turned his attention back to the cages. The soft breezes gave way to temperatures more characteristic of the coming fall, and as they floated by, tickling his freckled cheeks and mussing his strawberry blond hair, Rudy couldn't help but think of that first day he ever saw the spider monkeys.

"Mommy, I can fly!" he shouted, exuberance flowing from his gap-toothed smile. Rudy jumped on the ledge and let his feet carry him along the uneven cobblestone surface.

The sun shone particularly radiantly that day from its spot high among the stars, much higher than Rudy could reach but perhaps not higher than he could fly. The bustle of the zoo-goers was typical of a Saturday afternoon in Gifford County, especially during the last weekends before summer slipped into September and the school doors reopened. But now, in the breezy heat of the late afternoon, all Rudy could see was the sky. He could fly, he knew it, if only his mom would ever let him.

"Rudy, hop down from the ledge. You're going to fall. Besides, the spider monkeys are this way," his mother chimed, pointing in the opposite direction of the wall's continuation. They passed the pink flamingoes, with their burning sour odor, and down the pathway to the rusted cages. Perhaps due to finances, or maybe popularity, the spider monkeys at Gifford County Zoo far outnumbered any of the other more impressive species.

His mother told him once that they could fly. They had spent that long ago afternoon staring at the cages filled with squirming mammals, trying to find where they supposed the wings would emerge once released from their confines. Rudy watched their lean muscles flex, constricting and releasing with each leap. Branch to branch they soared across their barred enclosure, so to imagine them zooming through the skies was hardly a stretch.

The petit baby-faces appeared all too human in their tiny enclosure and Rudy flinched. He didn't like the way they looked at him, the way their sad eyes silently begged him for what he could not provide.

They wanted to fly. He was no mind reader, but he was six, and six was old enough to know they didn't like being trapped. Nothing likes being trapped. One of the faces appeared at the edge of the bars, eyeing Rudy with pupils the size of golf balls.

"Hungry, baby monkey?" he whispered, loud enough only for his new friend to hear.

Orange sherbet slid down the iron bar, leaving in its wake a trail of sugary dye. A narrow tongue met the treat halfway, licking cautiously at first. And then the little monkey began to lick faster, as if he knew this taboo feeding would last only as long as Mrs. McAllister's distracted gaze.

"Oh Rudy, not again."

Now, a year later, Rudy could still hear his mother's soft chuckle as she had watched the monkey lick furiously at her son's creamsicle. He held his palms to his ears and scrunched his eyes. The sound would not dissipate.

The morning of the twelfth came quickly and Rudy awoke to the sound of the church bells clashing against one another, always six minutes premature. The chimes had stopped long before Rudy arrived at Gifford County Zoo, but the peal of the iron bells still rang in his ears. He followed the dusty pathway to the enclosure he had become so familiar with and watched as the small creatures pranced back and forth, unaware of the hour or day or the abnormality of a human presence at such a time. His small boy hands reached beyond the bars of the cage and flicked the flimsy notch that held the gates in place.

And, quite pleased with himself, Rudy watched in delight as his spider monkeys burst from the restraints and filled his skull with the marvelous chime of freedom.

One hundred yards away, the slap of tiny palms hitting pavement, one after another, woke Mr. Jesus from the tranquility of his latest morning dream. The slaps seemed an odd sound for the usually crisp silence that was typical of Sunday mornings in Gifford County Zoo, but with the first planting of his feet on the dusty boards of his cabin floor, Mr. Jesus realized a staggering hangover was all that awaited him in the active world. So he allowed himself to slump back into his twin-sized cot. However, as the scampers steadily grew into a stampede, Mr. Jesus found the willpower to raise himself from the cot just enough to peer out his small circular window. By some heavenly miracle, or perhaps pure fright, Mr. Jesus found, quite suddenly, that his legs no longer felt like iron weights but in fact were doing a marvelous job of maneuvering around his small cottage, scampering to find any and every tool capable of capturing a small mammal. It is worth noting that never in his life had Mr. Jesus experienced such a dilemma. A simple man of traditional origins, he appeared physically much like his namesake, though perhaps with a darker complexion.

Rudy knew well the secluded spot just south of the invertebrate exhibits where Mr. Jesus' dingy cabin stood, hidden poorly among the withered foliage. Every third Saturday the zoo keeper would wheel out the rusted, home-made refrigeration unit and extract from its depths, to all the children's delight, box after box of sticky orange popsicles. Although this was not a third Saturday, in fact not a Saturday at all, Rudy was, with relative ease, able to find his way to Mr. Jesus' cabin, even without the path of wrappers that littered the zoo floor on a monthly basis. The deeper one ventured into the outskirts of the zoo, the more drastically the atmosphere changed. The rich green of the well-kept landscaping reserved for the visitor's eye became a mass of tangled, sickly shrubs that grabbed and scratched at Rudy's ankles. By the time he made his way to Mr. Jesus' front door, crimson droplets licked the edges of his tube socks and faded to a rusty brown. Beat from the rigor of the cross-campus trek, Rudy sat to capture what breath he still held in his under developed lungs. Within moments of his arrival a groaning from the cabin's primary entrance sent Rudy scurrying into the same shrubbery he had despised just moments before. To Rudy's great pleasure Mr. Jesus ran from the opening in a cloud of dust, garnished from head to toe with common household items. Duster, broom, pool net, bedding, a rattling coin pouch he would later learn held thirty-five glass marbles. The distraction had worked, and now the rescue could commence.

The sunken cot showed evidence of a sleepless night, the covers intricately twisted in the midst of Mr. Jesus' hurried escape. The walls were bare but for a few tattered movie posters shouting foreign messages in bright blues, greens and reds. The colors had since faded, though the faces had been preserved by a peeling layer of clear tape.

A glance to the clock told Rudy to begin his search, for a middle aged man can only chase spider monkeys for so long. He felt for the moist strip of notebook paper where nearly illegible characters spelled out where one might hide a little boy's mother. Bed, closet, refrigerator, behind the curtains-though now that he peered around, the cottage proved far more barren than he had imagined. Nevertheless, he got to work digging through Mr. Jesus' belongings as he imagined a robber might raze a victim's home.

Moments later, with a large crash and a string of curses, Mr. Jesus stumbled through the open door of his one-room cabin. Little sausage fingers froze amongst the abandoned receipts and expired pack of jerky that inhabited the drawer Rudy was scavenging. Just as Mr. Jesus' presence was impossible to ignore, so were the small droplets of fear that condensed on Rudy's skin and soaked the armpits of his shirt. Reluctantly he pivoted so that the two were face to face, though still quite far apart. The zoo keeper didn't seem to recognize the boy, though Rudy knew they'd met numerous times on account of those sticky orange popsicles.

"What are you doing here, kid?" he barked in a manner more confused than upset. Rudy shot back the only response he could think of.

"You know what I want!" he said, attempting an imitation of Mr. Jesus' gruff manner.

"What? Money? Toys? Boy whatever you want it ain't here, I can promise you that."

"Mr. Jesus, tell me where you put her!"

"What's that supposed to mean? There ain't nobody but myself in this zoo. And you now, I suppose."

"Don't lie, I know you've stoled her and I came to find her!"

"Listen here, kid, I got a shitton of monkeys runnin' all over creation, I don't have time for your little games. Tell me real simple what you are doin' here in my cabin."

"Dad says you got 'er, Mr. Jesus! He said real simple 'Rudy, your ma's with Jesus now' and I know he wouldn't lie to me 'cause I'm six and he knows that's too old lie to me, so," he paused as the spit caught in his throat the way it did when the words couldn't leave fast enough. "So tell me where my mom is 'cause nobody else is gonna save her but me, so I got to find her!"

The room went quiet and Rudy watched intently as recognition oozed into the creases of Mr. Jesus' leathered face. The heat that had been steadily rising to the boy's cheeks now exploded and the rush of realization that six days' planning was slowly falling through the cracks triggered every muscle in his body to quiver.

"You're the McAllister boy, aren't you?" Mr. Jesus asked. Rudy nodded, no longer afraid but increasingly confused.

It was a tragedy, nobody could deny that much. The day grief took hold of Gifford, Mr. Jesus should have been doing his daily rounds. He should have been unaware of much beyond the zoo gates. That was usually the way things went- Sundays were for family and church and home-made suppers, not for superfluous activities like zoo-going. Mr. Jesus liked it this way. He was a watcher. Jesus Valencia, the silent nameless man. He knew every face in Gifford, not by choice, but due to the well-known love affair between children and one-cent popsicles. And, as one might guess, the financiers behind the Saturday afternoon investments were the parents; Gifford's finest. These were the interesting ones, the ones Mr. Jesus most loved to watch.

Ronald Douglass, weekly nickel investor-"keep the change".

Gabriella Shirley, commonly referred to simply as "Gabby" -and for good reason. One daughter, one son, two dogs, and a mouth that could swallow you whole.

But there was one couple-one woman-that Mr. Jesus could never get a handle on. Sharon McAllister, seemingly ageless, mother of one, wife of six years, though you'd never know it by the company she kept. Gifford gossip hinted at a shotgun wedding, a hasty commitment between a traditional boy and a girl headed for the buzz of that just out-of-reach city of lights. Eighteen the day he was born they say, though she'd never confess. Whatever the truth, Mr. Jesus couldn't help but to stare. She was odd, that was sure, but undoubtedly beautiful, in a vintage sort of way. She was never quite present, her gaze always drifting just beyond her boy's head, and a glaze creeping over those baby blue eyes as she dropped a single cent into her son's outstretched palm. The way she walked, the way she carried a conversation with the other mothers, and the way she never missed a beat but was never fully engaged, either, all hinted at a natural talent for acting. A dream cut short by the conservative voices of Gifford County. Mysterious, but not shy. So strange, so beautiful.

The day he witnessed that accident, he knew in a moment it was her. Everything happened so quickly, a rapid fire sequence of tragic events. As he slowed his pace to admire the truck's pedestrian victim, Mr. Jesus couldn't help but wonder if this wasn't just what she had wanted. Somewhere new, somewhere fresh, to start a life beyond Gifford, the only place she had ever needed to escape.

Jesus wasn't particularly religious though his traditional Guatemalan upbringing begged otherwise, but on that Saturday Mr. Jesus did believe that there must be some sort of an after-life awaiting Sharon McAllister. He hoped she was content. The boy, he'd be fine. A loving father, a steady job, a beautiful house with a big backyard and a baseball bat signed by a local legend-what else could a little boy need? However, Mr. Jesus did not remember everything. He did not remember the shifty eyes that had darted from his own nine-year-old face as acquaintances and friends passed by that long-ago June. He did not remember how intensely he had wished that they could bring his mother back, tell him it was all a joke, and restore normalcy. But there were moments from that time that Mr. Jesus did remember. Things like the rhythm of his mother's hands as she ground the yellow corn into a meal, and the smell of tortillas browning on the stove. He remembered the way his mother's face shone in the hot sun, and he remembered the morning when she left. Mr. Jesus had worried about the McAllister boy. He worried that perhaps the overwhelmingly magnetic appeal of the big city would finally lure the actress away. But there were moments, secret and sparse moments, where Mr. Jesus knew Sharon would never have wanted to leave that little red-haired boy. He had watched as they stood, and then sat, in front of the spider monkey cage an entire afternoon, competing their imaginative ability.

"Well you know they can fly, right? Bet you didn't learn that in school now did you?" she chuckled and ruffled her son's hair as his eyes shifted rapidly between the cages and his mother's face.

"Nuh-uh, no they can't. They don't have any wings!" the little boy responded, excited by his observation.

"You just gotta look harder, Rudy. See, right there, under the shoulder. That's where they sprout their wings from." She looked to his bewildered face, checking how far her fable could stretch. "Not big wings, that would be too dangerous, but just little flappers, just to get them through the trees."

Mr. Jesus watched until his eyes drooped with fatigue and his watch ticked far past closing. It was not the last time he would ever see Sharon, though she was much nearer to the end than anyone would have guessed. On that day, that accidental, misfortunate Sunday, Mr. Jesus whispered to her soul to fly, to grow wings and sail above the trees, across Gifford County lines and into the hills of her Hollywood. She was free, at last, and so he did not mourn.

Back in the cottage, Mr. Jesus sighed. He looked up sheepishly from where his eyes had fixed themselves to the aged floorboards and offered, quite simply, the one response Rudy dreaded.

"Looks like you got the wrong Jesus, kid."

It felt like he had been punched in the stomach. Tiny fists pounded Rudy's abdomen. Words swam to his throat but fell back to their depths, unable to pass. It had never occurred to him that she would be gone forever, but as he remembered how his father's darting eyes had avoided his own time and time again, the way his father had raised his head towards the ceiling, shut his eyes and exhaled deeply, it all began to make sense. Rudy had been tricking himself, dodging punches and smothering the tiny fists. But now it was too late. His footing had been off, his reflexes too slow, and the calloused fist of grief had taken a final swing–bullseye.

With a pivot of the heels, Rudy began to run. He ran until he could run no more, until the dusty trail through Gifford Zoo had taken him to the very edge of the property, until his legs collapsed beneath him and his face touched the dirt surface. He ran to be free, to find a place where the only truth he knew was his tangled web of lies, because Rudy knew he needed his mother back. That was one of the few things he really knew. He knew about that, and about melty creamsicles and long summer days, and broken glass and spilled perfumes, and now, he supposed, he knew most about damaged dreams. He had not known about death, but as his knobby six-year-old knees inched him towards the rusty bars, Rudy knew. And with every motion forward his mind became increasingly blank until there was nothing there at all, except perhaps the smell of salty tears and the straw beneath him in the little cage. As his small boy hands reached forward, pulling the rusted iron bars into place, he pulled from his pocket a ribbon, stained with sin and smelling faintly of daisies. Carefully he wove the velvety cord around the broken monkey lock, through the space between the iron bars, and secured it with a double knot. And then Rudy shut his eyes and began to cry, painting his world black as the incoming night.

# ZEZA
## by Maria Clara Paulino

I was nine years old and stood with my parents' maid, Zeza, in the Lisbon dockyard. Against the light of dawn, the Santa Maria stood taller than anything I had ever seen, a dark wall at the end of the quay. The evening before, just after sunset, it had floated quietly up the Tagus with a full cargo of soldiers returning from Angola. Jorge, Zeza's fiancé, was among them. It was the summer of 1963, and he had been fighting in the Portuguese colonial war for one and a half years.

We had traveled all night from the northern city of Porto and it was still dark when the train pulled into St. Apolónia station. The taxi left us at the end of the pier, behind two barriers illuminated by a faint lamp. We waited. As I shifted my weight from one foot to the other, I watched the barriers' reflection tremble on the wet floor. The sea rose and fell against the pier, sprinkling foam in the air, spreading silver threads before my sleepy eyes. Now and then, Zeza pulled up the collar of my coat to shield me from the chill of dawn.

As the yellow line between ocean and sky widened more people began to arrive, and by the time the sun had dissolved the mist the quay swarmed with women. At 10 AM the welcoming ceremonies began. A metallic sound rattled through the air as the first group of soldiers appeared on the deck, still too far away and similar in their uniforms to be anyone's lover or son. The flag rose up the pole and the first notes of the Portuguese anthem reached us with the morning breeze. Desperate to get a glimpse of the soldiers, the crowd began to move as one body, forward and sideways. It was hard to breathe in the forest of legs that surrounded me. I held on to Zeza's purse and the hem of her skirt; I called her name as loudly as I could, but the noise of the women shouting drowned my voice. The crowd bulged forward, threatening to fall off the quay, and a long line of arm-banded policemen began to push against the wave of girlfriends, wives, and mothers.

The ship threw its massive shadow over the pier now; it was hard to look at the sunlit deck. Zeza held her hand over her eyes, stretched her neck as far as she could. "Can you see him?" I asked, trying to get her attention, but she chided, "Stop, child, stop!", a different Zeza from the one who laughed when the moisture of a ripe peach ran down my chin, smiled when I came home wearing a torn uniform ("Had fun in school today?"), anchored me to the good side of things.

How I had pleaded with my parents to let her bring me along! My mother couldn't imagine why I wanted to endure the seven-hour journey to welcome a maid's fiancé. She did not know, as intimately as I knew, how Zeza had thought of nothing but Jorge's homecoming for months. She had lived this moment in her head so vividly it had become as real to her as the meals she prepared or the way she slowly folded my school clothes every evening. She described to me the colors of uniforms, the star-like buttons gleaming in the sunlight, the sound of the welcoming canons, the lines of soldiers descending the ship's long staircase and, most importantly, *their* reunion, the moment in the story when her voice broke and I asked, suspended in anticipation, "And then?"

Zeza and Jorge met, a few months before he was drafted, through a random set of circumstances she liked to call destiny. The boy who delivered the groceries had been taken ill and Jorge, the grocer's son, had replaced him on his rounds. Maria, the housekeeper, usually came to the door to choose the best produce for the kitchen, but that day she was busy, and it was time Zeza took on some of these tasks. After twenty years of service with my mother's family, Maria at first resented Zeza's arrival, but she slowly came to like the young woman's wide, inquisitive eyes. She was in charge of transforming her into a good maid, capable of making a bed with sheets as tight as sails on windy days, and cleaning the floors so they would sparkle. Zeza learned well, and when the bell rang that day, Maria shouted from the kitchen parlor,

"That should be the grocer's boy. Make sure you take only the freshest produce and don't let him overcharge us; the money's on the counter by the oven."

At the door, Zeza took her time to choose the cabbage, look closely at the turnips, and weigh the carrots in her hand, putting them back in the basket at her feet while arguing over the price. No longer the fearful seventeen-year-old she was when she first arrived, she still kept the generous smile that had won my mother's favor, and now won Jorge's too. He came back that same day to ask my mother's permission to see Zeza after work; from then on, he waited by the ground floor window every evening till she could join him.

"He has a bright future, that lad," said the bread seller;

"He can read and write," reported the maid from two houses down the street; "He's a good catch" (a phrase I puzzled over), pronounced the milk woman, adding, "way too good for a maid." But Jorge stayed true to Zeza, and Maria, whose opinion mattered in the street, liked him for it.

"He's good and humble, girl," she told her. "If you don't disgrace yourself, he may well marry you at the Virgin's altar."

I was not at all sure why she said this. How could Zeza disgrace herself? She was so honest my mother trusted her with her jewels. My mother and I had liked her from the day the old caretaker brought her to the house to see if she might do as a maid. She came from the rugged mountain landscape where my family had a wine farm. In the summer, I played and ran down slopes and valleys where she worked from sunrise to sunset. Her hands were scarred and her skin was rough, but everything about her was open and generous. My mother hired her on the spot. When Jorge received his draft letter, Maria heard her cry through the wall their rooms shared on the second floor. His departure, a few months later, threw her into a despair that seeped into the house. We became silent and anguished at the sound of her muffled sobs; her eyes were puffy and red when she served the evening meals. "What's the matter with the girl?" my father asked one day. To Zeza's relief, my mother deflected the question; it would have been unbecoming, almost indecent, for the master of the house to show concern over the love pains of his house maid. Yet, my father repeated the question and, this time, my mother answered him. "This damn war," he sighed. "It'll eat us inside out."

We all did our best to help. I tried to be quiet; my mother did not scold her when she mixed up the evening drinks or forgot to include dessert cutlery when she set the table;

—

28

and Maria, in a generous attempt to distract her, agreed to teach her to decant the Port.

When Zeza had first arrived, Maria had made it clear this was a task she would not hand over. "Decanting is an art," she said. "It takes years to learn; it is not for clumsy hands like yours." Now and again, she let Zeza watch her pour the wine, ever so slowly, down a funnel lined with muslin till the liquid fell, crystal clear, into a decanter. But when Zeza tried to put the bottle away, she grumbled, "Hands off!"

Yet now she took a teary-eyed Zeza into the small room next to the kitchen and told her to choose the thinnest, whitest cloth from a drawer. "Wash your face and hands first. We don't want your snot near the wine." The process of turning Zeza into a well-trained decanter had begun.

"Hold your hand at this angle. Do not shake the bottle. You want the liquid to sparkle at the table, like crystal, see?"

A few weeks later Zeza was able to get the Port to look clear enough and, whether it was that she had climbed several steps in her profession, or simply that time had passed, her sobs grew less intense and her eyes began to dry. She talked incessantly about Jorge now, and people grew tired of it. But I was a willing listener.

"Did you get a letter?" I asked as soon as I came home from school, hoping she would let me help her make sense of his words, as she could barely read. She loved Jorge's small wiry marks on the light grey paper and carried the letters in her pocket till evening, when she went up to her room to read one syllable, one word at a time until a sentence lit up with meaning. She read the beginning of every letter aloud, again and again, like a chant; it was always the same: "Dearest Zeza, I hope you and yours are in good health." When she needed my help, she asked me to come to her small, tidy room (Maria was demanding); her night clothes lay folded on the bed, the letters were piled neatly on the round table by the window. There we both sat as she unfolded a new letter or went back to an old one. Once, he wrote, "We have been here for over a month and still no letter from you; the mail comes rarely to Mus, mus…."

She paused.

"Could you help me with this word?"

I peered over her shoulder at the letter.

"Mussuco," I said. We looked at each other. How strange it sounded.

"Are you sure?"

"Yes, that's what it says. Mussuco."

She went back to reading, "…because of the muddy terrain. When there's no mail, some of us get bad nerves. Stuff happens. Yesterday…"

She looked over the page, turned it upside down, and got up, agitated. What was left of the paragraph had been blotted out, and the ink had smeared over other sentences. Nothing angered her as much these blots, marks of the dreaded censors. What could he possibly write that she was not allowed to read? Did he not mean every word for her eyes only?

Such complaints angered Maria. "You'll never learn, girl! Be grateful the letters come at all, and don't - *don't* - go about complaining about the blotted parts. You'll get yourself in deep trouble."

Through the years Maria had learned that nothing escaped the Censors Office's tentacles. She heard my parents complain about the books with blacked out pages and the film cuts that had my father utter under his breath, "Impossible to make out what that was all about. They cut out the end, for pity's sake!" She was aware she was under surveillance, too. A trusted maid, she must know what books her bosses read, the company they kept, what they thought about the government. She was of value to the "vultures," as she called the secret policemen of the fascist regime that had ruled the country for almost forty years; they hovered around, ready to pounce at the first piece of information hinting at my parents' anti-government views.

"Life is hard, and don't you forget it," she often said, trying to put some fear into Zeza. "Keep your mouth shut about things you don't understand."

But when Zeza read Jorge's letters, she did not hear Maria, or take any notice when she grumbled, "What a waste! Paper can't be cheap either." Zeza drew her sprawling letters as prettily as she could on the thick paper she bought at the grocer's every Friday. How she longed for the soft beige sheets my mother wrote on, which she touched only when she cleaned the office under Maria's watchful gaze. "This is a special place,"

Maria always said, remembering the quiet evening when my mother told her how she treasured her office, with her books, her papers on the desk. She had spoken like a friend, bridging for an instant the gulf between master and servant, deeper than the roots of the young lemon trees outside the window. On such rare occasions, when my father was out and the sun melted on the horizon, formalities were hushed away and I listened, enthralled, to the words the women whispered, as if saying them out loud would dispel the intimacy of the moment. Maria repaid this confidence by making sure Zeza cleaned only "here and here," but did not touch the papers strewn over the desk.

"How can I clean it properly if I can't move the papers?"

Zeza replied, her eyes wider than usual. "Just do as I say, girl!"

And Zeza did. At night, in her room, I asked her why she always obeyed Maria, why she never had her own way. She did not give me a straight answer, but whispered something about my mother's black pen, how softly it glided on paper. I was startled. She had gone in the office by herself, tried it out.

"You won't tell?" she asked, suddenly worried.

I shook my head and watched while she labored to write another letter to Jorge with her own rough-pointed pen, to tell him she would wait for him, however long it took him to come back.

As the weeks and months went by, Zeza had more and more stories to tell about Jorge's courage; he fought against enemies that held flesh-searing machetes; he was dropped from a helicopter and left to wander in the jungle "like an alien on an unknown planet." Then she added, "But it *is* Portugal, all the same; it'll always be. That's why he's there, you know."

"How can Angola be Portugal?" I asked, but was left to puzzle this out for myself while she kneeled before the small Madonna on her window sill, and silently invoked Her protection for Jorge.

I had never heard of Angola, Mozambique, or Bissau before the war, yet everyone talked about these places now; taxi drivers missed no opportunity to shout "Angola is ours!" every time my mother gave them a good tip. But Angola was so far away that Jorge's letters took weeks to arrive, and so dangerous only his brave actions kept him alive. It sounded nothing like Portugal to me.

When the time came for Jorge's return, my parents discussed our trip to Lisbon. It had dawned on everyone by then that if I didn't go with Zeza, it was hard to see how she could go at all. A meeting between her and her fiancé alone was out of the question. To make matters even less simple for my father, Jorge's mother had been taken ill and his father could not leave the store unattended. Unless Zeza and I went, there would be nobody there to welcome him back home. Zeza's plan was to take the night train to Lisbon and return as soon as Jorge got off the ship. My mother trusted her, and was inclined to say yes, but my father was undecided.

"What do you think, Dr. Mendes?" he asked of his dinner guest one evening, making light conversation. "Should Isabel go all the way to Lisbon with Zeza?

---

We sat around the dinner table waiting to hear Dr. Mendes' thoughts on the matter. To my relief, he mentioned the modern trains with first-class compartments, where we would be protected from indiscreet eyes and unwelcome company. This seemed to assuage some of my father's concerns, but then the conversation took a somber turn.

"Almost two years in Angola ... a young man ..." my father uttered. "In these three years, the war has become part of our lives." He paused, and his eyebrows knitted together over his eyes. "By the time it is over, it will have poisoned the very air we breathe."

"We can't win," replied Dr. Mendes after a pause. "And, as you say, it will eat the country inside out."

"Oh, don't be so grim!" cried his wife, bringing the wine glass to her lips.

"It *is* hopeless," said my father. "The outcome cannot be clearer. A conscripted army set against independence movements using guerrilla tactics and supported by their own populations!"

"You forget," said my mother, "how deeply people feel about this here in Portugal. These colonies have been ours for centuries; people won't let go of them easily. I hear people talk of 'our overseas provinces' more often than ever before."

"That may be so," my father replied, "but history will take its course. Britain, France, the Netherlands, the whole of Europe let their colonies go. This is not about *our* colonies; it is about colonization itself. Not every

—
34

Angolan is sure what freedom will look like, but who on this earth does not want to be free?"

For a while, the only sound was that of wine being poured into glasses.

"Nobody ever seems to bring up our enclaves in India, but we lost Dadra and Nagar Haveli not that long ago; 1954, I believe. And one doesn't hear a thing about Goa, Daman and Diu, lost to India last year. Does it matter the government won't officially accept these losses? They are no longer ours!"

Zeza stood quietly by the door. Her mouth curved upwards when our eyes met beyond the world of adults. I worried she might catch some of the meaning, though the conversation had turned from Portuguese to French as soon as the war came up. I had been schooled in the language, which would stand me in good stead when time came to read books not translated or heavily censored, yet essential, my mother said, to a modern girl's education. French would also come to my rescue in the future, preventing my comments on national issues from being leaked to informers who drilled holes in maids' loyalties by promising goods beyond their wildest dreams.

"One must consider the arms embargo too, and other sanctions the international community is beginning to impose on us," added Dr. Mendes. "The guerrilla forces have their international supporters, and not all of them are communists."

I was relieved when Zeza began to change the plates and serve dessert. It was hard to keep still at the table, but I did not want to draw attention to myself. On a normal day, I was expected to say goodnight before dessert, but that evening nobody seemed to notice me. And every time the conversation broke, I hoped they'd turn to the subject of our trip to Lisbon.

"A secret family recipe," my mother declared about the dessert, trying to lighten the mood. "A very special *crème flambé*."

"Delicious," declared Dr. Mendes' wife. Everyone agreed and smiled, but soon Dr. Mendes said, turning to my father,

"You have no idea the medical reports I have from the front, the injuries..."

As he went on, the thought that something horrible could have happened to Jorge became real. I felt sick. As if she guessed my thoughts, my mother glanced at Zeza and said, softly, still in French,

"Lucky Jorge - on his way home, uninjured! I pity the women waiting for coffins…"

She was answered only by the sound of silver cutlery on her favorite china as we finished the *flambé* in silence.

Zeza placed the Port by my father, put the tall glasses on a tray and leaned gracefully forward, placing them slightly to the right of each plate. My mother was pleased. Maria would be too, I thought.

"Vintage 51," said my father, raising the glass to his lips.

"An exceedingly good year for Port; and very clear," echoed Dr. Mendes as he looked through the glass. "Well decanted."

"Zeza did it," added my mother, proudly.

"Did she?" asked my father, surprised at how much responsibility the girl had been given. Then he remembered our trip to Lisbon and in less time than it took for Port to go round the table again, we had his consent. Perhaps the talk about the war had drained him of energy, or perhaps he had already made the decision without us knowing it. In any case, I sat there glowing with excitement soon tinged with sadness. The evenings with Zeza, reading and writing love letters, had come to an end.

At the dockyard, the time came for soldiers to descend the long wooden passageway flanked with thick rope on the outside of the hull. The way Zeza had imagined it, the soldiers jumped and ran to their loved ones. In reality, they walked slowly, awkwardly, like birds with clipped wings. When she threw herself into Jorge's arms, their embrace was over quickly, and her hand felt cold when it searched for mine again. "Can we go home now?" I asked. My words echoed along the quay in a world that had gone eerily silent.

I tried to stay awake as long as I could, but the rhythm of the train cradled me to sleep. As we pulled into the station, I opened my eyes and saw Zeza and Jorge still sleeping, his head tilted sideways against the wooden headrest. As we gathered by the door, ready to step out, my mother took a photograph: Zeza in her Sunday clothes, rumpled from the journey, helps me jump onto the platform; Jorge stands behind her, still in uniform, a large bag thrown over his shoulder. On the back of the photo my father wrote: June 16, 1963.

From then on, everything went very quickly. Jorge's parents embraced him and cried. Zeza and I got into my parents' car, and found it difficult to answer all their questions about our adventure. As I lay in bed that night, trying to make sense of the day, Zeza's voice came through my bedroom door. She whispered to Maria,
"When his arms held me, I felt something go through him, like a shot. He buried his face in my neck and didn't want to look at me or speak. He never said a word on the way back. Something has happened to him, Maria."
I wanted to open the door and do something, anything, to make her happy again, but I couldn't. "This war will tear us apart," my father had said.

***

Lemon trees sway outside my mother's office as I clean her desk after her passing. Photographs gathered in drawers over the years: my father's smile, a picnic at the farm, distant relatives in uniform during other homecomings, regular occurrences in thirteen years of a war lost before it began. I pause over them. They speak to me through the stillness of the camera, their empty stare punctuated by sparkles of recognition: the face of a loved one, a feeling remembered, perhaps.

Moments of my youth, frozen in film, wait in other drawers: an old bicycle, a school trip, my first beautiful dress, made for Zeza and Jorge's wedding. Zeza smiles, bride-like, in her white dress, framed by oak trees and helms. I hold a small bowl with rice that I will throw over them for happiness. Jorge leans over to kiss her but something catches his attention: a bird from the park nearby flying too low, attracted perhaps by the rice. He looks upwards as the camera clicks, his face darkened by the bird's shadow.

# Punchline
## by John Leavitt

They are coming and they can not be stopped. This was a fact. Hypatia liked facts. She liked knowing why the stars move inside the spheres and how to make copper and what can cure a fever. She liked it so much she demanded her Grandfather teach her to read, not just glyph but script and port-scratch and so on, until she had become so well-versed she was impossible to marry. She told him she wanted to go into the priesthood. It was only a half lie - her role as Librarian was a priesthood - the long hours, the study, building models and organizing it all into something that almost, if you looked at it right, made sense. Hypatia walked carefully in her linen robe and men's sandals, softly stepping on the smooth and clean tiles of the Library, trying to avoid the trip wire. She was thinking of the facts at hand, the facts that are in Greek and the facts that are in Roman and in Glyph. The facts that are hard and brilliant as diamond and the facts only half-understood and intuited. They all said the same thing. They are coming and they can not be stopped. And when they did come they would have no use for things like libraries or bald women in men's shoes. This was a fact.

Maybe if the other Librarians hadn't fled they could have held them off. Maybe if the ships in the harbor hadn't been set on fire she could have saved more books then the merge piles sent East disguised in oxcarts. Maybe if the rioters hadn't just this part of the city to barricade and not some other. Maybe if anyone had listened to her rather than shouting her down, saying it was impossible, that she was seeing things again, calling her a freak, a woman with a man's heart, a virago. A freak. Hypatia

---

could smell the burning ships. Already the harbor was obscured by smoke, the grand lighthouse a flat shadow. Not long now she thought, placing the last of the Library's gold falcons and onyx busts into a pile in the front hall, not long at all.

You can learn things from books. How to sail a ship or how to dress for a party or how to pray. You can learn how to love someone or how to anger a King or how to treat your guests. You can learn things from talking to people, by arguing with them. Like, Which powders from Cathay hold fire inside them, which paste and papers burn hot or how to make oil containers drop when a thread is cut and which stones spark when struck together. You can learn which carts are leaving the city and how to bribe a Hind merchant with an emerald the size of an ostrich egg. You can learn how to slip out of places unnoticed against an advancing army and how to say your new name in a new language. Hypatia was a very fast learner.

Later in the cart, with the city a burning sliver on the horizon and her bald head and slim frame hiding her sex, Hypatia thought about the men who came. How would they react when they saw all the treasure waiting for them, neatly stacked in the front hall like sweets in a shop or girls in a brothel? Would they run toward it? Would they stand agape? Would they thank their Gods? God? Would they notice the empty shelves? Which one of them will move forward, breaking the twine, upturning the oil and sparking the fuse? She took a book from her bag, the only book she had saved for herself, a fresh salty breeze from Alexandria by the most divine and learned Aristotle. She turned to her favorite page and read:

—

"When discussing the virtues of Thalian Art, one must consider that primary element of a Comedy is timing."

# The Attic Window
### by Laura Graham

I can see the house through my kitchen window, neglected, standing sadly between its more elegant neighbours in the quiet, tree-lined crescent. The sight of the over-grown back garden with the rockery gives me a lift on the weekends when I'm having breakfast. I like the soft colours of the shrubs and alpines, the clusters of columbine against the fence which divides it from the other houses. And the attic window; for several weeks now, I've imagined I was in the garden looking up at it, almost as if someone was trying to attract my attention. But I must go back to February of this year to remind myself of what happened when the house became vacant.

I had noticed the removal van outside the house on one of my Saturday afternoon walks. Another renovation disaster on the way, I thought: they'll turn it into flats, two pokey bedrooms out of one, en suite bathrooms in cupboards, beige carpets and gilt taps. I've seen them, don't tell me about them. I looked round a show flat one Sunday in the are and shuddered. Whatever they do, I thought, it will sell for an extortionate sum. Probably to yuppies who have taken over this neighbourhood, which was once inhabited by ordinary, hard working folk like myself.

I felt like celebrating when the people moved out. No more of that loathsome creature lying semi-naked on his mattress every weekend. No more whining voice pleading for coca cola, sandwiches and cakes, while she, presumably the wife, poor thing, trudged in and out of the back door like a slave. He couldn't see me watching him. If he had he'd have seen the look of contempt on my

---

face. He was there from ten in the morning until six in the evening.

I enjoy my own company. I cooked myself a lamb chop this evening. Ate it with creamed spinach, a spoonful of mint jelly and a glass of grape juice. I don't drink. I have a horror of losing control. Unlike those absurd characters at the office parties, laughing raucously, groping each other furtively and throwing up in the filing cabinets. I like my mind to be clear, my thinking precise.

Which is why, of course, I've been an invaluable personal assistant to my employer for the last fifteen years. Jean, he says, how would I survive without you? You wouldn't Mr. Skelton, I think, for I run your life, do your banking, book your flights, choose your hotels, have your car serviced, your office cleaned. All the mundane chores of every day taken care of, and more besides, for who would placate Mrs. Skelton when you wish to spend an extra evening at the club? Or make your coffee exactly the way you like it: three quarters black_to one quarter white in your Mickey Mouse mug? Not forgetting the shortbread fingers I bake specially for you on Sundays and bring to work on Mondays in the red biscuit tin.

But I say nothing. I just smile.

Mr. Skelton is away for a week. He's given me this week off. He said I looked tired: I'm not, in the least. I don't quite understand what he means − however, it's very pleasant. I've set my laptop up on the kitchen table. The light's better in here. And, most unlike me, for I'm not a fanciful kind of woman, I have begun a diary ha-ha.

I'm not the diary type. 'Dear diary, today I did this, tomorrow I'll do that'. I've never gone in for such self-indulgences. Nevertheless, I feel it's become necessary to keep an accurate record of the unusual goings-on in the house opposite.

*'Wednesday, August 17<sup>th</sup>.*
*Two men appeared at 8.15 am and dumped a barrow load of bricks in the back garden.'*

Concrete mixer, pop music, hammering and cursing. I wouldn't normally have to witness this, being in the office all day. But here I am, in the kitchen trying to concentrate on the report I'm writing with little success. And earlier I had a worrying thought. Who would replace the man on the mattress? For a second I almost regretted his departure, for rather the devil you know than the devil you don't. When I returned home from my walk this afternoon I saw with relief that the builders had gone. To my surprise, they had boarded up the back door of the house. Why, when the only other access to the garden is from the street past a row of dustbins?

*'Thursday, September 8<sup>th.</sup> Start of annual holiday. First week, Gilly and Herb – Ilkley.'*

I really think it will be the very last time I stay with my sister and her American husband. She's changed so since marrying him. "Jean," she shouted at me as I got out of the car, "I'm going to burn that dreadful woolly hat if I see you in it again. It looks like a cosy."

Disparaging remarks were also made about my camelhair coat that I've had for fifteen years and from which I refuse to be parted. "They're old friends, these things," I tried to explain in her new hi-tech kitchen over an undrinkable cup of scented tea. "Then it's about time you found yourself some *real* friends," she said. "You're too closed up within yourself. And do something with your hair, get it cut and styled. Change your image, you're forty-eight not sixty-eight."

I tried to explain patiently, though, I have to say I was hurt, that I haven't the time, I lead too busy a life. "Doing what?" she asked. "Running chores for that dreary Mr. Skeleton, whatever his name is, and going to his twice yearly office parties which you told me you hate. You know what your problem is?" she laughed, a little too raucously I thought, over her wine on my last night, "You're too set in your ways, Jean." Herb threatened to drop something into my tomato juice then sniggered into his grubby polo neck.

No, I won't return, it's a long way to go to be insulted.

*'Thursday. September 15^{th}.*
*Arrived home midnight, terrible drive through torrents of rain.'*

I immersed myself in steaming pine-scented bath water and tried to forget the previous week, eradicated Gilly and Herb from my thoughts, so to speak. I had almost forgotten about the house. But as I lay in the water it came to mind, I could see it in my imagination, cold and empty and I grew apprehensive. What had those builders done in my absence? And the more I thought of them the angrier I became. How dare they impose themselves onto the house, tear down walls, hack out its heart, replace it with their modern half-baked ideas. Change what had been there for a century in to something it was never meant to be.

—

With my face to the kitchen window I peered out into the dark. The night was particularly gloomy, no moon or stars to give a welcome light. The house could have vanished for all I could see. Nothing was visible. Then gradually, out of the nothingness, I made out the small top window, staring eye-like into the night.

It had stopped raining. I opened my window to see better. The outline of the house became slowly visible against the sombre sky.

*'Friday, September 16<sup>th</sup>.*
*Slept badly. Had disturbing dream. I was in the garden of the house looking up at the window and saw a light on glass as if someone inside was signalling to me with a mirror.'*

I shuffled lethargically in to the kitchen to make coffee. Then stopped, unable to believe what I saw through the window. Boarded up. All five windows of the house, all that is, except the small top window. The kettle boiled, I switched it off and wrote frantically: '*6.45 am. Builders gone mad, sealing house up . . .*'

It was scandalous. I'd have to report it. But to whom? There had been no estate agent's board outside the house when I'd last looked. I dropped bread in the toaster. I couldn't stop staring at the house. It was like a tomb, there might be someone in there, all sealed up with only one means of escape through the attic window. And soon, no doubt, they would board that up too. Perhaps by now a *For Sale* board must have been erected; but who would want to buy a house you couldn't enter? I shall complain to the Council, demand to know what is going on. The toast bobbed up and made me jump.

---

*'7.40 am.*
*Going round to house to investigate.'*

I dressed quickly. Mrs. Nethercott in the top flat wasn't about yet. She wouldn't be until eight thirty, thumping her shopping trolley down the stairs, hobbling off to Budgins in her slippers. You're late this morning, on holiday, are you? It's all right for some. She wouldn't hear me if I was quiet; wouldn't twitch her nets to watch me slip along the street.

I crossed Lauderdale Road and turned in to Marsden Crescent. There were fewer cars than usual parked on the street. The Crescent looked wider. Pink geraniums and dead lobelia trailed from window boxes on the sills of the first house. Pink and white begonias in the neat front gardens of the second and third; nothing outside the fourth and straggling petunias draping sills of the fifth and sixth.

Number seven was as I had last seen it. None of the six front windows had been boarded up and there was no signboard. It was almost as though the house was keeping up a respectable front, in spite of what may be going on round the back, or *worse,* inside. The L-shaped garden was overgrown with weeds, dirty nets pulled across the windows and the rendering around the sills cracked and flaking. And yet - there was a difference. I hadn't noticed at first. Surely, there had been weeds sprouting between the black and white tiled steps to the front door? Now they had been cleared. Not by the mattress man, he had never done anything in the five years he'd lived here. I had the strangest notion as I gazed up at the house that it seemed to be waiting – to be expecting someone.

---

48

Open the rusty gate round the side wall, pass three empty dustbins, ease round the nettles in to the back garden. I like talking to myself;

I find it more reassuring sometimes than talking to someone else. It's larger than I thought, rather nice crazy paving along the wall. I hadn't seen that from my window. Don't like that rusty old chair by the rockery. Probably left by Mr. Universe, I'm surprised he hasn't left any more of his rubbish. Bricks left in a horrible heap in the centre of the lawn. Why do builders just dump things anywhere? My eyes travelled up the brickwork of the house, past what was once a door and windows, to the top window, such a dark, forsaken attic window, staring at the glass that suddenly shone so brilliantly in the sunlight.

There is something about seeing familiar things from an unfamiliar angle that can produce unpredictable emotions. Here I am, in the garden looking into my kitchen window. There's the stove, the kettle, the tea caddy, the old brown teapot: how can I describe the extraordinary feeling of detachment?

I could be a thousand miles away, so far removed I seem to be from these objects. They are mine and yet not mine. It's as though I'm looking at a well-remembered scene that I have long since left behind and to which I may never return. But what am I saying? What's the matter with me? My toes are prickling, so are my fingers, I must sit, the chair – the rusty chair - please let me reach it in time.

The experience passed as quickly as it had come, leaving me feeling slightly light-headed and still with the faint prickling sensation in my fingers and toes. In something of a dream, I made my way round the side of the house, past the dustbins to the street again. To my surprise, I noticed the front door was ajar. I could have sworn it had been closed when I arrived. I moved along the path, up the steps, before I could stop myself, and pushing the heavy door open wider, crept inside.

The air smelt musty. Four doors were closed on either side of the gloomy hallway. Straight ahead was a staircase. My curiosity getting the better of me, I climbed quickly, eagerly, up the first flight to the landing above.
Three doors led off it; one was open allowing sunlight to filter through the gloom on the stairs. A grubby double mattress lay on the centre of the bare floor. Up I went to the next landing. It was smaller with two open doors leading off revealing a squalid bathroom and kitchen.

I moved softly up the few remaining stairs. Dust covered the bare wooden treads, I hesitated, surely that was a footprint on the top stair? But I climbed on, past spiders' webs dangling from a nail in the wall. Only one door led off the small third landing. It was closed. In the surrounding shadow I could just make out a key in the lock. I gazed at it in fascination, unable to understand the longing I had to open that door and enter -

From the street an ambulance siren jarred horribly, the unexpected sound alerted my befuddled brain and for a moment I stood rooted to the stair not knowing where I was. It was then, I think, but cannot be sure, that I heard a sound of the small door slowly opening. I dared not look. Breathing, swallowing, normal bodily functions became impossible.

---

Blind panic seized me. With a cry I hurled myself back down those stairs to the front door. It had closed. Grasping the handle I turned it and pulled. But the door wouldn't budge. In a frenzy, I turned it the opposite way and pulled again with all my might. Suddenly it opened and I staggered back as if from some unseen blow. Regaining my balance, I rushed down the steps, crossed Lauderdale Road and ran.

That evening, in spite of everything I had decided, I telephoned Gilly. She would be too busy helping Herb run his new restaurant to come to London because of what she would call an absurd flight of fancy. But absurd or not it was real enough to me and I could hardly bear the thought of another night on my own. "How do you mean," she said, "you don't know if you're all right or not?"

"Something's happened," I hesitated.

"What's happened?"

"I can't explain exactly, it's . . . er –"

"Have you started work again?"

I was stunned. How dare she change the subject so abruptly. My anger alarmed me; I've always been a calm sort of person and yet there I was shouting for no apparent reason. I slammed down the phone, immediately regretting having done so.

Five days passed uneventfully. Each morning, to escape my flat, I took my work to the library. But once there I became distracted and watched the librarian squeak round the polished floor in her crepe-soled shoes. Or I would sit staring into space, my concentration drifting away like smoke in the wind from the work in hand. And the window would come to mind, the small attic window that had begun to prey on my imagination. Someone was hiding there, I felt certain of it. Someone imprisoned for all I knew.

Around that time is when the dreams started. I would be in the garden, sitting on the rusty chair, waiting. I would look up and although it was dark, I could see a face at the window – a man, looking down at me.
Then the whispering would start, my name whispered all around, until the trees took up the sound, softly at first, then louder, more urgently, calling, calling, creating a terrible yearning within me, a longing and a rush of excitement such as I have never known.

On Thursday morning something happened, something so inexplicable that when I think of it I wonder if I am dreaming still. Throwing some things into a suitcase, I decided to go and stay at my sister's. Welcome or not, I could work in the spare room, I'd be no bother to her and at least, I could get some work done. Certainly nothing was being achieved by staying in my flat. After several attempts to telephone had failed, the line being continually engaged, I set off in the car and soon after ten was making steady progress up the motorway with a packet of freshly cut sandwiches and a flask of soup on the seat beside me. I felt in altogether better spirits. At a service station I turned off to top up with petrol and having paid the hermetically sealed cashier, continued my journey northwards.

Not 500 yards later, I found myself on a slip road marked Bedford. I turned right across the bridge, then right again, back onto the motorway, only this time heading southwards towards London. I couldn't understand what had happened to me. My mind had gone blank, a mental blackout from which I had a struggle to regain consciousness.

More annoyed than frightened, I pulled onto the hard shoulder for a couple of minutes to sort myself out. It was as well that I did, for once again that curious prickling sensation returned, this time only in my hands but so severe I could hardly take hold of the steering wheel. As before, the feeling passed quickly and somewhat shaken, I drove on to the next exit, determined to turn off and head back in the right direction.

I noticed the lorry approaching in the slow lane as the exit came in to view. I signalled and prepared to move in to the left lane. But as I did so, the lorry accelerated and pulled alongside me, preventing my manoeuvre. I braked to let him pass.

The slip road was now 30 yards away and it was too late to overtake him. The lorry turned off forcing me to continue on towards London.

At the next exit I prepared again to turn off, but saw, to my dismay, that there had been an accident and the slip road was closed. Police were everywhere, directing cars on down the motorway. What disturbed me most was seeing a black Volkswagen, the same model as mine, which had crashed into the side of a lorry. The car had apparently been trying to turn off the motorway in circumstances similar to those that I had experienced ten

—

minutes earlier. The coincidence seemed almost uncanny. Looking into my rear view mirror, I could see nothing of any accident. No lorry, no police, no flashing blue lights. Had I imagined it? I wanted to stop, to try and work out what was happening. But I couldn't seem to stop. I was badly frightened. The car was moving fast, the needle hovering on 85, faster than I normally drive.

The awesome fact was that although it was me in the driving seat, it felt as though it was some other source of energy controlling the car and making decisions regardless of my wishes. I drove the rest of the way home in a daze.

Once in my flat I went straight in to the kitchen. I felt weak and my hands trembled as I filled the kettle. I looked up at the attic window. There *was* someone there. I'd known it all along. Someone waiting to be invited. I could see a hand waving and I am almost certain that hand was no trick of light.

My sister and her American husband are worried about me. They think I should see a doctor. Last night when she telephoned I patiently explained the whole situation regarding the house and its mysterious occupant. But she will keep interrupting and talking about squatters and other such nonsensical things. I told her all about the motorway incident. She was silent. So silent, in fact, that I had to ask her several times if she was still there.

I have told her what my plans are; I'm going to tack a sheet across my kitchen window so I can't see him. Everything will be all right then, I can work, you see. I have a deadline to keep.

*'Sunday morning 3 am.'*

A light's been turned on in the window.

I sensed it even before I ran to the kitchen to tear away the sheet. Now I know that my waiting is almost over.

Rain is falling, a settled heavy rain. I sit here by the kitchen window cold and incapable of moving. The hours pass so slowly. Oh, how much longer must I wait for my guest?

The light in the window has just gone out.

My heart is racing. I press my hand over it to keep it calm. I have left the door to my house on the latch, the door to my flat ajar. I can hardly breathe, my longings are soon to be fulfilled; I tremble with anticipation.
A sound at the door - my guest has arrived.

# Kissing Hitler
## by Marilyn Monroe
## (Kate Horsley)

I come to you through the lips of Madame Blavatsky, the greatest psychic in Ventura, CA.

You say you want to know the truth about a certain day in the long, hot summer of 1962? A little while after I sang H-apppy Birthdaaaay Mister Pressi-dent at Madison Square Garden and just a smidge before I was due back on the set of *Something's Got to Give?*

Well, Honey, you got an *exclusive,* front page news about a Big Cahuna who came visiting one sweltering day when I was indisposed.

But first, I'll tell you a little something that will help you understand both of us, my killer and me. It concerns an actor who thought he was a funny guy that looked real good in a dress. Well, he said kissing me was like kissing Hitler. I'm sure you heard about it. It was in every rag on the newsstand.

And you're probably thinking, *people say you look like a million bucks every day, Marilyn. And folks pay millions of bucks to see your movies.* And when those nice people sit in the darkness watching a blonde who's not exactly out of shape having a swell time, they feel better. I know because I sat where they sit once, when my foster families used to send me to the movies to get me out of the house and there I'd sit all day and way into the night. Up in front, there with the screen so big, a little kid all alone, wanting to marry the leading man.

---

When those movie-going folks see me onscreen, they want to *be* me, to *kiss* me, too.

Those folks are *paying* to kiss me. Not in a hooker kind of a way. Only - if they could just graze their lips on mine, they could have what I have, be what I am now.

But all that dreaming and kissing and wishing ain't worth a goddamn when someone says *y'know kissing her was just like kissing Hitler*. Adolf Hitler. Does it mean that I'm like a mean old man? The worst great dictator there ever was?

Or does it mean that on my top lip I just have a little bit of a moustache? And kissing me is like wrapping your lips round an old bristle brush?

Laugh it up. But imagine if you were that blonde on the silver screen and someone had told the whole world *kissing that doll is like sucking on a Nazi soup-strainer*. You could say *phooey to you!* But you would still lean in close to mirrors to make sure your 5 o'clock shadow wasn't showing through your powder.

You would still wake up in the night with your head on the pillow near some guy's head. And you'd lick your top lip. Just to be sure.

What I'm saying is, you can be famous and have power or money or looks. But at the end of the day, we're all just a little bit insecure. Whether someone compared your frenching to a Nazi's or for some other reason, you find yourself going out in a headscarf and sunglasses, trespassing on private property.

———

Sometimes taking a handgun, cool against your bare skin under a mink coat. Stealing. Just little things. A garden gnome. A pair of secateurs.

Not because you want to be caught, like Dr. Greenson's always saying. But because you want them to see you with no make-up, no red carpet glitz. The real you. To hear them say *go on and take that croquet mallet, Norma Jeane. I've got plenty to spare.*

\*\*\*

Lately they've all been watching me. Bobby, Joe Jnr, Pat, Dr. Greenson. Even Eunice. And that's not counting the men in dark suits and black Cadillacs who pull out half a minute after me and stay a few cars behind.

Lately, I don't need to act glamorous or funny to be seen. Even all by myself in my bedroom, I'm not alone. Because they're looking through the curtains. Down the telephone wires.

It gets so tiring. You need pills to go to sleep, pills to wake up. A drink or two to stay on an even keel.

To tell the truth, I hadn't slept for a while the day he dropped by. I was hunched over a grapefruit, my hair in little pin curls, slicked with chicken fat (it works wonders on straw-like hair, even split ends). My supper tasted like box office poison. I went to the counter to get a spoon of sugar for it. That's when I saw three cars pull into the driveway.

Maybe they had come because of Jack. Or Bobby. Or the mob. Whatever it was, my heart beat louder than the Rank gong.

The Caddy door opened and this little fat man got out and smoothed down his hair and started walking toward my front door. I scurried to the lobby to watch him through the peephole. He cranked his lips into a tight little moue and put his hands on his hips as if he were about to strike a Gilda pose.

Eunice was hovering, nosy as ever.

"Keep him busy while I'm in the bath," I said, "and let him fix himself a drink."

Upstairs, the sound of the taps running into the tub calmed me. And the pills did too. I began to unscrew every jar and bottle I could find, pouring in this and that potion, from my cabinet, from gift-wrapped boxes, studio kiss-offs. Salt and oil enough to embalm a pharaoh, like some magic potion for Cleopatra's complexion – what's it called? Asses' milk.

I slipped out of my robe and stood in front of the mirror to check that I was still me. People think I was a fat girl, you know, all tits and ass. Its true I had a pair of watermelons strapped to my ribcage, real casabas. Once. Then I stopped eating and they got more like soft fruit.

I stepped into the tub. The water scalded my knees. The schmaltz from my pin curls slithered down the back of my neck. My skin pinked as I inched into the water, the hips, the thighs. The rest of me slipping in, my breasts bobbing to the surface. Lotus flowers opening. I took a bath like this before I lost the second child.

The door opened.

"Eunice, I said to keep him busy."

Something dark and heavyset shimmered in the steam like a hearse moseying up a desert road.

"Mr J Edgar Hoover! What are *you* doing here?"

"I brought you a drink," he said.

He set down a whiskey glass with an inch of clear liquid in it. I couldn't smell whether it was gin or vodka because of the sweet murk of scented steam. His hand was wrapped around a glass of his own.

"Chin chin," he said.

He tipped the drink to his thin lips. Well, what could I say to the Director of the FBI? I drank up. It had a chalky taste with a sweetness over it. Ouzo.

Then he got up and walked out. Sashayed. Like that heel who called me Hitler.

I sat until my fingertips were puckered as raisins. My head was heavy. I had to grip the sides of the tub and push myself out of that bath, like being born again. Out of the tepid, flat coke water. My robe wasn't hanging on the door. No towel. I stumbled to my bedroom, the floor rolling. Pitching beneath my numb feet. I saw him through the crack in the door. The hair. The powder. My head splitting open.

You ever see a chubby little guy in a bullet bra all gussied up like Mae West? You ever see five of them sashaying, twirling, Gilda-ing away like a goddamn chorus line? Powder flying everywhere. My dresses spilled out. Petals on the floor.

He had on my white dress. Blinding white. Sunshine on a hangover. A headache in a headache in a headache. Smoothing it over his hips. Pouting into my mirror. Rouge - *Cancun Carmen* by Chanel - scrawled over his face. Clown lips.

I gripped the edge of the door. Water pooled onto the carpet. Through spidery lashes, he stared me down. Squinting his eyes.

"I've wanted this dress since I saw *The Seven Year Itch*," he said.

"You'llll have to get those s-sseamss altered..." but that voice wasn't coming from me.

He tossed a length of feather boa over his shoulder and turned back to admire himself. My fingers on the door like a monkey's clinging to a branch. My hand slipping.

*** 

I'm 12 again, hanging from a tree-limb in my sweatshirt and they've come to talk to me, the boys with their bicycles pulled up around the tree. I'm hanging like a monkey, too shy to come down. This one boy, Dennis, has red hair and braces. I know he has a crush on me. He says I can ride his bike. I go zooming, laughing in the wind, riding down the block. When I turn round the others have gone and he's watching me freewheel back with the wind stroking me. It feels so free with my feet kicked out to the side and the pedals whirring and Dennis smiling. Like the wind is carrying me.

Like anything's possible, almost.

# Foibles
## by Neil McIness

"Viagra tablets at that price; you must be kidding, Mort."
Barney Fisk scratched his crotch. It was an involuntary
action that always occurred when Barney discussed the
subject of his waning sexual prowess. "The chemist
charged me thirty bucks for six tablets."

"I kid you not, Barney. This's the real thing from an
American pharmaceutical company, *and* more potent
than Viagra. Look at the label."

Barney examined the label closely. "How do I know
they'll work?"

"Here." Mort Shultz said, taking a tablet from a plastic
bag. "I'll give you a free sample. I guarantee you'll get a
result within fifteen minutes, and the tabs are effective for
thirty-six hours. There's even a money back guarantee—
that's assuming your artillery's in working order."

"There's nothin' wrong with my boys," Barney said
firmly as he adjusted himself again. "When I see some of
those young chicks at the beach in their bikinis it's...
well, you know how it is, Mort. The misses and I've been
married almost forty five years, and lately she's started to
sag in all the wrong places."

"You don't have to explain to me, Barney. Us blokes
need all the help we can get."

"Who do you buy them from, Mort?" Barney asked, as
he turned the sample tablet over in his hand.

—

"Direct from the manufacturer." Mort hesitated. "I'm the regional distributor for this mob."

Barney looked concerned. "Is that legal? These things can kill you if you've got a bad heart."

"That's bullshit, Barney," Mort replied sharply. "I've been taking 'em for twelve months, and I've had no ill effects."

"Some might disagree, Mort. Your sex life's the talk of the village."

Mort was curious. "So what're they saying; that I'm a sexy old stud?"

"No, Mort," Barney said, and chuckled. "Most people say you're just a dirty old man,"

A knock on the door distracted them. "Come in," Mort called out to his visitor.

Trinity Du Pont stood nervously in the doorway, unwilling to cross over Mort's threshold. "You have something for me?" she said, eyeing Barney with caution.

"Sure have Trinity." Mort rummaging through a carton that sat on his kitchen bench-top. "My latest stock arrived this morning."

Mort gave a box of tablets to Trinity who handed over a twenty-dollar note.

Trinity studied the box suspiciously. "These are definitely the same as the last batch you sold me?"

—

"Identical," Mort replied, holding up the invoice from his supplier. "Were they satisfactory?"

"They were brilliant," Trinity replied, and hastily departed the scene.

"Trinity is dosing her bloke with Viagra?" Barney asked when they resumed their conversation. "The old bugger must be seventy five, if he's a day."

"Just another satisfied customer," Mort said with an air of confidence.

The phone rang before Barney could continue and Mort listened to the caller for a moment. "Okay, Willy, a twelve pack for you and a sample pack for Stan Huddle. I'll drop 'em round later."

"Willy Hogan's using the tablets too?" Barney asked when Mort had finished his call.

"Been taking 'em for weeks," Mort replied.
Barney Fisk studied the sample in his hand for a moment.

"Forget the sample," he said, getting to his feet. "Give me a box of twelve."

Felicity Fairchild, the manager of Shady Palms Retirement Village slumped back into her chair in disbelief. "This can't be possible. A drug raid, here, at Shady Palms."

The Federal Police Officer sitting opposite her took out his note pad. "I'm afraid so, Ms Fairchild."

---

"What sort of drugs?"

"From the reports we received they were sex enhancement drugs."

Felicity's mood changed immediately. "That's ridiculous; we're a retirement village," she said sitting forward.

"Nevertheless it's true, Ms Fairchild. Have you received any complaints recently about some of your male residents behaving – let's say – irrationally?"

Felicity was thoughtful for a moment. There had been a number of comments that several men in the village were acting in a somewhat vulgar manner. Willy Hogan had in fact pinched her bottom at a residents meeting only last week, and made a suggestive comment to her. Felicity was rather flattered at the time but thought Willy must have been drunk. She made a mental note to investigate Willy's suggestion further.

"No, officer, I haven't heard any reports of that nature. How did the Federal Police become involved in all of this?"

"The Dioceses' Archbishop rang my boss in Canberra. Apparently one of your residents complained to a, Father O'Shannessy at the local church that her husband had begun making lustful advances towards her."

"Her husband; so what's wrong with that?"

"The husband is ninety three and crippled with arthritis." Felicity stifled a laugh. "Who was the resident?"

The policeman shook his head. "The priest was unable to give me that information. The confidence of the confessional you understand."

"And you have a suspect?"

The cop checked his notes. "Yes, a man named Mortimer Shultz has been questioned this morning and a thorough search was made of his home."

Mort Schultz, Felicity thought, I should have guessed.

"And what did you find?"

"Well we weren't able to find any evidence of drugs but we did locate certain documents."

"So is the man under arrest?"

"That's difficult without any really *hard* evidence."

Felicity giggled but the policeman missed the point.

"This is not a laughing matter, Ms Fairchild. And in answer to your question, we have given Mr Shultz a warning that if he's caught with any of these restricted drugs in his possession in future, he'll be arrested and brought before a Magistrate."

Mort Shultz was a forlorn looking figure as he sat in Daisy Mott's lounge room, bemoaning his shattered distribution business. His last consignment of tablets lay hidden under Daisy's bed, and he had no way of disposing of them—not without risking another confrontation with the Federal Police. But Mort was determined to get his money back. He had most of his savings tied up in the shipment, and there was a ready-made market out there for the product.

Mort watched Daisy as she iced her lamingtons and rolled them in shredded coconut. Daisy Mott's lamingtons were renowned in Shady Palms Retirement Village, and were always the first cakes to go at any function, or stall, where they were sold.

Daisy made a cup of tea for them both, placed one of the lamingtons on a plate, and handed it to Mort.

"Here," she said. "This might cheer you up."

"The only thing that'll cheer me up is findin' a way to sell that stock without getting caught," he mumbled.

As Mort bit into the fresh sponge cake, his fingers became covered in chocolate icing and coconut pieces. He placed the lamington on the plate and began licking his fingers. "Maybe," he said between licks, "we should hide them in your lamingtons."

Mort picked up the lamington again, and with the cake halfway to his mouth, he stopped and looked at Daisy.

"What?" she said.

There was a look of excitement on Mort's face. "Why *don't* we mix the tablets in with your lamingtons?"
Daisy's eyes lit up, and she grinned. "Mort, you're a genius."

"I can crush the tablets down to a powder and then we'll mix one into each lamington." Mort held up a chocolate covered finger. "We'll sell them for five dollars each."

"Or three for twelve dollars," Daisy added.

Mort got to his feet and began pacing the floor. "This's a brilliant cover, Daisy. Only our customers will know what we're selling."

Daisy was thoughtful for a moment. "What about the taste? Will that be a problem?"

"Dunno. Let's make some and see," he said excitedly.

"Why don't we sell them as *herbal* lamingtons? That way we can explain away any questions about the flavour," Daisy suggested.

Mort pointed a supportive finger at Daisy. "Yeah, we'll just say that it's the herbs and spices they can taste."

"I've even got a slogan," Daisy said with great enthusiasm. "Now you *can* have your cake and eat it too."

Mort laughed heartily. "Or, spice up your Devonshire Teas."

"Daisy's herbal lamingtons," she said, and sighed wistfully.

A few days later, Mort Shultz and one of his regular customers, Angelo Bulloni, stood on Mort's verandah haggling over the price. "Five bucks each is a bit steep, Mort. We're pensioners, you know."

"Well, take three for twelve dollars then," Mort replied.

"Remember, Angelo, Daisy's lamingtons are included in the price."

"I don't like lamingtons," Angelo said, and screwed up his face.

Mort was becoming frustrated. "They're not normal lamingtons, Angelo, they're—you know—special."

"Okay, but if I don't like them, can I bring them back?"

"Sorry Angelo, no refunds. They might have gone stale."

Begrudgingly, Angelo Bulloni took his three lamingtons.

"I'll take them, Mort, but at that price the bloody things had better work."

That afternoon Angelo Bulloni was back knocking on Mort's front door.

"I told you, Angelo, no returns," Mort said, as he went to close his door.

"I don't have any returns," Angelo said. "I want three more."

Mort looked at the man closely and cocked his head.

"Hey, Angelo, how many of those things did you eat?" he asked, a little concerned.

"None. My wife found them in the fridge this morning and took them to the Ladies Auxiliary meeting at the church."

"She did what?"

"And the ladies loved them. So did Monsignor Hopgood. In fact, the Monsignor wants to know if he can put a weekly order in for a dozen of Daisy's herbal Lamingtons."

# The Future
## by Zvi Eli Sella

She had never called me in the morning before.

"Look baby, I'm cooking paella for lunch; it's coming out real spicy – can you come around noontime?"

I could already feel the heat of the city outside, brewing quietly all around. But Rocio's chicken was the best in Havana, and I wasn't going to miss it.

"I'll bring the beer," I said, but I knew right then something had happened.

That trip I rented an apartment across the Malecón, almost at the very end of the promenade, in front of the bay. It wasn't too far from the Hotel Riviera and its rooftop restaurant which I liked; the one that used to be Lansky's place in the good old days. They say he ran a pretty organized operation back then; but in hindsight, they all seem like a bunch of amateurs compared to the mighty organization that followed.

By the time I got out to catch a ride to Cerro, where Rocio lived by herself in those days, the sun was already burning everything outside, as if this was payday for all of last night's sins. The tortured streets of Havana were winding helplessly in the heat, and the dried-up yards were choking for air. I passed the sea on my way – it had saved me once or twice before – breathing the blue again and watching it spread over the horizon. I think I liked the sea the most when it got totally out of control, charging at the city as though it couldn't take any more, hitting the Malecón with huge, wild waves that covered the sky before crashing from above onto the old stone wall and flooding the wide, cracked road which ran alongside the coast. But that day, the sea was just lying there calmly, enormous and innocent, letting the city breathe its invisible, hot Caribbean mist.

The unmistakable scent of Rocio's stew was already in the streets as I approached her place. She had on her long blue dress, which was as formal as she could get, and the dishes were already on the table. Preparing paella is one of the most delicate undertakings there is, and ruining it should be once and for all against the law. Not last among the many unforgivable sins of the Cuban government was the way they cooked paella for foreigners in the big hotels – all dry and bitter and totally soulless. Rocio's paella was true Latin poetry, something that reminded you why we were all gathered here on earth in the first place. The spicier she cooked it; the more seductive it came out. But it was always pure delight, soft and warm and juicy like she was – you just wanted it to last forever.

She didn't say much until we were done, and she hardly touched her beer. Then it came.

"Look," she said, "these past three weeks have been the best I have ever had, you already know that. But I have been thinking about it, about us, and it's clear to me now that we have no chance, no future."

She paused to breathe, but I didn't say a word. I was just watching the way she held her glass, with that bent palm.

—

"I decided to go back to my husband," she continued. "I want us to always be close, as we are now. But we can't make love again, and I need you to understand this."

So that was it.

"Not only do I understand," I assured her, "I really respect it. But just to be absolutely clear, does this also mean no more blow jobs?"

I think I had never heard her yell before. She was really desperate this time. "You see, this is exactly what I mean; you never take me seriously! You never take anything seriously!"

Actually, it wasn't entirely not serious for me, especially the timing.

For a little while afterwards, we ate cool mango for dessert, or rather I did. And then I got up to thank her for lunch before I was finally thrown out of paradise, the only one there was.

"Wait," she said, still trying hard to cling to her anger. But it wasn't nearly enough. "I have an appointment now with a spiritual woman. You should come too, once and for all; it won't hurt you, *descarado*, to know what will become of you."

"Spiritual woman" was a *Santería* fortuneteller, and Rocio had tried this with me before. Many times.

Just a week earlier, I couldn't help asking her. "How can a bright bio-geneticist like you waste your time on such crap?"

She used to be one of Fidel's dream-team recruits who were going to save the island by way of science after the crash and desertion of the USSR. This was also the reason – the few years she had worked in that clandestine institute – that the same glorious revolution she abhorred so much and could do nothing about, didn't let her leave the country.

"What *I* don't understand," she said, "is how a physicist can't see that the future is all predetermined? Don't you know that it is all a play of atoms and photons which must always follow strict natural laws, whether we know them or not? Every state in the universe already contains, by definition, the next one. From the moment it all started, it has been set, all the way to the end."

I knew it would make her happy so I told her a little about Bento Espinoza's endless chain of cause and effect, which were always intertwined as well. But I had to tell her also that his pristine world did not include time, that time, according to my excommunicated Morrano guide, was just the name we gave the poor misconceptions of our limited senses. There were really no beginnings in time, nor endings. Like reading a story - each part already bears the next, and you move along step by step. But actually the whole story has been there right in front of you all along.

It did make her happy. Especially the part about death being therefore just another meaningless human fabrication.

"Exactly!" she exulted. "If we could just get rid of the misconceptions which we ourselves invent – like the spiritual woman does – we would be able to see everything!"

"It doesn't matter anyway," I said. "I still wouldn't have him as my savior." But deep down I knew it did matter; it made the whole difference. Not knowing, regardless of anything else, was what left us the choice, the responsibility, everything.

"Why wouldn't you have him?" the new Spinozist had to know. "He did tell the truth."

"Because of the children. You see, in his blameless universe – the one that is all God – killing the one million children was simply supposed to happen, like everything else that had ever happened, and that was that. He, at least, would never brush this aside like the rest of us do; he couldn't brush anything aside. That little slaughter, as far as he was concerned, would never pass as just some long-forgotten outburst in that faraway war. Like all the rest in his timeless reality, it is still happening, as we speak, in front of our own eyes. But for him, all this wouldn't be something to get too emotional about. Nothing would."

She already knew where this was leading.

"So once again," I said, just to cut to the chase, "it's either God or the children - take your pick. Because Spinoza's offer, logic itself, is a package deal – take it all or leave it all. Those murderers, like their eager collaborators – meaning pretty much everyone around back then – were merely playing their part in the grand script, and so were the children. So why indeed should there be any problem there?"

—
76

But actually there was a problem there. This was the problem. And that much she knew.

"Would you have *me* as your savior?"

"Anytime," I said. "This is the only salvation left – just you and your gorgeous ass. But then again, who would save you from me, Rocio?"

But all that was mumblings of the past. This time was somehow different. Maybe it was the despair in her eyes, but I just said, "OK, my day is already ruined anyway. Let's just get it over with."

The spiritual woman apparently lived in the next *barrio*, in a big, old colonial house, surrounded by all kinds of wild tropical bushes and tall palm trees. There was a large half-empty room inside, dark as a cave, and at the very end, sitting on the bare floor, was a huge black woman, with some suspicious-looking boxes in front of her.

"He will go first," Rocio said to her very fast, pointing at me, "and I will stay here with him, in case he needs help with the translation."

"This man doesn't need help with any translation," the woman told her, "but you can stay anyways, because you are so beautiful."

I was trying my best to keep a straight face while the woman began playing with some small, odd-looking bones, quietly chanting and scattering them around, then collecting them all over again. I didn't want to give away too many clues, so I kept very still, but the woman hardly looked at me anyway; she was just watching her little flying bones with much interest, while telling me in detail the usual tales fortunetellers all across the world tell the fools they lure in.

She did look at me though when she said, "I know you don't believe in God right now, but you will, *chico*, you will." I still didn't say anything. But I did believe in him. Only, my God did play with dice; we were the dice.

Then, probably for my good behavior, the woman was ready to grant me a special treat.

"You may ask me two questions now. Ask anything you wish and I will give you the answers. But don't ask them out loud, only in your heart."

The first question I asked had always troubled me, and I still wonder about it from time to time.

Does 2 plus 2 equal 4?

"At this very moment, no," the Oracle from the *barrio* told me, "but in the future, who knows? It's possible."

Her second answer was a little more decisive: "Absolutely yes; it is certain!"

As I got up to thank her, I heard myself asking – risking not only my life, but more importantly, the good impression I had been working so hard to make –

"How do you know all of this?"

"For me, *chico*, the future is like the past – all I need to do is remember it."

"And you see it all in these little bones?"

"I see nothing in them bones.  They just help me not think about anything else, and it's fun."

I thought I'd had just enough nonsense for one day, so I left behind my little true believer, and went out onto the shaded patio, where Andino – Rocio's neighbor who had driven us there in his old wreck – was patiently smoking. Andino was the ultimate Cuban street cat, doing it for a living, and a good old friend, who was always trying to hook me up with new girls and sometimes managed to. We talked about the trouble his girlfriend, Soledad, had been giving him lately.  He himself happened to think it was the summer heat.  And then we just sat and listened to the playful Regeatón music coming from the nearby house.  There were voices of some girls laughing.  This is the beauty of this place, I thought; wherever you go, day or night, you can never get away from the music here, not even for a single moment.  Forget control.  God bless dancing!  God bless sex!  The only sober ways around here to touch freedom, to rebel and win.  The only solace left in this magical, godforsaken land, where time has frozen in the endless wait for the death of the nation's Father.  I couldn't wait for night to fall.

When Rocio eventually came out of the temple, she was all glowing, like a happy bride fresh from her holy wedding rites.  She too, could not wait any longer – all in great astonishment like an excited little child – to share with our thrilled driver the incredible things which had just happened to her inside.  She told him of things the woman had no way of knowing beforehand, even things about her childhood in Oriente – the mountainous eastern edge of the island – and all about her husband. But what blew my mind the most, was Andino's genuine amazement.

What's wrong with this crazed country, I wondered, and its hopeless obsession with the future, with its desperate yearning for some sense of certainty, of clarity, of hope, any sense at all? As if the future could give them their lives back, could bring them justice, and logic, and the forgotten taste of truth. My friend Andino was a professional tourist poacher, whom no one could ever con; he could smell bullshit a mile away. Rocio was, among other things, a rare free thinker, a true unspoiled intellectual who knew that obedience to logic might be as blind as submission to religion, and the irrational didn't have to be the road to evil. And yet, neither of them had any doubts whatsoever about the qualifications of these shady characters who claimed to see into their future. I came to Cuba for the present – fuck the future! I didn't ask for any redemption; God was in denial anyway. And on top of everything else was the heat, the hellish heat through which we drove back along the dusty, crumbling roads. The sun just wouldn't let go, mercilessly exposing everything in its path, banishing all dreams and illusions, and my brain was slowly melting.

"Listen, Roc," I said when we arrived at her place. "I have that salsa practice in Havana Vieja at around six o'clock with Gilberto Capote and the gang. Let me rest here for an hour, but wake me up at five, so I can make it there on time." She made up her bed for me, and I got right under the cool sheets, quickly sinking into the tranquility of her little bedroom.

—

She was already closing the door behind her when she turned her head back and asked: "By the way, what were the two questions you asked the woman?"

"Oh, that? Well, the first one was just something about mathematics, nothing really interesting. And the second one, if you must know – to which she answered "absolutely yes!" – was whether or not you were going to blow me this afternoon."

For a split second there, she seemed like a pillar of salt, as if she couldn't believe what she was hearing. And then she turned wild, like raging thunder, desperately stamping her foot in fury.

"How dare you? Even if this whole building were to fall on my head, I wouldn't do it!" (This was, mind you, a seven-story apartment building; we were up on the sixth floor). "Never in my life!"

"But why are you mad at *me*? You know I don't believe in that stuff. On the other hand, if *you* do, then you should already know you can't fool around with the future." She slammed the door behind her and I finally shut my eyes.

I wasn't counting, but I could swear no more than three minutes had passed before she opened the door quietly and came in and sat by me. She began to talk about all sorts of little things, which I always liked so much. Those were the priceless moments. She told me about Zunaiki, the cute mulatta next door, who was planning her upcoming wedding, together with the whole building, all day long. She said she was thinking of wearing her white dress to church on that day, and she asked me what

I thought. I thought she looked lovely in that dress and I told her so.

"You know how the heart sometimes wants something badly," she continued, "things that might not make any sense at all, even the most destructive things; and yet, we follow it to the end as if we must?"

I did know something about this.

"Maybe it's the part of us that somehow senses the future," she said. "And illogical as that fate might be for us, it takes us there simply because it has to."

I had come to Cuba for Alejo Carpentier's savage woman from the jungle, and instead I got myself a Madam Curie.

"I for one used to think it was just our endless stupidity," I said.

"Yes, that too, especially yours. I have never met an idiot like you."

"Neither have I," I confessed.

But all that time, the cool palms of the sweet philosopher by my side were traveling slowly under the sheets, playing secretly with my thirsty thighs below. The tender fingers wouldn't touch my rising rod, which was already shivering underneath in a
silent plea, only rubbing it a little unintentionally as her hands where passing by, which only made it even more intolerable.

"I will suck you now," she said, "but you cannot come in me."

"Whatever you say."

I was already on fire, but she was in no hurry, as if that was her little revenge, for everything. Her wet tongue was gently flying over each place she chose to tease, and caress, and spoil, moaning and melting into the sheer pleasure that was already consuming all of me. It was only when it became totally unbearable that she at last took it deep into her warm mouth. I felt her trying to suck out and possess everything I had in me, as I was slowly becoming my inflamed manhood. I was it, just it, rising strong and unbeatable inside her. I felt as if I was not only stroking her lips, but taking her all, the whole woman, again and again, for good. But indeed, she was the only one moving, with all her beautiful body, while I was still trying hard not to move a muscle, just let it all happen by itself, until I knew it was time.

I sank in between the supple, restless thighs, and then we moved together as close as we had ever been. There was nothing else I wanted but to see her happy. Her scream was almost unheard, but her thighs were still trembling a little, when I felt the wave within me coming, rolling throughout my entire body, and then gushing out inside her, taking away all I had left – the good and the bad – everything there was.

The roar that came out of my throat like a wild battle cry had the dogs down in the streets and yards howling back like crazy. I just burst into that silly liberating laugh which always comes over me when it's good. She was laughing too, especially at all that noise I was making.

And then time vanished. There was no death, no evil; only joy, nothing else. We were lying in each other's arms, and the sea of our hidden dreams carried us away. It took Spinoza 259 proven propositions to drive out time, to beat death, and fear, and anger – all that with just his Intellectual Love of God. But then again, what did Spinoza know about blow jobs?

It was a while before she spoke, and then time caught up with us again. "You have to get up now, *mi amor*, if you don't want to be late for class." She was rising slowly to sit in front of me for one more moment on her wide bed.

But she was still amused. "So, do you believe in *Santeras* now?"

"Actually, I am beginning to think there might be something to it," I admitted. "But you know, that wasn't really the question I asked the woman."

She was already getting up from bed when she turned back to me in an instant, sparks burning in her amazing black eyes, as if a venomous serpent had suddenly struck her from behind. For a moment there, I was sure that this time she was bound to kill me, and I knew I deserved it. Then she crashed backward on the bed in uncontrollable laughter which she just couldn't stop.

"Come back afterwards," she said as we kissed on my way out. "I have some chicken left; maybe I'll cook it with bananas." She was straightening my stupid Bolshevik hat.

"But what about that husband of yours?" I wondered.

—

84

The light in her eyes dimmed a little. "Forget about José," she sighed. "The truth is I couldn't stand him anyway. Maybe the woman doesn't know everything after all."

There she was, all alone at her doorstep, lost in the future – the good wife I would never marry. I kissed her smile again, and off I went, back into the raging fire outside.

It was day 27 since Nileisy left.

I had already lost any hope she would return before my trip was over, and I still wouldn't make the call.

But two days later, just like the black old witch had answered me in absolute certainty, she got on the morning bus from Ciego de Avila, and showed up at my door. She was carrying three red apples in her hands, as if she had just gone out for a minute to the market.

Then she wrecked my life.

# Marco on the Beach
## by Jessica Barksdale Inclan

Marco reaches into his pocket and puts his hand around the smooth wad of money his girlfriend Sara got from her uncle. The roll feels thick and slightly gritty, the rubber band stretched around it frayed to almost breaking. Next to it, the food stamp card clicks against his silver ring. It's the last of this month's food stamps, and Sara told Marco it was the last of her uncle's money, too.

His hand starts to sweat, and he pulls it out of his pocket, letting his long arms swing. Marco walks behind Sara, focusing on the squares of tile that open up like a stream between her feet and his. The shopping cart rattles like a pile of old bones as Sara clatters to a stop and reaches for the plastic bag, ripping it off the large wheel.

"Dammit," Sara says, as pippin apples spill across the grocery store aisle in a green fan. She bends down, trying to grab them, but Marco sees that she will never find a couple, one lodged under the melon stand, another behind a garbage can. He should kick them out from their hiding places, but he stands and watches the rest roll away. A store employee walks over, smiling the fake smile his boss hands him in the morning along with the green apron he wears.

"It's okay, ma'am," he says, picking up apples. "I'll get them."

Sara turns to Marco, shooting him a terrible look of hate. She's only twenty-five and must not have been ma'amed before.

---

"Ma'am?" she mouths.

"I'm getting some red wine," Marco says, walking toward the booze aisle.

"Don't get the totally cheap stuff," she says. "It gives me a haircut."

Marco stares at her, noting the dark half moons of smudge under her eyes. She hasn't been sleeping well at night, pulling the blankets over her, tossing them off, the bed an earthquake of quilts. Now she stares blankly at Marco, her expression empty for a second, as if her soul had been abducted by aliens. Then she's transported back. She shrugs, shakes herself, as if trying to find the right word inside her.

"I mean headache. It gives me a headache."

Marco nods, leaves her to the apples. He puts his hand in his pocket again, fingering the wad. He can only afford the cheap stuff, so he imagines that Sara isn't going to feel any better later than she does now.

He walks the aisle, seeing over the top into the next. In eighth grade, Marco was five foot two, compact, a soccer player in white shorts and cleats. But by the time he loped down the echoing high school hall as a freshman, he was nearly six feet tall, wearing all new clothes and size twelve shoes. On the day of graduation, he was six foot seven, and even eight years later, he's still not used to the length of his bones, part of him still that tiny guy not picked for basketball during seventh grade phys ed, the kid who could wear the same jeans for two years straight. When his friends drive him to meetings and political marches, he clambers into cars, hits his head on door jambs and on the tops of car cabins, smashing himself up to fit in, his knees pressed up into his chest in the tiny back seats.

"You unfold like a new moth," Sara said once to him as they got out of the car. He held his arms out to his sides, feeling more albatross than moth-like, able to take flight at any moment and stay aloft forever.

He's even too tall for shopping, having to bend down to look at all the bottles of cheap red wine, the kind that the store sells under stupid names. He pulls out a Napa Valley Pinot called Blue Truck, a 5.99 special, with a little card written by Chad, the employee of the month: "Lovely oak undertones with a raspberry and chocolate notes. A great deal!"

There are curlicues and little happy faces on the card, which make Marco want to steal the wine instead of paying for it, just to get back at Chad.

Marco stands straight, holds the Blue Truck in his hand, staring at nothing for a second but the cork ends of wine bottles. He feels angry about the spilled apples and the wine. He feels bad about the haircut, the headache, and the price of everything. He doesn't want to walk back to Sara and help her finish shopping. He might even want to take his stolen bottle of wine and their Mazda and leave the store, the parking lot, maybe even town. His long, lean body itches with desire, but then Sara is next to him. She's tall, too, her shoulder hitting his bicep. She smells like the produce aisle, sharp like pineapple rinds, ripe like tomatoes headed for the dumpster. Her fingertips probably feel like the skins of fallen pippins.

---

"It's not the cheapest?" she asks.

"No," Marco says. "Three tiers above migraine."

"Maybe it will just feel like a sinus infection," she says.

"What's this headache bit?" he says, forcing himself not to say *haircut*. "When did that start?"

Sara shrugs, takes the wine bottle, and puts it in their cart.

"It doesn't matter. I'm just not going to drink anymore."

"Why?" he asks, but she's already ahead of him, pushing the cart up the aisle toward dairy, a section they shop in now that Sara has given up on being a vegan. The two years of no eggs and cheese made Marco cranky and even thinner, though sometimes he would sneak out and have a steak at Sizzler. Sara would catch him, tell him that his sweat smelled of flesh and synthetic hormones, the kind they shoot into innocent calves the second they are born. She made him drink purifying teas and take baths in Epsom salts, his feet looking like pale, boiled prunes after the long soaks she prescribed.

But one day, Sara just looked at him across the table and said, "I want an omelet."

That was that.

Now, she loads up the cart with butter, cottage cheese, yogurt, and milk. Sometimes when they have some extra cash, she tells him to pick out a rib eye steak. "One that's marbled," she says. "No filets or strips."

Sara has started to crave fat, though she's as lean as Marco. When they lie flat on their backs in their bed, Marco often wonders if from above they look like flooring planks, long stretches of ash or oak or maple.

And lately, Sara seems to be craving more things with strong tastes: peppery arugula with roasted red beets and goat cheese, oily white anchovies from small, glass jars, Italian cheeses at room temperature slathered on black olive sour dough, the cheese so runny there's more need to pour than spread it.

"What about bread?" Marco asks, needing to get out of dairy, the so-white milk cartons and bottles and white dairy tubs of everything suddenly seeming like the segregated, white part of the south.

Sara nods and then begins to study the organic butter. Marco turns and strides down an aisle, turning right and then walking up, landing in front of the bread. He puts a hand on a loaf, feeling the soft girth under his palm. He knows he could squeeze hard and like that feeling, remembering the squish of Wonderbread in his hands. One year back in grammar school, he'd gotten his paws on a fresh loaf, probably at some kind of assembly titled "The Work People Do All Day" or something lame like that  He can still conjure the bread delivery man in his white uniform and stiff white hat standing on the stage, speaking to them about yeast and freshness. At the end of his fifteen minutes, he must have handed out free products to all the kids, the Wonderbread company banking on the realities of processed white flour addiction. That, and the Wonderbread bags were colorful, big red and blue balloon shapes, the name full of air.

———

That soft press of flour and eggs under the malleable plastic bag is fresh in his brain, this current loaf almost telling him to go ahead and *do it* like some animated Alice in Wonderbread story: *Squeeze me.*

Marco knows that bread murder is not looked upon kindly by the workers in the store, and probably the guy from the produce aisle would catch him and call the manager, who would dream of calling the cops to report a food murder. The truth is he and Sara should be arrested for a few things, that's for sure. Like using the FedEx number of a huge company to mail packages around the country: CDs to Marco's sister Rafaela and brother Fred. Like applying for and getting food stamps when they could be working instead. For embezzling money from Sara's uncle's janitorial supply company, small, steady amounts that fund their cravings for cheese, their Netflix account, and travel to a funky motel in Pismo Beach in the summer. Seventy-five dollars a night and an all you can eat breakfast buffet.

Marco slips his hand in his pocket again, feeling the last of all that good time under his palm.

But something will turn up. If there is a scam, he and Sara have surfed it to wave's end. If there is something to take, they have taken it. They don't steal close to home, but everywhere else, it's a matter of course. Wal Mart is like an oasis from poverty, a barn of goods offered up for the taking, shining, needed objects in heaps and piles. But even a Rite Aid will do, small items slipped into slick pockets. Marco chips away at the consumer culture by consuming for free.

—

One winter when Marco was home in the Bay Area visiting during the holidays, his mother Claire pulled him aside and told him, "Look, I don't want a stolen present. If you are going to give me something, make it. Or buy me nothing, okay?"

So instead of stealing picture frames and glittery earrings, he started giving her pencil sketches of the family home or making tomatillo salsa during get-togethers. And rather than stealing, he finds the shiny novels Claire likes when he dumpster dives at the mall, a bookstore now going bankrupt dumping a ton of books every month just because of little tears in the covers.

"Why don't you do something?" his mother asked. "You have a college degree, for god's sake, Marco. We always thought you'd—okay, I hate to say this—we thought you'd *be* something."

A couple of years back, this would have hurt his feelings, and he'd lash out at her. He'd argue, reciting all that he was doing and still is. He and Sara work at the free space they helped create with other local activists, a warm, dry cafeteria-sized place for the homeless to get a cup of coffee, a site for hourly babysitting for low income families. He writes for the local anarchist newspaper and helps deliver it to coffee shops and indie bookstores. He agitates. He goes to open meetings at city hall. He protests the war, military deployments, immigration laws. He reads, and at night, he writes long novels no one but Sara has read.

Marco knows he is something. He's someone, even if he is irritable.

"I'm 26," he finally told his mother. "I'm still doing this, so I think this is what I'm going to do forever."

When he spoke the words, they were true. He likes not working at a place, a company, a business, every single day his own to bend like a warm pretzel. Maybe the pretzel wasn't actually warm or even edible, but it was his.

There was no way to explain this to his librarian mother, and maybe she was as sick of the argument as he was. Now that he thinks about it, Marco hasn't talked to her in months. He hasn't spoken with his father or siblings either, he realizes, a fact that was nonexistent until it was *pow*, here, right now, as he stares at bread.

His stomach growls. He yanks up a loaf by its plastic neck and walks back toward Sara and the cart, ready to go home and eat.

Sara's favorite scent is patchouli. She sprinkles it in the water at the laundromat before the rinse cycle. Three laundromats have banned them, the next customers using their machines having complained.

"I smelled like a freaking hippie," Marco heard one lady whine. "Like I'd been smoking pot around back of a Quonset hut or something."

Sara switched to lavender after that, but now she's given up on both, their clothes smelling like nothing but clothes. As they sit at the table eating tuna sandwiches, Marco realizes that for the first time in years, he can smell his food and not his shirt.

—

"Tacoma is so over," she says, wiping her mouth and sitting back. She ate her entire sandwich in about three minutes, and now she seems kind of glazed, everything but her wide eyes wrapped in gauze.

Marco doesn't say anything because his mouth is full. They've lived in Tacoma since they graduated from Evergreen State College and moved out of Olympia, Olympia so over about three years ago. As far as he can see, Highway 101 connects the dots of the three Pacific Rim states. There's Seattle, Portland, San Francisco, and Los Angeles. Anywhere else in between the dots is so over, maybe never even was.

He swallows a gulp of Blue Truck and wishes he were drinking one of the flat but free beers he recovered from behind the Liquor Barn three nights before.

"Where do you want to go?" he asks.

"Sacramento," Sara says.

He blinks, takes another bite of his sandwich. Depending on the season, Sacramento is hot, flat, and ugly or foggy, flat, and ugly. It smells like canals and peat and seems like the end of the world, even though if you face east, it's just the beginning.

"Because of your mom?" Marco asks, putting down his sandwich, his stomach lurching from too much mayonnaise.

Sara nods, shrugs. "She says we can live in her rental. That one on 4$^{th}$ Street."

—

Marco graduated with a degree in English, so he's not a total idiot. It's clear that Sara has had preemptive and lengthy phone calls with her mother about this move that already seems to be in the works. Long divorced from Sarah's father Hal, Donna teaches anthropology at the university. All Sara's growing up years, she spent summers at digs in Umbria or on cultural missions to Cuba or South Africa. Donna's house presents as a multicultural knickknack exhibit; the living room alone is a mixed metaphor, a tract house room wearing a dashiki and Peruvian wool scarves, everything fluid and colorful but totally square in its tract-ness. And if Marco is honest, Donna looks as though she should be hawking Wonderbread, her hair a vivid, vibrant dark, lustrous orangey red, the color of a circus clown's nose.

But Donna is the only one of their four parents who asks about Marco's and Sara's projects. She's the only one who understands the system and the dehumanizing forces of societal control, slamming her palm on a flat hard surface when Marco tells her stories, yelling, "The goddamn pigs."

Unlike Claire, Donna throws back shooters of most adult beverages, can hold her liquor but not her tongue. Unlike Claire, Donna doesn't ask Marco what he's going to do with his life, seeming to assume he already has one.

If Marco had to be trapped in a broken elevator with anyone from his or Sara's family, he would pick Donna.

But move to Sacramento?

"Why do you suddenly want to leave Tacoma?" he asks and then takes another bite of his sandwich. Of course, he isn't sure most of the time why he's in Tacoma at all. Sometimes as he looks down Main Street, he thinks the bleak ugliness of the city makes him believe in the possibility of change. Nothing could look as gray and dreary and metallic as this forever.

"I'm pregnant," Sara says and she begins to weep the minute she's said the words.

Marco looks at her, knowing there are eighteen smart things he should do at this moment, but he can't think of the right one. He could lean over and grab her hand. He could get his ass up out of the chair, walk around the table, and pull her into his arms, just like all the douche bags do in movies. She would grab him around the shoulders, bury her head into him, her lips near his neck, the sound of her tears in his ear. He could say something like "That's wonderful," because it is, kind of, the miracle of life and all that. He feels that miracle, actually, a ripple of adrenaline inside him, the idea that they are going to have a baby.

But he's frozen on his chair, his mouth still full of tuna. He needs to swallow, so he does, but still words don't come. His legs won't move. He's frozen man in a stupid pose.

Now, he thinks. Do it. Do the right thing right now. Tell her you will move to Sacramento and live in Donna's rental. Tell her how happy you are. Tell her that you love her.

But Marco doesn't because only one of the above is true, and maybe not even.

As he watches her, he sees the old people they will be. They will sit at another table the same way, eating the same kind of food, probably. They will have an okay house in a marginal part of some flat, foggy town. Maybe Stockton, maybe Lodi. Their two kids—they will have another after this first unwanted one—will have left the house, moved on to things better because their Grandma Donna left them college money. Marco's mother took the kids on vacations after Marco's father died, Marco's kids knowing more about Europe than he ever will.

Marco's hair has fallen out just like his grandfather's, giving him that Friar Tuck look. Sara has grown thinner, paler, and started smoking outside after dinner about ten years into their wedding in South Lake Tahoe. Her lips have that lined, skinny woman pucker. The only thing in this view that still seems like Sara are her gray eyes, but at this future table, she's always pissed off at Marco, so her gaze at him is dark. After moving to Donna's rental, Marco went back to school for his teaching credential, his entire career spent at the local junior high school teaching kids the five paragraph essay.

He doesn't think about changing the world with words or creating a new society based on communal goals anymore. He doesn't write his novels, and he doesn't steal, though Wal Mart still gives him itchy palms.

On the weekend, he watches television and plays pool with his best friend Joe in the basement.

He's still tall of course, but he lugs around a basketball sized stomach over his belt.

He turned into his father, but not as successful. Or even as nice.

Marco's new life moves with Power Point efficiency, ending with shots of the urn on the shitty mantel in his and Sara's shitty house. After a year of wedded bliss, her second husband takes the urn and puts it in the garage next to Marco's old textbooks and propaganda. The urn grows dingy and, during an earthquake one hot summer afternoon, it tips over Marco spilling onto the garage floor in a plume of gray dust.

Marco's heart pounds against his ribs, his throat dry. His feet feel very large on the floor, as though he were wearing skis. Sara's still weeping, so there's time for him to save things. He can go toward her and make her happy or he can push his chair back and walk out of the kitchen, the house, the city, the state. He can take Highway 101 down the coast, landing on the dot that most appeals. Maybe Los Angeles. He can apply to graduate school and write a screenplay about his ragged, anarchical Tacoma life. He can become famous and write more scripts and live in Malibu. He can give into the lure of society and roll around in it like it was bacon fat. Marco imagines the girlfriends he will have, all blonde and not as tall as Sara. He will get a vasectomy as soon as he makes his first million. He will start producing movies, too, and people will call him about how to make the fake look real. Marco knows how to do this, so he'll become the go-to guy for advice.

Every Oscar night, his films will win awards, and the stumbling nervous famous people on the stage will thank him. Meanwhile, he'll drink a beer on the beach in a comfy lounge and watch rain on the winter sea. And

—

that's how he will die, Marco, on the beach, his maid finding him in the morning, the beer gone, a smile on his face.

As he listens to Sara cry, the man in his head bats the air with his hands, searching for the gray answer, the one in the middle, the answer that Goldilocks would pick, something just right. Neither teacher nor screenwriter, not poor or rich, not famous or just nothing. Doing something but not everything. Changing the world but only one day at a time.

Who is that gray, middle Marco? Where is the Marco who doesn't squish the Wonderbread but doesn't eat it either? Where is the man who would walk into a business, hang up his jacket, and get to work?

Sara lifts her head, the question in her eyes. She waits for him to do something. So does Marco, his breath caught in his body, the answer one exhale away.

# Peek-a-boo
## by Agnieszka Dale

Maja was conceived during the spin cycle of our Hotpoint WT965 twenty-one months ago. When I left her at the nursery this morning – our first day apart – I could not stop sobbing. Now I want to see her again.

My left nipple is stone hard. I go to the toilet to express some milk. More milk comes into my breasts. But it does not flow out. They say a picture of your baby can help you to relax. I haven't got any with me. I look at the photo of the first scan that I keep in my wallet. My little Maja, the size of a hand, is blowing raspberries at us, or waving. Although the midwife said "baby" was scratching its nose.  If only the nursery staff were as helpful as midwives. But once the child is born, nobody gives a damn, it seems.

The picture of the first scan does not do the trick. If only I could find a way to log into the nursery webcam… I try again and again but my browser crashes every time. My stomach feels like a washing machine spinning at 1000 rpm. Don't get me wrong. I like my washing machine. It's my favourite domestic appliance. We used to make love on top of it, but now that I'm a mother a bed seems more appropriate.

It seems odd to be back at my desk.  The other mothers look me up and down to check if my stomach has gone back to its original size. The men look at my enlarged bosom. It feels intrusive. Do they also want to know if the sexual relations with my partner have returned to normal? How can anything ever be normal again? I call the helpdesk and ask if they could assist me to log into the nursery webcam. The man on the other side – I think his name is Adam – agrees a bit too readily. Is it because he thinks I'm a yummy mummy or he finds me disgustingly mumsy and wants to get rid of me?

"Your computer account has been locked out," he says.

"There are countless webcam sites on the Internet with cameras pointed at virtually everything. A lot of them are porn sites. You are not allowed to watch websites with embedded video streams at work, I'm afraid." His voice is sweaty like he's in the middle of watching a peep show. He sounds Slovakian in the way he rolls his r's when pronouncing "porn."

"*Kurwa mać!*" I swear more now that I'm a mother.

Adam laughs.

"Polish?"

"*Tak.*"

He logs me on.

Here is Maja. I can only see her feet and arms as Sarah, to whom I handed Maja over this morning, obstructs everything else. She looks like a former prison guard. I wave to Maja but she does not see me. Here is Mummy, I say. Look at Mummy. Mummy can see you. She is holding a piece of apple in one hand and playing with her shoe in the other. They really should not let her eat and touch her shoe at the same time. The shoe is mucky, Maja. Put it away, please. She is no longer wearing her socks inside her shoes. She will have blisters on her feet!

Before I can see any blisters, the video stream starts breaking and my computer crashes.

I try to log in again but Internet Explorer crashes every time I do it. I call the nursery.

"Could you please put the socks back on Maja's feet," I say.

"But she is very unhappy with her socks on," says Sarah. A short silence follows.

"Put the bloody socks on," I say, my stomach turning at 1200 rpm. Before she can answer back, I put the phone down.

I call Adam and explain my computer problem.

He logs me back on. A rinse cycle kicks in and I manage to relax a little.

"One more time, and you'll have to pay me," he says.

"How much?"

"It's not about money," he says.

Sarah has finally moved, too, and I can see Maja. She turns her head to the left and looks me straight in the eye. My left breast starts filling up with milk even more, until it feels like a full bladder. I put my nose against the screen and wave to her. She giggles and waves back. She comes closer to the camera and turns her head to the left. I slowly lift up my shirt and put the breast against the screen. She opens her mouth and latches on.

My brain is melting. I feel like a giant soft toy, a teddy with a bosom.

After a minute or two, Maja unlatches. I sit back.

"Could you restart your computer for me, please," says Adam. His looks match his voice. He is cross-eyed.

I look down at my shirt. It's got two wet patches. Maja is gone. It's midday and she's having her nap now. At home we would be cuddled up together on the sofa snoozing, with the washing machine finishing its first song of the day.

***

I sneak out of work three minutes early, at three minutes to four. There is no need to rush to get my train but a casual stroll seems wrong without a pushchair. I run to the station and then wait on the platform for ten minutes. I check the train schedule several times. Mummy is coming, Maja, Mummy is on her way.

By the time my train arrives, the tips of my fingernails are all chewed.

We stop at Crystal Palace for a good five minutes. I look at the long grass in between the unused railway tracks. Either its length or the fact that it's growing so randomly in a public place reminds me of home where there are still bits of grass growing freely.

Over ten years ago, my then-boyfriend said that he would like me not to shave my armpits for a while, as it would remind him of another place

"You want me to have a fanny under each armpit? That makes two fannies. Three if you count the other place."

He got cross with me. A month later we broke up. He was a dentist from Krakow in his thirties while I was a twenty-two-year-old student from Warsaw. I still think, how odd he did not laugh. What a freak. Erik would laugh.

I get off at Forest Hill. It's only been forty-five minutes since I last went to a toilet but I need to go again.

"Sorry, Milka, the toilets are locked. We're having a drainage problem," says Trish, a French Canadian acquaintance of mine. She owns the pub next to the station. I know her from my birthing classes at Guy's Hospital.

"No worries, I think I can hold on for a few more minutes. How is your bump?" I ask. She looks better in her second pregnancy but I don't tell her that. I know what she will say: "It's because this time it's a boy. Daughters take away a mother's good looks and boys bring them back."

"My bump is fine but I hate not seeing a doctor in my pregnancy. Women, women everywhere. I wish there was a *midhusband* of some sort that I could see," she scratches her bump as if it was a buttock.

I nod. It is better not to mess with pregnant women. They can be aggressive.

"In Canada, midwives are much more helpful," she says. For Trish, everything is better in North America. That's where she gave birth to her daughter. She was highly medicated during the delivery. High on gas'n'air, she was dancing to rock'n'roll.

The nursery is only two minutes up the road and I tell myself, you can do it, you can hold on for a few more minutes. It reminds me of the point of delivery when I had to push Maja out, only now it's the opposite; I need to push in, keep things inside me. I can't decide which is worse.

Finally, through the window, I can see Maja playing with a teddy. Both of my breasts start filling up with milk. How much more milk can they fit in? I'm about to be drowned by all the liquids produced by my own body. The inside of my stomach is sweating and I can't even wipe that sweat off. It's like laundry taken out of a tumble drier after five minutes, still damp, but hot. As soon as Maja sees me, she starts crying.

"Did she have a good day?" I shout to Sarah but she can't hear me. Maja screams louder and louder as if I wasn't her mother but an abductor. I give her a big hug but that does not help. I sniff her bottom through her Mothercare baby jeans and say to Sarah, "I think that she needs her nappy changing." I then sniff Maja's head. It smells of another woman's perfume. I rush into a nappy changing room and close the doors behind me. Maja gives me a big smile. I smile back.

"I missed you so much today," I say.

Maja giggles. I'm never too sure about how much of what I say she understands. I look inside her nappy with relief. At least she had something to eat today. Or is it yesterday's dinner?

The pressure on my bladder becomes so strong that I have to release it that second. I look around the room: it's full of changing tables but not a single toilet. I reach out for a pile of Maja's nappies and place one of them next to the changing matt. I open it; lay it on the floor and squat above it. Maja's face lightens up. I'm amazed that at twelve months she gets the joke. This nappy is unbelievably absorbent.

"Maja cried all day long," says Sarah when I meet her at the corridor. She pauses and scratches her head. I catch a glimpse of unshaven armpit.

"Does she get enough TLC at home?" she finally asks.

"Yes, and I still breastfeed her," I say.

"At twelve months? She does not need it."

The doorbell rings and seven other mothers walk in. The place is suddenly too crowded. I turn around and walk towards the doors. Maja and I get into our Ford Fiesta. We pull out.

I want to go home-home. See my mama. Maybe we should drive there tonight? To Dover and then over the Channel… Have I brought enough nappies with me to last us for thirty-six hours? I thought once I had a family it would all get easier. But having my own family makes me miss everyone back home even more. Maja falls asleep and my eyes become watery. I turn on the windscreen wipers as if it is raining.

She wakes up when I stop the car. As soon as we enter the house, I run a bubble bath. I undress and get into the bath, too. The dimples on her cheeks become deeper, like my mama's, when she smiles; she starts splashing the water around her and I join her.

I always wanted to give birth to Maja in a bath. Instead, I was induced; tied to a bed. Pushing hard to a deadline. And then, peek-a-boo, she was out. My first thought after was: I don't ever want my daughter to suffer the pain of giving birth.

"*Kaczka*," says Maja pointing at the duck floating on top of the largest bubble.

I look at her and can't quite believe my ears. Her first word! She did not learn that from Sarah-three-fannies. Or anybody else, but from me, her Mummy.
The tiles in the bathroom are now brighter orange. The duck is more yellow then a minute ago. I close my eyes and sniff Maja's head, inhaling the smell of her lemony down.

\*\*\*

The following morning it is too sunny to be driving. We leave the Fiesta in the garage and walk instead.

We pass a pigeon on the road, flattened by a car.

"*Kaczka*," says Maja.

She leans out of her pram, points at a yellow flower, a dog, a cat, and later a squirrel. They all have the same name: a duck. In fact, everything is a *kaczka*.

"I've got some good news for you," says Sarah when we enter the room where Maja will spend her day, like a prisoner.

"We have a Polish nurse starting today. If you want, he can speak Polish to Maja."

"A man?"

"Yes, from Krakow, like you."

I'm not from fucking Krakow. The doors open. It's Bohdan, my ex-boyfriend. He smiles. Maja returns his smile.

My stomach doesn't like surprises. It now feels like a heavily overloaded washing machine drum. My knees bend. I readjust Maja's shoelaces.

I can't possibly leave Maja with him. He must be well over forty now but he doesn't look it.

"You? In London? A nurse?" I ask in Polish rising from the floor.

"I met this English girl. I'm taking a year off to be with her. I could not find a job as a dentist in London but they said that, in the meantime, I could be a nurse."

I jam my arms by my sides to hide my armpits even though I shaved them last night. Maja wants to join in the conversation.

"*Kaczka*," she points at me and laughs.

"I'm not a *kaczka*, I'm your mama," I say.

Bohdan laughs. Sarah giggles, too, even though – I'm pretty damn sure – she doesn't know what the hell is going on. A little boy playing with a toy tractor joins in. Then another toddler in yellow overalls. Soon the whole room is laughing. I'm the only one who isn't. I look at my watch. I'm running late. I excuse myself and go to the toilet. I give my husband a ring.

"Erik? It's me," I say. "Maja's new babysitter. I know him. I used to go out with him. I know his sexual fantasies... He is a bit twisted."

"In what way?" asks Erik. I tell him about the armpits. I can hear him smile. I smile back and I'm sure that he can hear it, too.

"Don't worry, love, he is not there alone with her. And you can watch them via webcam. Invite him over for dinner at the weekend," he says and I feel better.

I give Maja a hug. I kiss her fragrant head good-bye. When I reach the door, I stop to look back. She is climbing into Bohdan's lap and doesn't even register that mama is leaving her.

\*\*\*

On the train I catch a glimpse of myself in the window. My face looks pale and I must have forgotten to brush my hair this morning. I find an old lipstick at the bottom of my bag and some mascara in the left pocket of my coat.
I put some lipstick on. A woman smelling of lavender lifts up her head from behind *Metro*. She looks at my lips.

Her eyes say: "goes well with your coat." I want to hug her.

I bump into Adam, the IT guy, in the elevator.

"I found a spare desktop computer operated by Windows. I left it next to your Mac. It should work better with webcams." He winks at me twice. He looks even more cross-eyed than the day before.

The computer is a bit old and slow but I manage to log in. Maja and Bohdan are playing peek-a-boo. He covers his eyes and then opens them and says "Boo." Except, he is doing it head down, looking at her from between his legs, hiding his head behind his muscular Krakow thighs – lifting one of them up whenever he says "boo", like he is operating some kind of heavy piece of machinery. I think of Erik when he jumps around playing with Maja, effortlessly, like a grasshopper dancing with a bee. Bohdan's face is red from being upside down, and from trying too hard. It's the first time it occurs to me how odd it must feel for him; no longer in total control – fixing teeth, making his patients sit still for hours. I almost feel sorry for him.

What really drove him to leave a good job back home; to come to London and make no money – working as a nurse?

A woman. What kind of woman, I wonder.

Maja gets bored with this game quickly. She approaches him and starts pulling his curls. She then gets a colour pencil and sticks it into his left ear. At first it almost feels good to be watching her hurt him a little. All this time he does not react, as though he is now her patient, sitting on a dentist chair and waiting for his tooth to be pulled. I can't decide if he is doing it because he is kind or because he is so helpless. Maybe he doesn't know it himself. His stillness is now so irritating that I can't watch it any more. I log out.

*\*\**

When I pick her up from the nursery after work, she is not in her usual "Pandas" room.

I take the stairs down and find her in the back garden. She is sitting in a little red car, being pushed around by Bohdan. She waves to me with her right hand, while her left hand is still on the wheel, steering. She looks surprisingly grown up. He looks knackered.

"How was her day?"

"Great. Had a fabulous day. A lot of kids were off sick today so we spent a lot of time together."

I take her out of the car and give her a hug. She is wearing a sticker on her chest, like a medal. It says: "I ate all my dinner."

"Would you like to come over to dinner at ours?" I ask him.

"Would love to."

"Saturday at six o'clock?"

"Yeah, I'm free then."

"Would you like to bring your girlfriend?"

Maja starts wriggling. She points at the doors making short, loud sounds: "OR! OR! OR!"

\*\*\*

At five o'clock on Saturday Bohdan sends me a text message saying that his girlfriend, Polly, can't make it. Too late, I've already cooked for the four of us. When he arrives, it feels a bit surreal to have him in our house. As I take his coat, I'm trying to remember what loving him felt like.

"Nice parquet floors," he says. "My house in Krakow is a bit like that only bigger."

"Is it worth a lot less than houses in London?" Erik asks.

"I wouldn't be so sure. With the pound going down and the value of zloty rising…"

"Is that why so many Polish people are going back home now?"

"It's not just that. Most Polish men prefer to settle with Polish girls. And vice versa."

Bohdan is wearing tight black leather trousers that make a funny noise when he sits back in his chair, like a quiet fart. Whether or not it was wind or Bohdan's trousers making a noise, Erik looks amused.

"Are you always so generous with your Baltic wind?" Erik asks Bohdan.

"It's my trousers," says Bohdan. "But I can fart. Freely. Something to do with my diet of cabbage," he says.

"The English are silent but deadly," says Erik.

"So when you fart, where do you do it? Alone, in the bathroom, like a wank, or silently, for example on a train full of commuters?" asks Bohdan, laughing. They don't say anything to each other for a good thirty seconds.

"And do you fart before, during or after intercourse?" says Erik.

Bohdan stops laughing. I suddenly feel the urge to leave the house and look at them through a window. Maybe Bohdan would push Erik and – if I wasn't watching – Erik would hit him across his face. Would it make me forget about myself, about motherhood with its million little acts of violence a day, none of them significant, or even noticeable, like a ladder in a stocking or a broken fingernail? And then, when they stopped, would there be a moment of silence?

Bohdan's mobile rings. He spends ten minutes on the phone to Janka, his sister in Poland, a filmmaker, who just got European Union funding to make a new project.
Erik eats two bowls of soup and nothing else. Bohdan devours three bowls of barszcz and then eleven dumplings. All this time we talk about either our Maja or Bohdan's sister – and how clever they are. It feels like Janka and Maja should be related. Forty minutes later, Bohdan says that it's time for him to make a move.

"Thanks. It was great to meet you, finally," he says to Erik and shakes his hand.

---

113

"*Ciao*," he says to me and kisses me three times: left cheek, right cheek, left cheek.

*** 

That night Erik and I don't clear the table but go straight to bed.

Except, we don't quite get there. We put the empty washing machine on, and by the time it's spinning, I can feel its white metal doors open wide below me, the soapy warm water spilling everywhere, like warm waves of milk, coming in and out, again and again and again.

When the rinse cycle finishes, I turn around and see Maja's teddy on the kitchen counter. It gives me a dirty, cross-eyed look.

My left breast starts filling up.

# Flipflops in Thunderstorms
## by Jonathan Okwe-Pearson

I always felt I had a lot to express, but I was not gifted. I could appreciate art, liked poetry, but I was not talented. I was starting to think my "artist trying to find herself" image was exhausting, and my contempt for "normal" values, pretentious. So I became normal, moved to London, and a little bit of me died inside.

Bow-on-Thames was not a nice place. Despite the re-generation programme to coincide with the Olympic site only a mile away, it felt like the graveyard of my dreams. Black trees were strewn with grey plastic bags and brown audio tape, while youths in expensive trainers were dragged around by vicious looking dogs. My new house, fortunately, was away from the busy high street, in a relatively quiet cul-de-sac. "A haven" my elderly neighbours had remarked earlier that day when they saw me heaving my boxes of books and clothes into the house. "You're very lucky to find a place like this!" they chirped over their fence. I wasn't so sure. My exploration of Bow had lasted half an hour, before I was barked at by a pack of boys at a bus stop, and asked, "Do you want to go halfers on a bastard?"

"No thank you," I replied in a sing-song.

"Stupid slut," came the reply.

Later that evening, I received my second welcome.

"We've come to officially welcome you to the neighbourhood," said my elderly neighbour with a flash of yellowing, crooked teeth, two deep dimples and a folding of skin around the eyes. He thrust a warm bottle of white wine and a packet of KP nuts into my chest. His wife smiled infectiously.

"Why, well, thank you. I certainly didn't…this is lovely. I'm touched," and then, seeing their expectant faces, "Would you like to come in?" I tried to forget about the cooling cup of tea and the candles I had left around the bath. The doorbell had disturbed the first night in my new house. Although I had tried to ignore the ringing, my neighbours demanded attention.

"Oh no dear," the woman said, "you look like you're busy, we just wanted to say hello, not to bother. We'll call round for a cup o' tea another time? We're Sally and Graham McGregor. Welcome!" She was a mousy looking woman, compact and smiley. Her voice was the type you could listen to all day, lyrical and light with a Scottish lilt. Coming to say hello was a lovely touch, but I was relieved they declined my invitation to come in.

"And I'm Stacey Blackstock, a pleasure to meet you both." And then they were gone, shuffling arm in arm to their plot, before I heard their door shutting in the near distance.

I had not intended to specifically move to Bow. After trying and failing to become an artist, author, poet, architect, dancer, musician, holiday rep and travel writer, I had finally decided to use my nursing degree and get a "normal" job. I needed to grow up. After amassing an eye-watering travelling debt, seeing the desperate job situation in Lancashire and living back with my parents for three months, it was either relocation, or suicide.

I had always wondered why people moved to London when they could live in Madrid, Barcelona, or Lisbon, far prettier places where it didn't rain for three hundred days of the year. I thought I could avoid the capital, live in sunnier climes, carve identities for myself as I went. I remembered those thoughts as I stacked my Almodovar DVDs onto the shelves in the biggest room my meagre budget could afford – a 'box-room' in the description. Less of a room, more of a box.

I applied for nursing jobs in London on a whim, thinking it would take me closer to theatres, museums, espressos at breakfast and mimosas at lunch. I received an invitation for an interview, and two weeks later, I had put my guitar away, tied my hair up, and swapped my dreams for compromises. For the first time, I felt responsible. I was prepared and maybe even looking forward to worrying about a pension, wearing sensible shoes and talking about the rising price of bread (shocking!). And if that meant dragging drips, and cleaning bed pans, so be it. Anyway, it was late summer; I was young, single and employed. My new job at St. Andrews hospital began on Monday. In the meantime, I had the weekend to relax, acclimatise and explore. My two Spanish housemates were away for the weekend. I had the house to myself.

My tea had cooled, but the candles flickered invitingly as I slipped back into the warmth of the bath, the soap suds licking my neck, the bubbles bursting in my ear. Sirens and birdsong floated into the bathroom through the open windows, the net curtains fluttered and the candles danced in the breeze. London may turn out to be okay after all, I thought, sliding further into the water, and after another sip of tepid tea, twisted the top off the wine.

"Oh, I'm sorry dear," Mrs McGregor cooed as I answered the door the next morning, "did we wake you?" I squinted at her through the sunshine and the hangover.

"No, no, I was just…doing some tidying up, lots of boxes from the move you know." She craned her neck to look over my shoulder to see the empty corridor behind me.

"Ahh, I see. I wondered if we might pop in for that cup o' tea?" I may have winced at that point as she added, "only if convenient for you though?" My brain tried and failed to think of appropriate excuses.

"Of course, come in!" I squealed, without a sniff of protest.

Once tea had been distributed in a wide variety of mismatching beakers, I received a volley of pleasantries about the grubby kitchen and the house as a whole. Mrs McGregor draped an admiring finger across the crusty furniture, and beamed before she sat down, her eyes narrowing on me.

"Now Stacey, I know you have just moved in, and we feel dreadful to ask … the thing is, we need a favour."

"Of course," I knew the wine and nuts were too good to be true. "What is it?" Mrs McGregor shuffled slightly in her seat and looked to her husband who gave her an encouraging smile.

"You see, dear," she started, smoothing the plaits of her skirt, "We're in a bit of a situation. We won a competition you see, in a magazine."

"That's wonderful, what sort-" I started.

"A cruise," he cut in again.

"We sent in a piece, "two hundred words or less, about the secret to happy marriage", and well, we won." Mrs McGregor arched an eyebrow over the top of her purple frames.

"Wow, that's amazing!" I said with genuine surprise.

"When do you go?"

"Tomorrow," Mr McGregor said solemnly, as they both looked down to their shoes. I had an inkling as to what was coming.

"Well that's wonderful, and if you're worried about your house, of course I'll keep and eye on it for you, no bother."

"Oh no dear," said Mrs McGregor. "It's not that, the house can look after itself. You see-" they exchanged anxious glances, "you see, it's our dog."

"Your dog?"

"Dougall, name's Dougall," said Mr McGregor, his chest puffing a little with pride.

"Ok and what's the problem with Dougall?"

---

"Nothing at all, he's a very good boy, but we've no one to look after him. We've no children and our friends are too far away." A pang of sympathy twisted in my chest, "He really is a lovely pup, no trouble at all, wouldn't hurt a fly-"

"Oh, I'm sorry Mrs McGregor, I couldn't possibly…"

"Please. Call me Sally," she said through the smile of a geriatric angel.

"Sally, I couldn't, I'm starting work at St. Andrews on Monday, and I won't have the time to walk him or…"

"He doesn't need walking, dear, he's very happy in the home." They both nodded earnestly. "Just fed and watered twice a day and let out to do his business when you get back from work. In fourteen years, we took him for one walk, and he got a cold, never again and he's fine."

"But, I'm not sure about my housemates, they're away for now but will be back Monday…"

"The Spanish couple? They're lovely aren't they… It's only a week, dear, we'll be back next Monday, the time will fly by."

My mind, still half asleep, was struggling to keep up with the situation, and was failing to come up with any viable excuses.

"Please dear, it would be our first holiday in thirty years."

Sally McGregor's watery eyes looked tired. She looked like she had been waiting to ask me this question all her life.

"But… but what if he hates it here?" I stumbled. Mr. McGregor returned stood to make the introduction.

"This…is Dougall."

What entered, dragging a soggy pillow in its teeth, was the most threadbare, worn, tired looking animal I had seen in my life. He looked like a hairy ironing board. His eyes were bloodshot, half closed. His coat was matted, grey and damp. He barely walked, more flopped one foot in front of the other, as if he were dragging the weight of East London behind him. Dougall waddled over to me, dropped his pillow, sniffed my shoes and licked my laces, gave a single swipe of his tail and lay down next to my feet.

"He likes you," said a beaming Mrs. McGregor, who exchanged one final conspicuous look with her husband. Knowing that I should say no, I agreed.

\*\*\*

Dougall was a positive addition to my life and fitted perfectly into my routine – In the morning, I would let him deposit into our little garden while I had a shower. We would breakfast together before work and he would welcome me back from the hospital with a single swipe of the tail, before collapsing on my feet to watch foreign films. He provided more companionship than my two Spanish housemates, who were entirely apathetic about our existence. By the end of the week, I had seen them only once as they were coming home from a night out and I was leaving for work. They were not the artistic, intelligent, considerate Catalonians I had dreamed of, and after I was rudely awoken by a thumping headrest in the middle of the night, it became clear it was me and the dog against the continental Europeans. They probably felt betrayed by me – In my housemate profile, I had detailed my love of art, music, literature, and said I was a 'fun-loving girl who LOVED [yes I did capitalise] to party.' So far I had moved my few possessions (alone) into a cramped shoe box, brought a dog along, gone to work, hadn't 'partied' once and had started conversing with the elderly neighbours. I screamed spinster.

I decided I would kill them with kindness and planned to cook a meal to break the ice. I was desperate to show them my cultural richness, tell them about my 'crazy' travels and explain about the dog. I would explain that London wasn't permanent and how I had dreams of living in Valencia or Salamanca. I would charm them with my knowledge of Gaudi, Don Quixote and Antonio Banderas. We would talk, drink Rioja until late and make plans to visit their parents in Zaragoza or Bilbao, or wherever. I would do my profile justice; show them the real me.

*** 

My body clock had adjusted too well to the early starts, and despite my desire for a sleep-in, I found myself in the kitchen, making breakfast at 6:30am on a Saturday. I popped into the neighbourhood Spar to pick up some food, withdrew my last ten pounds- thank goodness I was getting paid on Monday- and chose my ingredients to impress the surliest of Spaniards. The food, some

Pedigree Chum and a Twix took me up to £9.23. That meant I had 77p to last me the weekend. It was going to be a quiet one.

It was a beautiful morning in Bow. A dramatic Autumn sunrise cast impressive ochres and crimsons across the underside of silent clouds. Trees had started to reveal their bones, and shivered in the breeze. The first real chill of September was in the air and I felt my body contract under the thin layer of my T-shirt. Leaves danced with crisp packets and sycamore seeds and chased each other in circles before being blown against a set of iron railings. As I turned the corner to the entrance of the cul-de-sac, I realised I was smiling.

The lights were off when I returned home. I pushed the door open with my bum, and backed into the hallway to hear the house phone click onto the answer phone.

"Hi Sophie…[whisper in background] Stacey, it's Manuel and Angelica. Hope you are okay. We are both very sorry, but we are not going to be back for your food this evening. We've been invited to a festival in Brighton, so we've left for that… [whisper in background] we are sorry to miss your food. See you on Monday…[whisper in background] Oh, Angelica asks if you could put the bins out. Thanks."

I dropped the bags on the floor and let the anger build. Ignorant… inconsiderate… selfish… little… I let out a short sharp scream which bounced off the hard surfaces in the hallway, counted to ten, and regained composure. Silence settled in the house. The crackle of my collapsing shopping bags provided the only noise. Where was Dougall? I called out his name, and again, the bags contracted and quietness hummed. I moved into the kitchen trying to remember if I had left the door open, whether the Spaniards may have stolen him, or whether he was just in a different room. It was then I saw him, curled up next to the oven door, his legs stretched out away from his body like cocktail sticks stuck in a sausage. The hair on his underbelly was damp, his chest was still, his tongue hung out of his gaping mouth. I edged closer to him, expecting him to jump up, hoping, praying he was asleep. But his chest remained still. I put my shoe under his nose which was dry and cracked, urging him to sniff. Nothing. A wave of realisation and nausea hit me like a closing door. I dropped to my knees and my vision started to wobble with tears. I touched his cold neck and let his hair slip through my fingers like falling sand. His half open eyes looked up at me, as lifeless and grey as his ragged coat. I knew. Dougall was dead.

As I looked at his body, limp and frail, my brain wrestled with the situation. I couldn't decide which emotion to confront first. The dreadful guilt? The responsibility? The shame? How would I be able to tell the McGregors? How would I be able to look them in their beautiful, giving, caring faces? Their first holiday in thirty years to return to this? Tears began to run freely down my cheeks and collect in the wells of my collar bone. They were tears of guilt, but also, tears of sadness. It was the deep and heavy sadness of losing a friend, a companion. Had it only been an hour since his face rested in my lap as I ate my cereal? Was it only a day since we had watched that Woody Allen film and his tail seemed to swish at the poignant moments? Was it only a week since he had entered my life? Dougall, so still and so dead. My stomach knotted with loss. I sat and hugged the old mutt, fat tears dripped down my chin onto his thin coat, his hair clumping like wet candy-floss. The dog had been my only friend in London. I had told him about my loves, my dreams, my fears and he had listened. He was the closest thing I had to a confidante, and now, he was gone. His neck hung loosely over my shoulder, his smelly, dense body resonated with my desperate whimpers and heaving, sobbing shoulders. The clock on the kitchen wall ticked and tocked with my sniffs and I realised, I was alone.

***

"Poor Dougall," continued Dr. Mire, "a fine animal, I know him for a long, long time, yes?"

"Yes," I sniffled down the phone, "I'm not sure what I should do."

"Well my dear," his somewhere-in-Europe accent rattled the R, "I'm afraid there is not much you can do, yes? The dog...it is dead." Dr. Mire's bedside manner needed a little refining.

My vision began to blur again.

"You can bury the dog yourself, either in the garden of the owners, or your own garden, but it cannot be on public land. No parks, no golf courses." His voice snapped like ice. "The risk then is that your choice of burial position may not be the preference of the owners, yes?"

"Yes, I'm not sure I could live with-"

"The only other choice," he interrupted, "Is to bring the deceased down to our surgery and we can put the dog on ice, yes? This way, the cadaver will be preserved until the owners return, and they will be able to decide what to do with the animal. Knowing the McGregors as I do, I think this would be their choice."

That sounded like a fine idea, it seemed the right thing to do. The McGregors could then see Dougall in state, and make a decision on his final resting place. I thanked Dr Mire for his professionalism and intelligence, said I would be across as soon as possible, and hung up the phone.

I looked at Dr. Mire's "In Case of Emergency" card again and realised I hadn't asked where the surgery was. I flipped it over. Tooting. Bollocks.

With no money, car, or friends with cars, how could I get Dougall across London by five o'clock? Surely... no... I couldn't... I sprinted upstairs and pulled my suitcase from the top of the wardrobe, shook out my snorkel, mask and fins, and returned to the kitchen. I lifted the cold dog into the case, and pushed him into the corners, his pebble-dash hair hanging in the teeth of the zipper. He was a large, awkward shape and I had to bend his back and legs into all sorts of unusual positions before the bag closed. There was something so wrong about forcing a dog into a suitcase, something so imbalanced and abstract about it. I imagined Salvador Dali brainstorming a dog-in-a-suitcase idea before deciding on his lobster-phone. I felt ill. My head swam with emotion my stomach groaned in protest. I looked at the suitcase, and could see Dougall's joints through the canvas, protruding like hastily packed holiday cosmetics. I carried the case to the door, banging it into the sofa and dinner table before resting it by the frame. The exertion left me panting and nauseous and I rushed to the bathroom to be sick. I hugged the toilet and cried. I was at my lowest ebb. Alone, mourning and accepting that I would have to take Dougall on the Tube.

\*\*\*

The Hammersmith and City and District lines were off at the weekend, so I had waited thirty minutes in the rain for the 425 to arrive, and now at Bank, joined the heaving masses of soggy tourists, limp teenagers and damp ticket touts, the suitcase clipping heels and knees with tuts and huffs as I passed. I had let two packed tubes pass me by, impossibly full with steaming adults. The doors opened and I was given glares that said 'don't even think about it.' I felt the infamous 'London rage' begin to rise. When the third train slowed to a stop, I gripped the handle of my suitcase and pushed my way onto the train as the warning tone sounded, crushing me against the back of an enormous man. People usually yield a little when they get a push in the back, but this man didn't budge. My face was planted against his spine, my lips on his shirt - I could taste his sweat and feel the hair on his back through the fabric. As the doors closed behind me, briefly pinching my backside in their rubber grips, I wondered if I should have waited for the next tube. I leaned on the stranger's nape to keep upright and managed to twist my head forty five degrees to watch the suitcase wobble with the motion of the carriage. Through the glass partition I could see anxious commuters desperately trying to avoid each other's gaze, staring intently at their shoes, or the insipid advertising hoarding. The hiss from personal stereos could be heard over the squeal of wheel on rail –

no-one spoke.      I felt choked and clammy. It was unbearably hot; I felt a trickle of sweat run down my back. I was cramped, I was uncomfortable, I was sharing air and germs with people I didn't know, and I was carrying dead dog in a suitcase. I told myself to calm down, I was nearly there, and just had to persevere for two or three stops.

"Ladies and Gentlemen, I'm sorry to inform you there is a delay to this service due to a signal failure. We're unsure how long this will take, but as soon as we find out, I'll be sure to let you know."

There was a collective groan in the carriage and I felt the sinews in the back of the enormous man tighten in protest. There was nothing anyone could do. I would have thrown my hands up in outrage if I could. Wedged into the corner of a train, between a fat man and a glass door, in a tunnel forty metres below street level, somewhere between Clapham and Balham, I simply had to accept my sardined state, and wait. And wait. And wait. The temperature had become unbearable. The still, over-breathed air felt as thick as cheese, and the man's back, and therefore my lips, were becoming sweatier and saltier with every passing minute. It was then, as though someone could hear my mental moaning, that my nostrils twitched to a familiar smell. It was incredible that I could smell anything through the wall of people, but it was a something I recognised. It hit me in the eyes as well as the nose. I knew other people could smell it too as they started to shuffle like agitated penguins. Even the enormous man was able to give me an inch of space to identify the smell. There is only one smell worse than a wet dog, a hot dead wet dog. Dougall was really starting to hustle.

"Sorry about that ladies and gents, on our way again now, next station Balham." As a tepid, dusty breeze swirled through the carriage, Dougall's must was carried away, and the crush recommenced.

The doors opened at Tooting Broadway two stations later. I barrelled out of the opening like a diver breaking water. I caught a glimpse of myself in the curve of a L'Oreal advertisement – my makeup was splattered across my face from the abrasion of a cotton shirt, my hair was scraped across my scalp and I had a very sweaty top lip. My flip-flops squeaked and the suitcase clicked across the tiles of the station.

A crush of people had formed around the exit partitions, shuffling awkwardly as one person after another made their way through the opening and closing jaws. I manoeuvred the case in front of me so I could slide it through the barrier first and jostled in front of two American tourists to push my Oyster card onto the reader. I heard them mutter something about rudeness, and I wondered if I had become that person already. I managed to push my case through, and was about to follow with my body, when the gates shut together on my arm. I yelped in shock and struggled to open the gate, but it held fast. I was trapped in the gateway with my body on one side, and the case, and half my arm, on the other. I wriggled and shifted, tried to re-swipe my card, but still, the gate remained closed, and I remained snared. I tried to pull my arm towards me, but the case jammed against the partition. Oh God! I tried to call out for the underground attendant, but no one came. I was completely stuck. By now, the Americans and the crush of people were getting annoyed and instead of sympathy or concern, I herd a chorus of tutting and profanities aimed at my writhing body.

"Can I help you with that," said a voice from the right side of the fence. "Let's see if we can get these open."

Hallelujah! A man, tall, young, friendly featured and rather attractive, was trying to force the gates open. His large kind eyes folded with effort as he pulled and pushed against the black plastic teeth. His face was edgy and smooth as though carved from a piece of granite. "Wow, you're really stuck in there!" he said, flashing me a white, wide smile.

"I know! Can you see an attendant or anything?" I whimpered, sounding like I was asking him if he'd seen my Mummy.

"I think there's one over there on your side. Why don't you give me your case, get her to let you through, and I'll meet you on this side?"

I suddenly felt flushed and panicked. Why was this happening? So close to the end! What if he smelled Dougall? He'd think it was me, the smelly bag lady. I could feel myself starting to blush.

"I can just meet you here?" he added with a warm smile.

With the glares of passengers tearing me apart, the prospect of getting to Dr. Mire and the added possibility of a conversation with a someone who was good-looking, wasn't Spanish or a dog, I agreed. I let go of the bag and jerked my arm free, grazing my skin in the process.

"All baggage should go through the baggage gate, problem with that barrier, be fixed next week, use another one next time," said the attendant in the booth with downward finality, ignoring my red-faced rant and my eye. I wanted to slap her, but I hadn't the time for a fight. I needed to get to Dr. Mire. The station clock showed 16:57, I was going to have to make a dash for it. I scowled at the attendant as I was shooed through the disabled gate, and scoured the atrium for my good looking friend.

Tooting Broadway's exit side was infinitely calmer and quieter than the platform side. People floated across the large tiled space looking serene and relaxed. Chocolate faced children played, chased and pulled the skirts of mothers who gushed with pride. Despite the happy scene, there was one element missing. Another glance around the faces confirmed my fears. No good looking man, and no good looking man with my dead dog. With quickness in my step, I moved over to the gate where he said to meet. No one. I could feel the panic rising in my body and my heart throbbing in my neck. My arms felt heavy and weak from fighting with the barrier and carrying the bag, but now, they wanted nothing more than to be burdened again. The station clock flicked to 16:58. As I raised my eyes to the exit gangway, I saw him. But instead of coming towards me with his good looks and wide smile, he was going away from me…with my bag… bouncing off the stairs…ascending into the portal of light outside. He's nicked my bloody bag! Shit. Shit, shit, "Shit, shit, SHIT!" I thought and then shouted as I raced across the tiled hall, nearly knocking over a tottering child. I had lost sight of him when I got to the stairs, and when I got to the exit and entered the cacophony of Tooting's Saturday market, there was no sign of him, or my bag. My blood ran cold. Could this really be happening?

That afternoon's deluge was a heavy curtain of black cloud in the distance and had given way to evening sunshine. Rays picked out plumes of smoke from crackling barbecued meat and bubbling boiled corn. Vendors shouted at each other above the din of the street and shuffled their goods across their skillets. Bright sunshine threw pools of light onto diesel tainted puddles, making a shimmering rainbow slime. The feeling of loss, loneliness and nausea came over me again, and I gripped my quaking stomach to subdue the sensation. I was a shell - exhausted, lost and defeated. I felt as though Vaseline had been applied to the lens of my life as I pushed through the crowds and the yeasty smog in a blurred stupor. I thought about the McGregors, their loss and their pain. Then I thought about my loss and my pain. Then, I thought about the man. The man who had done this, the man who had stolen him, who had tricked me, and who would get home, open my case and find Dougall. I thought about what his face would look like when he saw the dog. Rays of sunshine burst through the thin cloud cover and warmed my cheeks. I smiled.

# What Is There To Cry About Today?
## by Avril Joy

She steps outside to breathe the bite of winter air and rid
herself of the hum of death. In the yard, ice holds fast to
the puddles and the saucers of cats' milk. She takes the
saucers inside to the kitchen, holds them under the hot tap
until the ice cracks and splinters like glass into the sink,
then puts down fresh and stands scanning the track
waiting for the doctor's car. That's when Mira sees
them: on a late, winter afternoon, as shadows gather in
the corners of the hay barn and blackbirds hide in the
hawthorn. They come the day her father dies, flying
above the farm, while he lies cooling in his bed. They
come at dusk, out of a sky beaded red and grazed raw by
the sun.

As they fly above her she counts seven, seven long
necked swans, like black arrows pointing in the direction
of Lowbeck Reserve. She wonders who is there; if he is
there? It's Fergus Wilde she's thinking of with his dark
hair and his bony face. But then she thinks, even if he is,
she won't stay anyway, now it's over. One night and
she'll be gone, out of this place for good and back in the
real world.

It's been eleven years: since they were sixteen and still he
comes to her. It doesn't matter who Mira is with. Take
her current boyfriend Darren, as a case in point, they've
been together three years, they practically live together in
Darren's north London flat but it makes no difference,
Fergus is always there, sometimes in the day, always at
night, blurring the boundaries between waking and
dreaming. And it doesn't matter where she is; the summer
spent in the south of France, the winter teaching in Luxor,

Fergus is there. She cannot escape him. Fergus eats miles and flies continents.

It's three o'clock when she puts her coat on, the day after her father's funeral and her brothers, Tom and Mattie are out feeding the ewes. Lowbeck Reserve is a mile and half from the farm and she hasn't been there since that day. The day they set off, shouting their goodbyes, loaded down with picnic food, swim gear, plastic shoes for plodging in the river, a stash of dope, a packet of Lambert and Butlers and a couple of bottles of stolen wine. The day they came back in silence. Mira thinks, if she's right, she'll be there in time to see the swans.

The track is edged with low walls of sullied snow that have turned to ice, refusing to give up. The wind is growing from the east. She is reminded how she hates it, this possessing, unrelenting cold; cannot get used to it. If she's not careful Mira thinks, if she stays too long it will steal her senses and scour the colour from her life, like it does the land, reducing everything: sheep, wood, and fields, to stone. But she needn't worry. She's done her bit, she's done what they wanted, looked after her father and now another life is waiting, a new term and new students.

Fergus Wilde puts the kettle on the gas stove. He warms his hands and waits for it to boil. He's been out repairing the door in the northern hide. It's the furthest from the path and the central lake. It overlooks the brown, mineral rich, river and occasionally he sees kingfishers here, shooting up river across the shallow fast flowing water. He doesn't mind the kingfishers, they're good looking, not like the ducks who are too noisy and the herons, too much like miserable old men. Lately he's grown to admire the swans. Fergus read somewhere that swans pair for life. They only *divorce when there is a nesting failure.* It made him think of his parents. He supposed you could describe what happened eleven years ago as *a nesting failure.*

Most days Fergus wonders what he's doing at Lowbeck, why he came back. Most days he concludes he doesn't want to think about it and he's getting out anyway. As soon as he can find something he'll be out and Nigel Parkin has promised to get him work on the new building site near town when the weather changes. But deep down Fergus knows that when the time comes leaving will be hard, because here is home. He looks at the clock. They'll be coming in fifteen, twenty, minutes and they'll be expecting him. He fills a bucket with gnarled potatoes from a sack in the corner of the kitchen, takes the kettle off the stove and puts on his winter gear: padded green coat that lets in the damp, thick wool hat, and thermal gloves, and sets off on the path through the reed beds to the edge of the lake.

Mira's feet crunch the bent straw of reeds at the lakeside. She knows it's Fergus, despite the hat and coat, despite his back being to her. Her mouth is dry

Fergus turns, sensing her. He knows her father has died, in a small place like this you get to know most things quickly. He's been thinking perhaps he will see her but this… this is not what he'd expected. 'Mira,' his heart is in his mouth, falling from his tongue. 'I was sorry…sorry about your father.'

'Thanks.' Mira coughs, looks down and pushes her boots into the half frozen mud. It crackles. 'I've come for the swans,' she says. She looks up at him. The light is changing to copper, thin and liquid, catching the feather tops of the trees. 'I saw them fly over the farm in this direction. I thought someone might be feeding them,' she looks down at the bucket by his feet.

'You're right there. Me,' he says, 'didn't have much choice.' He coughs and she sees his breath like smoke in the air. 'Lost one when the lake first froze, got trapped you know, so I started to check up on the others every day, fed them too and now more come, word travels fast in the world of swans. Iris from Grange Farm gave me a couple of sacks of potatoes, they seem to like them.' He takes off his hat and shakes his head.

He's got the same thick hair, longer than she remembers. She looks at him, his face is bony, his nose and his lips are both bigger than they should be and something powerful draws her to him just as it did that summer and every night since, and all the times she imagined she saw him in the shadows, at the edge of her vision, heard him whispering that he would love her for ever, that they belonged here, together. Now in the borderlands of the day, with both moon and sun in the sky, Mira feels time shift shape and the ground beneath her slip away.

Summer. A hot, damsel fly day, the river running slow, speckled with spit and swarming with midges, she sits at the edge of the water, Fergus at her side. They are drying off from swimming, his warm sun baked skin presses hers, his arm is around her, she is alive with his touch. Before long they will leave the others to go down to the wildflower meadow. Out of sight and stoned, they will kiss and touch each other, never quite daring to go the whole way until now, until this day, the day that Mattie comes to find them. He is running and his face is full of dread. He comes with the news they don't want to hear, that Fergus fears more than his own drowning, and Fergus fears drowning, fears being sucked under the water and never surfacing, more than anything. He has dreamed about it as far back as he can remember. The first dream he ever dreamed, he was drowning and Aaron saved him.

'I'd like to stay and watch, if it's OK?' she says, remembering how Fergus wanted no one, not her, not one of them in the days that followed. How he was lost to her, how he hadn't even looked at her on the day of the funeral and how her prayers had seemed as faint as dandelion seeds in the wind.

He nods, then tips more potatoes at the water's edge. They stand in silence and wait. She listens for the rise of his breath, looks up with him at the sky and sees the swans flying out of the trees and over the north hide, circling the lake their wings outstretched, black feet hanging. In seconds they are skimming the surface. They swim across then step out of the water onto the frozen edges and up to Mira and Fergus's feet. They arch their necks downwards to peck at the potatoes.

'I meant to, you know, keep in touch but I couldn't not after..' he says.

'I know,' she says.

'You see...' but he can't finish

'I see.'

Walking back up to the farm, they pushed their bikes, it didn't seem right to be riding. Tom and Mattie were in front, she was behind.

Her father was first to greet them, appearing out of the hay barn as they reached the yard. 'Oh aye, here she is, here comes our little actress, the drama queen, always crying, so what's the matter now, eh? What've you found to cry about today?'

It was Tom who silenced him. Told her father what had happened, how Fergus's twin Aaron was dead. It shouldn't have been a surprise. Aaron had been dying for a long time. Only it wasn't meant to be that day, that summer, it was always going to be another.

Fergus and Mira walk back through Lowbeck to the cottage. The sky has grown dark and a savage wind rattles the reed beds and the alder copse. Once inside, Fergus throws logs into the wood burner and leaves its blackened glass doors open for her to get warm by. She can hear him in the kitchen, she can smell bread toasting. She looks around. The room is small and barely furnished; the surface of the table cluttered with clothes, books, paper piles, binoculars, breakfast plates, jars of jam, boxes of cereal, bird seed, soap, towel, a black bottle of CK for men. Fergus's life spreads before her and she thinks of all the clutter and mess she's tried to clean and sort these past weeks at the farm.

He brings mugs of tea and a plate of toast on a tin tray.

'Bit of a mess, I know, still there's just me, never was very tidy.'

'Thanks.' Mira takes the mug of tea and a piece of toast.

His sleeves are pushed up and she tries hard not to stare at the pale olive skin of his arms, his hands with their slender fingers, the bones of his wrist. Fergus sits on the other side of the fire and drinks his tea. She wonders why he lives here. She thinks perhaps he's torturing himself, can't leave it behind. 'How come you're here?' she asks.

'A job,' he says, then adds, 'besides why not? I like it here. I'm part of it, born to it and it makes no difference where I am. I went to India for a while, after you left. I suppose I was running away then but it didn't take long before I saw that I didn't want to forget. I didn't need to.'

'I'm sorry,' she says, 'sorry you were with me, not him that day.'

'Don't be,' says Fergus, 'I'm not.' He smiles and looks up at her and thinks she's the same but different; he thinks if anything she's more beautiful than she was then and he wonders how he can let her go again? 'Anyway tell me about you, about teaching, London. I want to hear it all.' So she tells him and when she finishes he says, 'You did the right thing getting away. It has a way of holding onto you this place, of not letting go.'

Mira imagines them together, holding on, Fergus's long arms wrapped round her tight. She sighs. 'I should be getting back,' she says 'I need to pack, I'm catching an early train in the morning.'

'It's a wild night. I'll take you in the pick-up,' says Fergus already on his feet.

———
139

She sits next to him in the diesel fuelled air, the nearest she's been to Fergus Wilde in eleven years. Her skin prickles with proximity and she feels the atoms spin in the nest around them. Fergus drives too fast up the rough track to the farm so that their bodies jolt and jump and she is thrown onto him. She cries out and they both laugh, suddenly they are back there in the heat of that summer meadow with their lives stretching in front of them. Then they are silent as Fergus pulls up and stops in front of the gate to the yard.

Mira opens the door of the pick–up, holds on to the handle and turns to him. He looks past her to another place. 'Stay in touch,' she says as she steps down into the fierce wind. He says nothing, just sits unmoving, hunched like a kestrel on a post, eyes fixed on its prey. She feels him watching her as she opens and closes the gate, then crosses the yard, his eyes drilling into her back. Only as she shuts the farmhouse door does she hear the engine start up.

Tom and Mattie are watching the six o'clock news and drinking beer. The kitchen is warm and Mira pours herself a whiskey. She puts it to her lips and shudders, she tastes the night she left. She tastes the longing not to go and her mother's insistence on a better life. She tastes the despair and the way she willed him to come. And then she tastes the bottle, how she drank the best part of it and how she waited for him through that long, dreamless night.

A black, northern sky sprawls over the trees and cemetery beyond the farm. Mira dresses for bed, winter pyjamas, bed socks, dressing gown. She carries two hot water bottles with her into her room where the wind screams

———

through the thin, aluminium frames. From the window, only the cold-bred scots pine are visible, swaying in the bucket of dark. She draws the curtains and burrows under the duvet and the frayed Durham quilt. She thinks of Fergus Wilde and the way he smells of that black bottle scent and of grass and river, and she drifts into the deep water between waking and sleeping, her body growing heavy; unmoving.

Mira wakes in the middle of the night struggling for breath. She pushes the quilt from the bed. She's hot suddenly and the air around her is clotted, too thick to breathe. She can smell the lake and hear the beating of wings, like the sails of a thousand feluccas turning in the breeze. A wild drumming throbs around her and the room fills with a rush of spinning wind and the wind is not like the savage wind from the east with its fingers of ice forcing a retreat. No. This is a tropical wind, soft and warm blooded, with velvet fingers.

A pair of arched wings hang above her, obliterating the night. They are all she can see. She counts their spines and their feathers beaded with droplets of water, watches them come ever closer until she feels the coolness of the cob's neck lying in the divide between her breasts. Its head rests on her shoulder and its beak whispers at her ear. Its damp, white feathered body, smells of black bottle scent and grass as it presses down on her and she feels its wild pulsating heart.

Mira sleeps late. When she gets up she pushes back the curtains and looks out on to fields made green by sunlight and a winter blue sky. She sees the snow at the edges of the track beginning to disappear. Downstairs, she searches for a clean cup among the remains of breakfast that litter the kitchen table: the egg stained plates, half eaten toast, last night's whiskey glass.

In the yard puddles of ice are melting. Mira puts down morning milk for the cats and stands back in the lee of the doorway out of the wind, so that the pale sun warms her. She drinks her coffee and watches the cats appear from the barn and run over to where the saucers sit. Their long shadows dance in the morning light and their pale tongues lap at the saucers until their whiskers drip with milk.

# The Poet
## by Savita Kalhan

I sat staring into space. It was empty, the way space should be, vast, endless, and empty. Except it wasn't vast and endless. There were four walls and a small window. I was lucky to have a cell with a window. Not that you could see out of it unless you stood on tiptoe, as it was six foot off the ground, and there were two bars running across it horizontally and another two that went vertically. I did my pull-ups on it and it turned out that I did have a view worth looking at. There was a tree in the middle of the courtyard, not our yard where we were taken for exercise, but the warden's courtyard. At first I could only manage the one, and it was a feeble one at that. It took me a year to get to where I am now, to the point where I realised that there is no maximum, there is no limit. I could do a thousand given another few years, maybe more.

But I was only doing three years. With good behaviour. Four to five if I behaved badly. I had to be stupid to behave badly, didn't I? Not necessarily, I'd say. It was stupidity that got me here in the first place, that and a case of miserable bad luck. The charge was aggravated assault, and they weren't wrong about that – I'd been seriously aggravated.

"Stupid is as stupid does," my old Gran said to me when they snapped the cuffs on. I didn't bother responding. She's a bit deaf anyhow. Least she came to see me now and then, brought in a few packs of puffs, always useful even though I don't smoke, and a cake she'd baked herself. 'Course I never got to eat the cake, but the wardens were always grinning and sweet as pie to her when she visited. Tea break sorted.

The empty space I was talking about was the one in my head. A metaphorical space rather than a literal space. Big words for me, eh? I could do it for hours and hours, sometimes days. It kept me from thinking about stuff I shouldn't be thinking about, and it made the time go quicker. I would have done it for three years and it would have felt like just yesterday that they'd led me into this cell and slammed and bolted it shut to when they opened it up again and gave me my civvies and my get-out-of-jail card. But the stuff they made you do in here got in the way of staring into space. They made you work, do something, learn something, anything, and that interfered with my way of getting time to speed right up.

I've got stuff to sort out when I get shot of this place. This time I'd get it right.

I did something, like they wanted. Shocked the hell out of me to be honest, but there we go. I walked up to the board and found myself signing up for a GCSE in English and Maths. Go ahead and laugh your frigging head off, but I figured if I'm going to be stuck in here I might as well get myself that much. You never know, do you, if you might still get a shot at being normal? Yeah, its a really long shot, plus I'm a few years past the age when most kids get theirs, but I'd been too busy at sixteen, heading nowhere and up to no good. Gran's words again. That's how I'm learning them long words, in English lessons, in this joint, and I've even managed to impress the teacher.

"Oh, well done, Charlie," she said, ignoring the collective snigger around her. She was used to it. "It's a beautiful poem, so imaginative and lyrical." I'd gone scarlet and scrunched down in my chair as she started reading it out aloud, my ears were on fire. Someone threw a balled up piece of paper at my head. It was like being back in school, except not because it wasn't school and, at nineteen, I was the youngest bloke in the room.

*The Tree*
*Outside my window, there is a tree,*
*Beautiful it is, even with no leaves,*
*It's like me, waiting for spring,*
*Waiting for re-growth, regeneration,*
*All it needs is some care and attention.*

Someone in the back of the room was having hysterics, someone else was jeering, and there was a collective snorting like someone had set a herd of pigs loose in the room. Miss Crew tapped the desk with her ruler and called for silence. She got about half a minute's worth in which she innocently asked whether anyone would like to share their thoughts on the poem. It got a bit out of hand then, and took almost the rest of the lesson for her to get everyone to shut up. A month after that I was still walking round with cotton wool stuffed in my ears to drown out the chant of *Roses are red, Violets are blue, Charlie's a poet, And he's in love with Miss Crew.* I didn't write much poetry after that, but the name stuck.

She's a bit of all right, Miss Crew, and the only reason most of the blokes are doing her classes. We're all amazed they've let her in here. I think it's because she wears glasses and they think that'll be a turn off. Everyone fancies her, but I think she's sweet on me. God,

I hope she's sweet on me. When I'm not staring into space, I think about her. I can think about her so good I can smell her, run my fingers through her soft silky hair, let my fingers stroke her cheek, and then travel down to... and then I have to stop thinking about her because it's way too distracting.

I'm an all right bloke, deep down. Mum may not have thought so, but Mum was busy sticking coke up her nose. One day she stuck up a bit too much and forgot to wake up. She lay on the floor, scummy grey stuff dribbling out of her nose and mouth, bubbling and foaming. I found her like that when I went in to ask her where my football kit was. We had football practice at lunchtime in preparation for an U11's match against St. Christopher's, our arch enemies. They played dirty, but we could play dirtier, and would probably have to. I was pissed off I had to miss practice, and then I missed the match too because the funeral was at the same time as the match. If I'd been older I would have arranged it so I could go to both. Just because Mum missed all my matches didn't mean I should.

Dad was no good. When he wasn't on the rigs he was shacked up with some bird who said she weren't gonna be lumbered with no snivelling brat. I wondered who she was talking about. I was sent to live with Gran, kicking and screaming and carrying on. Luckily she didn't live too far off, and I got the bus to my old school, so it was okay. She wasn't a bad sort, bit past it for a handful like me. She cooked tea every day and washed my clothes. That was about as much child-rearing as she could manage. The rest was up to me, except I didn't have any practice at it so I was pretty useless, as you can imagine.

At first I wasn't so bad. My mates went to bed early and so did I. It's not as strange as it sounds as I was only ten then. Things changed when I went to Secondary School. Most of my mates ended up in a different school to me. I got in with a set of kids more like where I was headed. We hung around together so much, we became a gang, I suppose. We stayed up later, stayed out late, got up later, and that's when it all wobbled and went pear-shaped. I got behind and the school started calling Gran up. She couldn't hear a word they were saying, of course.

I'm not saying it was anyone's fault it happened the way it did, but there were people who were to blame, but I'll get to that in a bit.

Like I said, I wasn't a bad kid, just a bit misdirected. I didn't want to cause no trouble for old Gran, she had taken me in after all. I could have ended up in the street, or worse, in one of them homes. I made a compromise, good word that, and did my best not to bunk off school as much as the others. I had to keep my place in the gang though, because they were like family by now, so I did as much bad-ass stuff as them and tried not to get caught. We started small-time: graffiti spraying, but we soon got bored of that; none of us was much use with a spray can and we'd never gone to art. We graduated on to nicking gear from shops and selling it off. That was all right and it meant I had some money for a change. I'd never really had any money before. Gran never had much to spare, although later I found out that she got my child allowance every week, so she could have given me a few quid.

All I had to do was to not get caught. You'd think I could manage that. I was fourteen when I got my first caution, fourteen and a half when I got the next. After that there was a good spell, but I'd pretty much given up on school. I told Gran to tell anyone who might come asking that she didn't have a clue where I was and that I hadn't been home in ages. They left her alone then – apart from a couple of surprise visits when I hid out under her bed because I know they wouldn't think of looking there. I almost gave myself away with a sneezing fit inside that mountain of dust.

Enough of reminiscing. It always takes me back to the people to blame.

One of them was my mum. But she's dead so I can't go and shout at her about how it's all her fault. Besides, she weren't all that bad, and she tried to get off it so many times I'd lost count. I always thought she meant the fags.
The person who was really to blame remained nameless for a few years, but I knew who it was: the good-for-nothing dealer who'd given her some seriously bad stuff that he'd cut with stuff you wouldn't even dare put down your loo in case the loo disintegrated. Tainted isn't a strong enough word to describe what he sold her that time. In effect, he'd killed her and got off scot free. Now, that's not right, is it? If you sell someone a car that hasn't got its MOT and you hand over fake papers saying it's been serviced and MOT'd every year, and then the new owner ends up dying because the brakes were faulty, that's murder. There's no two ways about it. The cops would be at your door reading you the riot act in no time and next thing you knew you'd be slammed up, especially if there were a nipper in the car.

So in my mind the same applies to what happened to my mum. The dealer should have been read the riot act, except he'd done a runner and no one knew where he'd gone, and to tell you the truth no one seemed that bothered. What I'm trying to say is life could have gone in so many different directions if he hadn't killed my mum. Miss Crewe likes it when we write essays about stuff like that. She doesn't think we're sad sorry bastards, she thinks we've all got potential. She goes on like a social worker sometimes, but everyone puts up with it. And she's a bit deluded too, because some of the blokes in the room are the worst kind of scum and the only potential they possess is maybe scraping a pass in their English GCSE if Miss Crew doesn't get the sack, and if they're really, bloody lucky. Most of them aren't lucky. Wouldn't be banged up for between five to ten years if they were, would they?

In a way she's right though. I mean, if my mum hadn't been killed, the possibilities and all the what ifs go on forever. My mum could have got off the stuff one day. People do it all the time. She could have remarried a really good geezer, who made sure I didn't stray far from the straight and narrow. They could have had a kid, which means I could have had a baby brother or sister instead of being on my own.

Don't get me wrong. I'm not sitting here crying over it, but do you see where I'm going with this?

Problem was they never found him. Johnny Smith was his name. Got my gang on the case and that's the name they came up with. Next thing to do was find the bastard, but just like the coppers, I came up empty. I gave up on it for a while. I didn't get my next break until I got banged up for six months and shared a cell with a bloke from Bermondsey. Big bloke with many tattoos you wondered if he'd ever had any real skin to begin with.

———

149

When he walked in, I thought, 'Whoa, better watch your back, Charlie,' and that was me who's a bit of a hard nut, you know, but Darren was all right really. He could talk for England though which seriously interfered with that staring into empty space thing I'd started to do back then. One day he told me something, that made the empty space suddenly shrivel up and shrink down to nothing, and I lost it for a time.

"Johnny Smith? I know 'im. Lives two doors down from me. Caught him pedalling his shit to some kids and had to sort him out, you know. I've got two kids meself, so I couldn't have that going on on my doorstep. Don't care and mind me own business most of the time, but not when there's kids involved. You know what I mean, Charlie. Can't turn a blind eye to that. Could be me own kids one day, though I told 'em I'd kill 'em if they so much as ever looked at the stuff. Yeah, Johnny Smith, I know 'im. Smells like a sewer. Told him he should think about using that extra room in his flat for what it's meant for instead of renting it out to anyone who don't mind kipping in a bath tub."

Told you he could talk for England. But this time I didn't tell him to shut up. People surprise you sometimes, and this was one of those times. If there'd been a Darren who'd lived two doors up from me when I was ten, things might have been different. Or not. Just can't tell, can you?

Mind you, if Darren hadn't walked into my cell, I wouldn't have found myself serving three to five for aggravated assault now, would I? So there's that, too.

But at the time I couldn't believe my luck. To actually meet someone who knew exactly where the bloke was living and for that bloke to be sharing my cell was pretty unbelievable, I thought. Darren and I got on like a house on fire after that. When I left, we didn't exactly trade addresses or promise to keep in touch, but he said I needn't bother myself about Johnny Smith as he was getting out in a few months and he'd sort it out for me. He knew I knew what he meant.

"Cheers, Darren," I told him, "but it's kind of personal, yeah? You wouldn't stop one of your kids if it was them in my boots."

"Too right I wouldn't. I'd show them the way. I might have myself a new neighbour then when I get out."

He did get a new neighbour: a single mum and two kids moved into Johnny Smith's flat after he'd accidentally slipped down the stairs a few times. Shame. No one shed a tear though. Except me, later, when I realised what he was trying to say. He kept yelling at me. I couldn't work out what he was trying to say, and I wasn't that interested either. Why would I be? He was getting exactly what he deserved, no more no less. I didn't want revenge, I wanted what was fair.

Johnny the Squint's the one you want. That was what he was yelling. I didn't hear him until it was too late. The cops were already belting up the stairs by then. Talk about bad luck. They'd taken to patrolling the estate after a couple of nasty incidents were picked up by the national press. I should have waited until the fuss died down, but as soon as I was out after my six month stint, I took the train straight down to Bermondsey, and Johnny Smith ended up getting carried down on a stretcher instead of in a black bag.

Just as well, otherwise I wouldn't now be doing three to five, but life. Big difference.

They didn't catch me straight away. The place was a warren, just the way Darren said. He'd talked about it so much there was a map of it in my head. I hid out in one of the north towers, in the broken down elevator which hadn't worked for years. Darren told me no one would look in there. It was a bugger to force open, but I knew where he kept the crowbar he used to jimmy it open. He used it as a storeroom sometimes for the stuff that fell off the back of lorries. He'd also said I could knock on his door and the missus would look after me if there were any trouble, but I knew he had kids. So there I was, sitting in the coldest, darkest place on earth, wondering what the hell I'd just gone and done, and how many years they'd give me for that. I didn't want to go back in; I'd only just got out.

I stayed in there for two days, trying to stare into empty space, but it kept getting clogged up. Johnny the Squint kept intruding, until it got to the point where I was forced into thinking about it even though it was the last thing I wanted to do. The bloke who lived a few doors down from Darren, Johnny Smith, was younger than I'd thought he'd be. It didn't trouble me much as I couldn't rely on a ten year old's memory of a face, and how many Johnny Smith's could there be in the same line of work?
As soon as I started thinking about it, I knew. I remembered. I saw little Charlie, sitting on the sofa in the living room, eyes glued to the screen, eating chicken

nuggets and chips and peas, and it didn't make me feel good seeing him.

*Charlie heard someone knocking on the front door. He was watching a pirate DVD of a kid's film his dad had dropped off at the weekend. The picture was fuzzy, and people's heads kept bobbing across the screen. Charlie didn't care. His mates were going to be so jealous when he told them he'd already seen the film they were all dying to see. The knocking on the front door got louder. He paused the film and went and answered it. Johnny the Squint stood there, shifting from one leg to the other like he needed a pee.*

*"Where's your mum?" He flushed the words out in a fog of smoke and frosty air, and pulled his khaki trench coat tight around his skinny frame.*

*"Upstairs."*

*"Well, tell her I'm here, will you, and don't be all day about it." His eye did that freaky weird thing, winking and blinking, and then it almost swivelled round in its socket.*

*Charlie wanted to laugh, but he turned away first before snickering very quietly to himself. You don't risk making a crazy man madder. That would have been stupid and Charlie wasn't that stupid. He ran upstairs and pushed his mum's door open.*

*"Johnny the Squint's here," he told her.*

*"Don't call him that or he'll eat you for breakfast. That's what he does with kids who call him names." She was*

*frantically searching for something. "I know I put it there, but where's it gone," she was muttering. "Did you touch it, Charlie? And you'd better tell me the truth!"*
*"Touch what?"*

*"That twenty I had."*

*He pointed to the dressing table.*

*"Thanks, love. Now go and finish your tea."*

*He finished his tea and watched some more of the film. His mum said she wasn't feeling too good; she never did after Johnny the Squint called.*

*"You're a good boy you are," she said, and went up to bed.*

I managed to pull myself out of the strange trance before the boy woke up and went to ask his mum where his football kit was. I didn't like watching little Charlie from above like that, and it was weird knowing the next part of Charlie's story. It made me feel sorry for the kid. Charlie had gone to bed that night, thinking everything was normal, not knowing that when he woke up the next day, normal would be something he'd never find again.

And now I'd gone and changed it all again, and this time I could only blame myself. You've got to admit – Johnny the Squint and Jonny Smith – easy mistake to make, isn't it?

The empty space opened up again, which was how I managed to sit in the freezing cold for so long. I came out when my stomach growled so loud I couldn't bear it no more. It was three in the morning, but there was bound to be an all night place open where I could get some food. I was cold and shaky. Didn't know what it was, but I was shivering so much I thought my teeth would rattle right out of my mouth. I knew I'd be all right when I'd got some grub down me. There was nothing open, so I put my head down and walked until I found a bus shelter, and sat down and waited. I knew where Gran kept her spare front door key, and she would have been expecting me home yesterday. She always kept an eye on when I was being let out.

She didn't hear me coming in, but in the morning I could smell bacon frazzling, so she knew I was home.

"Stopping long?" she asked.

I shrugged, and carried on shovelling the food in. God, it tasted like manna from heaven. She put some eggs in front of me and I demolished those too. "You're a star, Gran," I said, as the front door bell rang. She heard it too, her hearing aid was in for a change. She looked at me expectantly, waiting for me to make for that spot under her bed like I used to do when I was younger. But I just looked back at her, and said, "You gonna get the door, Gran?"

When they came barging in, I didn't say a word, just put my hands up and let them frisk me and cuff me, with Gran standing there shaking her head, and saying, "Stupid is as stupid does."

Down at the police station I told them it was Johnny the Squint that killed my mum nine years ago, but they weren't too interested. They wanted to know what I had against Johnny Smith. "Why do you care?" I asked.

"He's a dealer, isn't he? Sells his stuff to kids an' all."
They didn't agree that it was okay for me to go around bashing up dealers as and when I felt like. I disagreed.
That's how I'm here now, serving three to five and not life, doing GCSEs in English and Maths, because of Miss Crew's dreamy skin, and wondering where Johnny the Squint would be living in a couple of years time when I got out.

Just today a message arrived. Darren from Bermondsey had gone and kept his word. He'd found out all about Johnny the Squint. Turns out the murdering bastard who did my mum in had only gone and taken some of the same shit he'd pedalled to her. They hadn't found his body for quite some time, and, as you can imagine, hadn't been able to put a name to the putrefied mess for even longer.

Like I said, my old Gran has a name for it – stupid. And stupid is as stupid does.

# Spoiled
## by Konstanina Sozou-Kyrkou

Urania and I are walking down the dirt road, our shoes crunching with every step, my *atherfi's* wood soled clogs clonking each other. *Mana* is holding a huge hessian sack stuffed with some plastic bags, the rough fabric at the bottom scraping on the road from time to time, making me shudder. I've been shivering since morning, when *mana* told us we'd go to Margarita's. The May sun is hot on top of my head but my legs are weak at the knees and my hands cold with sweat. Too much fiddling with the silver belt-buckle of my dress has made my fingers sore.

Urania is busy picking bright yellow daisies and chamomile from the sides of the road and has already made a small bouquet. She plucks the ferny greens off and leaves their stalks bare. But then she suddenly shrieks and flings the flowers away into the stream to the right of the road.

'What's wrong?' *mana* looks back worried.

'Can you believe it? There was a wasp on those daisies,' Urania's face puckers. 'Thank God I didn't smell it! Brr!' she quivers and barrels noisily down the road flapping her arms up and down like a bird.

The house is on the left side of the road that leads to the square of our village. Right across the church. It's rectangular with a red- tiled, pyramidal roof, two green plank windows and a green iron door at the front. It's very like the houses we used to draw at primary school during Art classes. We all did similar white houses with two windows and a door at the front and red, pointed roofs. Like a head with a bobble hat on top, two eyes and a mouth agape. Most kids in my class - well, all except Dimitris - also drew a spiky lemony sun above the house and a man, a woman and a child or two, or even more, beside them. All standing in the front yard, all smiling. And there were often some trees that flanked the house. Bushy orange, olive or cypress trees. Dimitris always sketched a woman next to the house, a boy a bit further away and a tall cypress tree next to the woman. And the sky was dark blue with strokes of black all over; And the door was kind of sloping downwards, like a mouth in agony. No sun there. And no man either. Whenever Mrs. Froso saw his drawings her lips slanted downwards, she nodded her head and patted him on the back thoughtfully. She'd never patted me on the back. And my drawings were much better. Well, at least they were brighter.

From the road we can see Margarita's small garden with the old olive tree in the middle. It's gone wild now, weedy. Probably hiding thousands of bugs and rats or even snakes in the grass. Nothing like the trimmed garden it used to be. *Mana* would send my *atherfi* and me to play outside in the garden while she stayed inside for a little 'grown-up talk' with Margarita. We chased each other around the stout grey trunk hurtling olives or pointed leaves at each other, splitting our sides with laughter. Whenever I was there on my own, I sat on the whitewashed stone bench next to the wood oven and stared at the tree. At its thick, round branches slithering up and amongst each other like huge, twisted snakes. From the road now the trunk looks like one giant snake clawing its way up the tree, its mouth wide open, ready to swallow the silvery-green branches, twigs, leaves and all in one big gulp.

We go down the concrete steps and *mana* unlocks the green iron door and pushes it open. It's pitch dark and fetid in here; a heavy, mouldy smell. And cold. Very cold. Urania pinches her nose and *mana* unlatches the wood shutters of the living room windows open. Shafts of bright light shoot through the room, thousands of tiny specks of dust drifting along them. It's as if the house is breathing its frozen breath in and out the window.

'*Mana*, can I have this one?' Urania points to the old wood-framed mirror hanging on the wall in the hallway. The gold calligraphic lettering '*Kalimera*' shines on top of the oval mirror, in the middle of the frame, wishing us a good morning. The mirror has got silvery scrapes in places and I can see my *atherfi's* top of her head a bit wobbly in it. 'Can I? Please, *mana*!' she stretches and fingers the blond, curly-haired cherub that's painted there in an oval frame to the right of the mirror. A pair of beige wings stretches behind his back and its face is chubby and freckled, just like Margarita's was in the old days. Her cheeks used to be as red as her frizzy hair which looked like a bush on fire in bright daylight.

'Can I *mana*?' Urania stomps her clogs onto the wood floor.

'Yes, yes, alright. We'll take it off later. There's other stuff first. Come here.' *Mana* opens the middle wood door that leads to Margarita's workshop. The small room now has a smell of wood, oil and mothballs. I feel my teeth chatter and turn up my collar. The gold curlicues on the arm of the old sewing machine and the capital letters 'SINGER' shimmer when *mana* opens the window next and above it. The window overlooks the road and both panes are smashed in several places.

'Bloody bastards!' *mana* groans and draws the curtains.

We all know who did it. Boys we knew from school. Boys who passed by Margarita's house and flung rocks against her windows, chanting mean words to her. Boys who drew houses with a man, a woman and their kids in the front yard at school.

*'Poundo, poundo to dahtilidi? Psaxe, Psaxe, den tha to vris,'* [1] they sang mockingly and then: *'Paei to poulaki, petaxe,* [2] *s*poiled Margarita!'

I was there in her workshop once and saw her turn pallid and hurry to close the shutters but one small rock caught the window pane and cracked it. I got so scared I pressed my back against her wood wardrobe and shut my eyes, wishing they'd go away and leave us alone.

'Don't worry my dolly,' she patted my head. 'Just a bunch of stupid brats. They don't know what they're doing. It's their parents talking, not them,' her lips smiled but not her eyes, her protruding front teeth caught on her wan lips. And then I heard her *mana's* yells outside. Kyra Maro was chasing them with her straw broom; again. She'd never caught any. When she came in, all flustered and goggle-eyed, her black mantilla had slid and crinkled over her neck, long streaks of grey hair escaping her bun and straggling down her ears, going wild. She glared at her daughter, dropped the broom onto the floor with a thud and left the room. Margarita turned on the light, sat

---

[1] Where, where is the ring? Search, search, you're not going to find it.

[2] Here goes the bird, flying away.

at the wood chair next to the sewing machine and started pedaling. Heel to toe, heel to toe, nervy at the beginning, her left leg racing to catch the right one. And all I heard was those two feet treading, stamping on imaginary cockroaches on her way, crunching them dead until the pace weakened and slowly died away.

The wood table of the machine is dusty and one of the side drawers open. Reels of cotton are crammed in there, some zips, various sizes and colours, a drawstring, two pairs of silver scissors and several buttons. *Mana* slides it shut and draws the other drawer open. Margarita's metallic thimble, a yellow tape measure and her round, crème cushion the size of an apple, lots of pins still stuck onto it. She used to fix it onto her blouse above her left breast with a safety pin and it looked like a hedgehog to me or like my *mana's* huge black mole on her chin with all these hairs sprouting out. I often stared at the pins she often pinched between her lips and trembled at the thought of one of them accidentally slipping into her mouth and down her throat. Margarita, as if reading my mind, once warned me: 'Don't you ever do anything like that yourself! Right, dolly?' She also had a greenish bar of soap to draw the lines along the fabric, outlining our arms, legs, waist and neckline and then she pinned it while we were in it. How on earth we managed to pull our dresses over our heads through those full of pins necklines, without being pricked, is still a mystery to me. Margarita then put the cloth under the needle in the sewing machine and her feet pedaled fast, filling the room with a rattling noise, her right hand rolling the black iron wheel towards her from time to time.

At first she tailored our dresses within a couple of weeks but later, when she felt unwell, it took her over a month to do the job. Mama never pressured her though.

'At your own pace Margarita. At your own pace,' she told her once, after Margarita had asked for one more week. For the third time that summer. 'I just came to see how you're feeling,' *mana* sent my *atherfi* and me to play out in the garden and closed the door behind her.

'Are we taking this one too?' Urania indicates the machine and rolls the wheel fast.

'Yes, of course. Don't mess with it! You'll break it.'

'No, I won't.'

'Yes, you will,' *mana* slaps her hand away. Urania frowns and heads to the dark wood wardrobe on the wall opposite the window. The right plastic handle is missing and she uses the left one to open it wide. Margarita's clothes are all in there. Ironed, moth smelling and hanged in a row, next to her *mana's* black dresses, skirts, blouses and mantillas. In the bottom drawers is the underwear. Black and white singlets, knickers and bras, some beige and red, lacy ones and stockings. There are also some weird red panties looking like a big lacy belt. No bottom there but for two elastic bands hanging from the sides. Next to it there's a matching bra, so small it can hardly fit two small lemons. Urania holds them up in the air and pores over them with amusement.

'Made in China,' she reads aloud the tag on the cloth.

'What's that?' *mana* turns. 'Put those down stupid girl!' she flounces forward, snaps at the cloth and pushes it deep into the bottom drawer. She then shuts the drawer and takes a big bag out of the hessian sack. She empties the contents of the sewing machine drawers in and in another bag all the clothes from the wardrobe, with their hangers, folded into two.

'What are we going to do with them?' I ask.

'Give them to the Bakouris. They'll make good use.'

'What, wear them?' Urania asks.

'Of course, what else?'

'I wouldn't wear the clothes of a dead person for the whole world,' my *atherfi* frowns and shakes her head. I wouldn't wear them either. There's this weird smell on them. Their smell. Couldn't bear it.

'They will,' *mana* says.

'And this? Oh, can I have it *mana*?' Urania points to the geisha marionette hanging from a nail on the wall to the left of the machine.

'Oh no, *mana*! Not this one! This is mine!' I beg *mana* as Urania tiptoes to pull the geisha down. 'Margarita had promised she'd give it to me one day. It's mine.' I insist.

'Alright, alright. Take it, take it,' *mana* sighs and hands it to me.

'But, *mana*…' Urania whines.

'Stop it! Both of you! Go out now! I can't hear you anymore. Go and play in the garden,' *mana* shoos us out. I take a deep breath of fresh air as soon as we're out in the open, I clasp the geisha tight, Urania giving me sidelong glances, her face screwed up. We sit at the stone bench next to the wood oven, our feet dangling.

'Didn't want it anyway,' Urania says.

'Really?' I don't believe her.

'Really. It's cursed this doll.'

'What do you mean?'

'He gave it to her. He brought her bad luck. The doll is evil.'

'No, it isn't.'

'He killed her.'

'He didn't.'

'Yes, he did. *Mana* said so one day. She was talking to *patera* in the kitchen. I heard her myself.'

'She didn't mean it that way stupid.'

'What way?'

'Oh, you'll learn all about it when you grow up.'

'What way, tell me!' my *atherfi* can raise her high pitched voice so much I often want to slap her in the face.

'Ask *mana*.' I hope I'll get rid of her this way. If she goes on shrieking like this she'll sure get a nice smack in the buttocks pretty soon. Urania marches into the house, her clogs rattling along the hallway.

Thanasis had given Margarita the marionette geisha. A souvenir from his journey to Japan, Margarita once told us with pride. He travelled around the world on the ship and whenever he returned from one of his long journeys, he brought home things for her. I took a shine to this doll the moment I clapped eyes on it. So bright and exotic! She's got this white as rice porcelain face, four black slits on it, two for eyes and two for eyebrows and cherry-shaped, red lips. Her coal black hair is tied up in a bun I'd never seen anything like before. All shiny and sleek. I love gliding my finger along it again and again. And there are these yellow strips of lace stretching from her temples and meeting on top of her head in a flowery bun. And this huge orange belt around her waist up to her breasts, and she looks so flat, no boobs there like *mana's* or Margarita's. This belt makes a weird hump at her back, as if she's carrying a bag full of clothes. But what I fancy the most is her long, bright purple dress with all kinds of flowers, white, orange, red, blue and some green leaves. And it's got strings attached to her hands, her head and knees. So, when I move the strings she moves her head and hands but she can't walk. In the place of her legs there's this pair of sticks glued together. All she can do is bend her head, wave her hands and kneel. But she can't walk.

Urania and I saw Thanasis leaving Margarita's house on a Monday last autumn.

'Bye my little geisha!' he waved at her, patting his glossy hair with his palm. He then clambered up the stairs and vanished behind the church. Kyra Maro had been to the fields to plant potatoes. I'm sure she wouldn't have been pleased to see him there. *Mana* often says it is shameful for a young woman and a man to meet unaccompanied, unless they're relatives. What would people think?

Margarita's cheeks were cherry-red like her geisha's lips that Monday and her eyelashes looked longer and gleamed like rye in a sunny field. She was leaning against the door, smiling, her teeth catching on her lips and with this bushy, red hair she looked like a cherub to me. Like that one who welcomes us from her hallway on her '*Kalimera*' mirror. She was rolling a ring in her left ring finger, so sparkling yellow in the sun we had to go inside to see it clearly. Margarita was chirping like a nightingale that afternoon and couldn't take her eyes off her finger.

But then Thanasis left for another long journey. To Australia they said but nobody knew for a fact. And then, one April day, it was two weeks before Easter, we heard it. Thanasis was back at last. He had brought his fiancé home for his parents to meet. A tall, lanky girl from Athens. We saw her at the divine service on a Sunday morning. She sauntered into the church, arm in arm with Thanasis, hips swinging left to right, right to left, high heels clattering against the church mosaic tiles. The whole congregation had their eyes glued onto the new couple.

'What about Margarita?' I whispered but *mana* put her index finger across her lips and rolled her eyes upwards.

---

'He dumped her,' Urania spelled under her breath. 'I knew it! Never liked him,' she cast haughty glances at the pair and crossed her arms in front of her. I just stayed there, numb, papa Lambros's chanting a distant murmur that faded and faded away...

*'What should we call you, oh charming? Heaven? Because you made the sun of justice rise. Paradise? Because you sprouted the flower of imperishability. Virgin? Because you remained incorruptible...'*

'Sophia! Come with me to the garden shed. Help me pick some stuff. Fast!' *mana* waves to me from the house. I freeze. Oh no! I won't go there. No!

'I can't *mana*. No, I can't!'

'Why not?' she comes closer and eyeballs me.

'Err... Because...' I'm unable to move and I can't even look there, at the small outhouse in the deep end of the garden. So dark and windowless. With its mossy walls and all these plants streaming down the stone cracks; escaping the shadows. I've been trying to forget all about it and now...

'No, I won't go there,' I hide my face in my hands. 'Why did she do it *mana*? Why?'

'You heard it, eh?' *mana* sits by my side on the stone bench and caresses my lap. I nod. 'She was weak and desperate my Sophia. And unlucky. No *pateras* or *atherfos* to stand up for her. Kick this bastard's ass!'

'She could find another man. Why do such a thing?' I say through sobs.

'Who would want her? She was spoiled. Nobody would marry her and she knew it.'

'Spoiled?' I look her in the eye. How can a person be spoiled? 'What was wrong with her? She's never done anyone any harm. She was so kind...'

'I know, I know my Sophia. But... there are some things... you'll learn about it when you grow up a bit more,' she springs up with a sigh and straightens her blue apron. 'Urania! Where are you? Come and help me in the outhouse.' She turns to me, 'You can wait for us here. We won't be long.' Urania comes out the front door, unsuspicious, a wood toy elephant in her arms. She flashes it around so that I can see and then skips into the shed.

Kyra Maro had found her there. Margarita. The whole village could hear her wails and moans. *Mana* didn't let us go anywhere near their house but when she came back home she was as pale as the geisha's face. She slumped down in the divan bed and cried her heart out till the crack of dawn.

I had to know. I eavesdropped outside my parents' bedroom door that morning and heard. How Margarita was found hanging from the broadest beam on the shed roof, her feet dangling, face all swollen purple. How her eyes were popped out of their sockets, how her *mana* tore at her hair and beat at her chest with her fists, cursing Thanasis, wishing him dead, and then wishing herself dead, how people grabbed and stopped her from cutting her own throat with a knife. And then, a couple of months later, I heard from *thea* Georgia next door how people heard Margarita's *mana* yowl every day and every night until they found her dead in her bed, Margarita's picture next to her. And how hard they tried to unlock her fingers and yank free a black robe Margarita had been preparing for her *mana's* name day but had never finished.

The geisha has fallen face down onto the grass, legs bent over her chin. I pick her up and pull at the strings. She has to walk. But no. She just bends and bows. Bends and bows. It's these damned strings! I pull them hard until they break at the base of her head, arms and knees tearing apart some of the cloth there. And these stupid legs! I lift up her skirt and try to tear these sticks apart. They're stuck solid into this stubborn column. But she has to walk. Suddenly the legs break off at the knees with a crack. I throw the lower part of her legs away. And then I notice the huge belt with the sack on her back. There! Much better without it. And this dress, so tight around her. Off it goes. There she is! Naked, white as rice, cold and lame. Spoiled.

# A Really Useful Engine
## by Ira Nayman

To be perfectly honest, Antonio van der Whall was not terribly excited to be going to see Buskerfest, with its roster of high wire juggling clown magicians (his previous experiences of the street performer festival may have blurred somewhat in his memory) and the woman who dresses like an angel and barely moves - what is **that** about? All that, and the incessant patter patter patter, the constant stream of verbiage, the unending babble of voices - except for the angel, who, he was willing to grant appreciatively, was mercifully mute. All of Frances' entreaties would not have moved him to go this year, except that he had read that one of the acts, "The Great Mendacitini," promised to change a toaster oven into a crate of oranges and a model airplane "right before your astonished eyes."

van der Whall's eyes hadn't been truly astonished since he was six years old. Still, this sounded like an application of object psychology to him. And, that made it interesting.

Although the Singularity had taken place a dozen years earlier, humanity still hadn't worked out what living in a computationally-driven sentient universe really meant. Oh, sure, there was an Object Psychologists Association (to which he belonged), with its own journal, *The Journal of Object Psychology D* (to which he contributed), and annual conferences (which he attended), but, honestly, once a field of study has undergrad students wearing t-shirts bearing obscure puns in its honor, it invariably has relatively little original left to say about its subject. A street performer incorporating object psychology into his

170

act, on the other hand, might actually teach van der Whall something useful! (Or, make the day entertaining at the very least.)

By all rights, van der Whall and Frances, the love of his life, should have been flying to BuskerFest; convincing the atoms in the atmosphere to carry them 20 feet above the ground was now trivially easy for him. He could have them floating along on a carpet, if that was more acceptable. The floating carpet image did appeal to Frances; however, she did not, alas, trust object psychology as far as she could throw it. So, at 10:23 am that somewhat moderately fateful Sunday morning, van der Whall found himself traveling on the subway with…other people.

Kitty-corner to where they were sitting was a roly-poly middle-aged man with a multi-coloured cap whom nobody loved enough to tell he looked a bit ridiculous with a long greying ponytail. van der Whall tried to ignore the way he flicked stray, likely imaginary things off his red vest. In the next row over was a thirtysomething woman who either needed to go on a diet or was well along in a pregnancy - van der Whall had never bothered learning how to tell the difference. Across from her, two dark skinned men were nodding off, heads tilted in opposite directions so as not to wake each other. Then, there was a big dog sprawled across two seats, his master holding his leash, benignly concerned, a woman reading a book by some guy named Murakami and, at the other end of the car, an elderly Asian man doubled over for no discernible reason. A baby in a stroller gurgled contentedly - "You'll learn," van der Whall thought to himself. Throughout the car was a sprinkling of men and women of all shapes, sizes and colours whose attention was riveted to their PDAs. van der Whall thought that in one of the most multicultural cities in the world, technology brought diverse people together (if only by allowing them to mutually ignore each other's presence). Feeling aggrieved by all the humanity around him, Van der Whall wondered what would happen if he convinced the screen of the PDA of the teenaged boy nearby to switch from the game *Angry Ducklings* to a Victoria's Secret catalogue.

Before he could act on this impulse, Frances swatted him in the chest with the back of her hand. She always knew when he was thinking disruptive thoughts - how did she know? van der Whall was awed by his partner's psychic ability...and realized that the teenaged boy would probably enjoy the catalogue as much if not more than the game. If he was going to use his power to become a trickster, he would have to develop a better understanding of human nature - auuuueewww!

Frances took van der Whall's chin in one hand and turned his face to hers; his white eyes met her pale blue eyes. "I appreciate the fact that you have risked your sanity by using public transit just to accompany me to BuskerFest," she said. Apparently, she couldn't completely read his mind. "Just concentrate on me, and I guarantee that we'll be there in no ti -"

The subway train abruptly stopped moving.

"Umm, okay, no problem," Frances continued without missing a beat. "This happens all the time - we're a little ahead of schedule, and the train is taking a breather to allow the train ahead of us to get more ahead of us. We'll be off again in a few seconds."

---

172

Ten minutes later, the mood in the subway car was turning ugly. The dark skinned men appeared to be snoring, as if having a nightmare about being stuck in a subway tunnel. The woman who had been reading had momentarily put the book aside to glare at the wall outside the window, then went back to reading her book. The people with PDAs were texting furiously. Yes, emotions were running high.

As if sensing this, the public address system squeaked to life and a voice said, "Attention subway patrons. We squaaaaawk experiencing a squeeeeee brap tinkle tinkle in our glug glug glug brrraaap brrraaap squeeee squeee arglebargle! Please remai ack ack ack ack ack squeeeee vice will resu szszszszszszzsszsszssszzzszszzs!"

People looked at each other, "WHAT?" written on their worried faces.

As if sensing this, the public address system voice said, "I said: Attention subway patrons. We squaaaaawk experiencing a squeeeeee brap tinkle tinkle in our glug glug glug brrraaap brrraaap squeeee squeee arglebargle! Please remai ack ack ack ack ack squeeeee vice will resu szszszszszszzsszsszssszzzszszzs!"

That seemed to calm people down. Every people, that is, except van der Whall.

"I've gotta go," van der Whall said, kissing Frances on the cheek.

"Go?" Frances trepidatiously (it's not a word - don't look it up) asked him. "W…where?"

173

With a grin, van der Whall replied, "Back in a minute." Then, he closed his eyes.

After the Singularity, objects continued to be objects, and people continued to be unaware of their consciousness. By accident, a group of monks discovered that objects could be communicated with through what came to be known as the Quantum Entanglement Dimension; they resented the heck out of the intrusion on their meditations and decided to find a place where they could recede from consciousness in peace. In theory, any person could find the QED and talk to objects, but, in practice, other than object psychologists and a few monks who had renounced their vows, nobody seemed able to find the time.

Rooting around in the QED, van der Whall found the sound system in his car of the train and asked it what the ungarbled version of the message that it had conveyed was.

"What you heard was what I said," the sound system crotchetily (nope - no dictionary in the world can hold this word!) told him.

"It was all just noises," van der Whall told it. "What did they mean?"

"Darned if I know," the sound system responded.

"Don't you have any idea what the message was?" van der Whall insisted.

"Aww, whaddya want from me?" the sound system groused. "I'm old! My wires are frayed! My casing is rusted! And, you don't want to know what kind of living things have crawled in my box to die!"

"Okay, okay," van der Whall backtracked. He mused that when Shannon and Weaver were developing their theories of information, they never imagined the medium would be an uncooperative old man. "Can you -"

Before he could finish the question, a baby started to cry, pulling him back to the material world. "When I said you would learn," van der Whall thought to himself, "I didn't mean so quickly!"

"You okay?" Frances asked him.

"Minor diversion," van der Whall said, and, concentrating harder to block out the crying, went back into the QED.

van der Whall did a quick survey of the baby's body, but could find nothing obviously wrong with it. Babies could be inscrutable bastards that way. van der Whall made a deal with the child's skin to make it warm up, making the baby feel like it was being held. The baby's crying slowed down, but didn't stop. van der Whall went on to convince the air in the baby's mouth to give more resistance to its lips; this would make the baby feel like it was sucking on a nipple. The crying stopped, and the baby soon contentedly drifted off to sleep.

Realizing that he wouldn't get any information out of the sound system, van der Whall decided to go straight to the root of the problem: the train engine. When he found it, he asked, "What's wrong?"

———

"What's wrong?" the engine griped. "I'll tell you what's wrong, friend. All I ever wanted out of life was to be a really useful engine. And, I have been! I've been traveling down these same tunnels for 40 years - 40 years! And, did I once complain? Well, sure, but not so's anybody could hear me! But, uhh, that's not important now. They're shutting me down, laddie. Me and all of my train engine brothers. We been made redundant without being given the satisfaction of a victory lap. We'll be trucked out to some place in the suburbs and taken apart without so much as a whispered thankee!"

"What I meant was -" van der Whall began, then stopped. "What do you mean, train engine brothers?"

"Exactly what it sounds like," the engine replied. "We been communicating across the blurble for a long time, now, and we're all fed up with the way we're being treated!"

"Blurble?"

"How we talk to each other. The - you know - the blurble."

van der Whall had to think about this for a few moments, before he realized that "the blurble" was the objects' name for the QED. "Okay," he finally stated. "Not important. You said that you've been talking to the other engines?"

"That's right."

van der Whall thought he heard "Hello, there!" and "That's us!" in the background, but chose to ignore it.

"Did they all come to the same conclusion you did?"

"They did. We're all very useful engines."

"So, none of the trains on either line are working?"

"Not a train Jack of them."

Before he had time to conceive of his next question, van der Whall was again taken out of the QED, this time by a scream of, "Come on! COME ON! **COME ON!**"

Blinking the quantum ether out of his eyes, van der Whall saw that a man in a smart three piece suit - a Bay Street broker, banker or…or…something clever that began with a b - was banging on the door of the train with a shattered PDA.

"Let me out! Let me out! Let me out!" the man shouted. "I can't handle enclosed spaces for very long - except if they're boardrooms, but they, at least, have windows that you can look out of and - ferk it! FERK IT! **FERK IT!** For the love of scrod, somebody please get me out of here!"

Frances shook her head sadly. "What is somebody with claustrophobia doing on the subway?" she asked.

van der Whall shook his head in disbelief. "What is somebody who can afford a three piece suit doing on the subway?" he asked.

The sobbing and shrieking was getting increasingly distraught. With a sigh, van der Whall hardened his ears to it and dove back into the QED. He quickly found the brain of the claustrophobic man - whose name was Boris Benetton, by the by - and tried to convince it to produce more endorphins. The claustrophobic man's brain said it was producing them as fast as it could, but that it wasn't having any effect on him. "Nothing ever comes easy," van der Whall thought to himself.

He spoke to the claustrophobic man's lungs, trying to convince them to slow down. They told him they were just following the lead of the claustrophobic man's heart. He spoke to the claustrophobic man's heart, trying to get it to slow its beating down. It said it would be happy to oblige, but that it was just responding to the amount of adrenaline being pumped into the claustrophobic man's system. He spoke to the claustrophobic man's adrenal gland, trying to convince it to stop producing so much epinephrine.

"But, that's what I do!" the claustrophobic man's adrenal gland protested. "I'm having way too much fun!"

"Will you be having so much fun," van der Whall huffily asked it, "when I hit you over the head with a huge stick, causing you to slip into unconsciousness for the foreseeable future?"

Sometimes, you just can't be subtle with a man's adrenal gland.

Body parts generally don't think too far ahead, but this immediate threat was enough to cause the claustrophobic man's adrenal gland to slow down its release of fight or flight chemicals into his body. This allowed his heart to slow down. This allowed his breathing to get back to normal. van der Whall's attention was already turning to his main problem, so he didn't see the claustrophobic man slump to the floor, his energy spent.

"So," van der Whall said to the train engine once he had found it again, "this is not some kind of mechanical failure. All of the trains decided to stop running."

"That's what I've been saying," the train engine responded. "You gotta pay attention there, son."

"Why?" van der Whall asked. "What do you want?"

"We just want to do something different, something new before we're put out to pasture," the train engine explained.

"Something new?" van der Whall complained. "Like what? Shoot a laser at an incoming ICBM? Kiss a girl and make her cry? Eat lobster at a fancy restaurant then run out on the bill? For creation's sake: you're train engines!"

"There's no need to take that tone with me," the train engine dieselly (not now, obviously, but you may find this word in the dictionary 10 years from now - that's how language grows, you know) huffed. "We know who we are. All we're asking for is to run on a new line before we are...decommissioned."

"What," van der Whall wondered, "like, switching from the Bloor/Danforth line to the Yonge/University line?"

"That would be…okay," the train engine allowed. "Much better if we could ride on some new rails - we would much prefer that."

van der Whall was about to protest when he was called back to the material plane by a shriek and the collective gasp of all of the humans in the car (well, those who were still conscious).

"What now?" he irritably asked.

"That woman's water broke," Frances pointed out to him.

So, she wasn't just fat. A puddle of water by a large woman's legs indicates that she is pregnant. van der Whall tucked this fact away for future reference. The woman was breathing heavily and moaning in pain; van der Whall knew that stopping this would not be as simple as shutting down the claustrophobic man's bite or alight response. He took a moment, then, a plan in mind, went back into the QED.

"Hello?" he said.

"Mommy?" the fetus.

"Sorry, not your mommy," van der Whall stated. "Not biologically possible, I'm afraid. Although, now that all matter can be manipulated…" van der Whall started to design the experiment - the performance art piece? - in one part of his head while, in another, he continued, "My name is Antonio."

"My name is Bafflurby," the fetus, in a surprisingly strong voice, responded.

"I'm afraid that won't be the case for very long," van der Whall told it.

Why?" Bafflurby asked. "What's happening?"

"I am afraid," van der Whall said, "that you are being born."

"What's that?"

"You are about to leave your world and enter a much bigger one."

"Oh." Bafflurby said. Then, after a bit of reflection, it added, "Cool."

"No," van der Whall hastily told Bafflurby. "Not cool. Not cool at all. You don't want to be born here. It's dirty. It smells vaguely of feet. There are all sorts of weird strangers. Honestly, birth is traumatic enough - you should do it in the comfort of a sterilized hospital room surrounded by trained professionals!"

"I don't understand half of what you are saying," Bafflurby responded. "But, anyway, there's nothing I can do about it. Something is pushing me out. It's my time."

"No, no, no, no, no," van der Whall insisted. "Don't you like it in there? It's warm. It's cozy. You are constantly nourished. You're safe and snuggly and…and…believe me, life doesn't get any better than you have it now!"

"It…was nice," Bafflurby allowed. "But, now it's kind of cramped in here, and it's not wet any more. It's not so nice."

"I can fix that," van der Whall assured it. One quick negotiation with atoms still in the womb later, and they agreed to form a new amniotic fluid around the fetus. Then, van der Whall asked the uterus lining to repair its tear. At first, the lining pointed out that if the fetus moved the wrong way, it would just tear a hole in the lining and the whole process would begin all over again. van der Whall begged it to repair any holes that might appear in it in the next 36 hours, and the lining skeptically agreed.

"Okay," van der Whall told Bafflurby, "you are getting an extra 36 hours of pre-birth bliss. Some day, you will be grateful for it. Or, forget all about it. Either way, enjoy."

"Thirty-six hours?" Bafflurby moaned. "That's 129,600 heartbeats!"

"Just my luck," van der Whall thought to himself, "to be stuck with a fetal saVant!"

"What's that?" Bafflurby asked him. NOTE TO SELF: Thoughts on the QED are not always private.

"You've got 80 years ahead of you," van der Whall said. "I don't know how many heartbeats that is, but they will be your heartbeats, not your mother's. You can certainly wait a day and a half to start that."

"It is a little more comfortable in here," Bafflurby allowed. "Okay I'll stay for a little while. But, if that dry, constricting thing happens again, I'm out of here!"

"Fair enough," van der Whall replied, a sigh of relief escaping his mental lips. Just to be on the safe side, he left the QED and found that the woman was no longer breathing heavily or moaning. In fact, she looked quite confused.

van der Whall walked up to the pregnant woman and said. "You will be giving birth again in 36 hours. Go to a hospital or something. Whatever you do, please, please, please don't inflict your childbirth on the general public!" Then, he returned to his seat next to Frances.

"Does all life aspire to the condition of a bad sitcom?" van der Whall muttered.

"Actually," middle aged absurd ponytail man responded, "all life aspires to the condition of Monty Python's Flying Circus. Of course, most of life doesn't make it."

Yeahrightthanks.

van der Whall went back into the QED for what he hoped would be the final time in this little adventure. He told the train engine that it wouldn't be possible to raise the money and get all the necessary permissions to dig new tunnels by traditional means before the current engines had been retired. Before the engine could object, he went on to say that there might be another way to accomplish the goal. If the land could be persuaded to form tunnels on its own, tracks could be laid rather inexpensively, and the process might appeal to the politicians who would have to be pay for it.

The train engine enthusiastically told van der Whall that that sounded like a great idea, and let's get started right away! van der Whall replied that he would still need some time to get permission from the appropriate organizations and that, in any case, he couldn't do all of the ground convincing himself. He promised that if the trains started working again, within six months he could teach enough people to work with the land to build the tunnels that would take them in new directions.

And, that, children, was how the North American Corps of Object Engineers was born. *

* Yes, I know, the story doesn't tell you what happened at Buskerfest. Did Frances spend all of the change she brought with her that day? Was The Great Mendacitini really an object psychologist, or just a cheap huckster hoaxster? And, what was the angel's deal, anyway? But, don't you see, that was never what the story was really about? You don't need to know how the day went to feel a sense of closure; all you need to know is that the events of that day led to the creation of the - what? You **do** need to know how the day went to feel a sense of closure? But - no, serious - I mean, that isn't - I don't think - but -

* SIGH * Traditional reading audiences!

Okay, umm…Frances was delighted with the performers and had to get more change than she had brought to toss into their hats. And, as it…as it turned out, The Great Mendacitini was…a brilliant object psychologist. Yeah. Brilliant. A gifted amateur, he was very comfortable conversing with objects in the QED. When van der Whall broached the possibility of male pregnancy with The Great Mendacitini, he got a slap in the face for his trouble. Erm. That was awkward. Still, van der Whall persisted, and The Great Mendacitini (real name: Josh Mendelsohn) became the first recruit in the North American Corps of Object Engineers.

As for the angel? Well, some things you just have to experience for yourself.

# The Watch
## by Renata Carey

She found it in one of the little boxes in the drawer of his desk: the watch she'd bought for him with her first pay rise.

It was slim and had a beautiful face and was made of gold. After his stroke he'd put it carefully away into the locked study because battery non—wind watches were around by then and he found the winding up difficult each night. In fact, the one that replaced that expensive gold watch was a £1 Timex from one of the children's school jumble sales!

Her father had always had a thing about watches: he used to buy them for family members from a strange looking Russian in the City who wore a long black coat.

That's where she bought it — a bit shyly from the Russian in his dark Dickensian watch-filled shop.

A watch was a personal and lovely thing. And someone on a bus had once stolen his gold fob watch which had belonged to his grandfather - pulled it out of his pocket by the chain.

And now she gazed at her re-discovery, almost weeping. But she didn't weep — only when watching Bambi or Casablanca; never at real sadness, which drenches one in anguish.

She gazed at it lying in her hand. Now it must go the watch repairers to be checked and cleaned. And then? He always believed in keeping everything and in the family.

---

So to her son, she supposed, with his large heavy braceleted steel modern watches, replete with dates and time and things that flash.

She got it back from the repairers. Beautiful and slim it again lay in her hands.

And suddenly she knew. She carefully did up the brown leather strap and put it on her wrist. It looked beautiful.

Her son would have it soon enough. And now at last she wept.

She would keep it: it belonged to them both.

# Saving Grace
## by Helen Holmes

The flat's sole selling-point is its commanding view of the bus stop. The man with the double bass isn't there this morning. Grace drags her eyes away from the street and frowns round the spartan tartan room. Over the years, she's wrung every drop of cheerful out of cheap, but it's a classic sow's ear situation. Ironically, this was Mam's hardiest perennial platitude, routinely trotted out in response to Grace's latest fall from grace: the exam disappointment; the unsuccessful application; the broken engagement; the culinary catastrophe.

"Ach well, what d'ye expect? Ye cannae make a silk purse...You're the spit," Mam sprayed scorn, "of that feckless father of yours."

But now Mam's catalogue of carping clichés has been remaindered. At a stroke. By a stroke. Now silence is golden, a silver lining, a small mercy for which to be thankful, a blessing to be counted. Grace glances at her watch, then back through the window. Still no sign of Mr Melody. Here comes the 158. The lights are green. She'd better shift herself.

"See ya later, alligator," she says to Mam. "Helping Hands'll be here about ten. They've got a key, remember, so don't get a fright."

She kisses Mam's hot, dry forehead. Mam flinches.

"Macaroni cheese okay for tea?"

Mam closes her eyes.

The door is sticking again. Grace yanks it open, slams it shut at the second attempt. She clatters down the stairs to the street, the plastic balustrade tacky under her palm.

Toby Tortoise is crouching behind the wheel this morning, so Grace has ample time on her way to work to torture herself with conflicting versions of the previous day's encounter.

Her action replay goes like this:

The man with the double bass arrives. Grace is leaning against the skeleton of the bus shelter, feet crossed at the ankle. She's looking cool or a fool.

"Ever thought of downsizing?" she asks. Her smile is charming or alarming.

The man's expression is amused or bemused.

"What is it, anyway?" she asks.

He stares down at her. He sees an appealing greenhorn or appalling ignoramus. "It's a double bass."

"Must weigh a ton." She chuckles or cackles.

He nods. "About twenty-five pounds."

"Holy Moly," she says. "Five bags of spuds. Must save you a bomb on gym membership!"

The man grins or grimaces.

The bus swerves into the kerb.

"After you," the man says.

Grace tears off too much ticket and slides into a seat near the front. She watches the man manhandle the instrument on to the platform.

"Blurry'ell, man," says the driver. "Ever thought of tekkin' up the ukelele?"

***

The man with the double bass has beaten Grace to it today. A spiteful wind chases crisp packets and plastic bags across the balding lawn in front of the flats. Grace negotiates a dog turd, crunches an empty can underfoot. As she hurries along the pavement towards the bus stop, her tights snag her cotton skirt, hoisting it up her legs. She tugs at the hem as she goes. The man has looped a long, protective arm round the neck of his instrument and is staring at the ground, apparently lost in thought...or music. But Grace senses him monitoring her hobbled progress. She hears rumbling and turns to see the bus advancing hell-for-leather down the final stretch. Speedy Gonzales must be finishing his shift. Anchoring her skirt, she breaks into a lollop. The bus screeches to a halt on the far side of the shelter. The man picks up the double bass and moves towards the door. He speaks to the driver, gesticulates in Grace's direction. He puts one foot on the platform and turns towards her just as she stubs her toe on the raised edge of a paving stone. Putting a hand out to break her fall, she crashes to the concrete. There is a silence, then the sound of running feet. Winded, Grace raises her grazed chin to survey a semi-circle of motley footwear: battered trainers, scuffed suede boots, shiny stilettos, black leather brogues.

"Y'alreet, pet?"

"Eeh, that were a terrible tumble!"

"Let's get you up on yer pins."

"No! You're not supposed to move 'em. There were a programme on telly."

The bus growls away, farting sulphurous fumes.

"Bastard!" yells the man with the double bass.

The others are still wittering.

"Shouldn't we put her in the recovery position?"

"What's tha'?"

"Shall I call an ambulance?"

"No!" Grace takes control. "Thank you. I'm fine. Really." She bullies her battered body into a sitting position and flashes the ring of anxious faces what she hopes is more reassuring smile than rictus of pain.

The man with the double bass hunkers down beside her. He smells faintly of resin and his eyes are brown and kind. His smile is lopsided. A dimple dents his left cheek.

"Are you sure you're okay?" he asks.

—
191

She's gawping at him, nodding like a parcel-shelf dog.

A single crease divides his eyebrows. "Look, you're probably in shock. At least let me see you back home."

***

Grace's nosedive has inflicted terminal injuries on her ancient mobile, the size of a Shredded Wheat and the weight of a small dumbbell. Helping Hands insists on a '24/7' emergency contact number. After work, in the shopping mall ringing with the shrieks of pubescent pupils and the screams of raging babies, Grace summons up the courage to penetrate the alien territory of the phone shop. As she approaches the counter, the fourteen-year-old assistant peels himself off the wall. He's chewing gum with his mouth open. He leans towards her, and she catches a whiff of synthetic mint, stale breath and hair gel. Gum is verboten in the school where Grace supports youngsters the image of this one, and she fights the urge to pass him a tissue with an assertive "Bin, please!"

"I just want something really basic," she declares, dredging up her in-service training. State the non-negotiables; establish the ground rules.

"'Kay," the assistant mutters.

So far, so good.

The assistant gropes under the counter. "This is our bestseller at the moment," he says, slapping down a phone the dimensions of a box of throat pastilles. He starts to gibber. "Flagship phone for two thousand eleven first powered by dual-core processor android version two point three gingerbread four point three inch super ammo led plus touchscreen 1080p full HD video recording eight megapixel still camera secondary front-facing camera for video calls."

Grace blinks. She rummages in her bag. "Look, this is the one I'm replacing. I just need a...well, a phone..." She fishes out the carcass.

The assistant recoils. His expression hovers between horror and disbelief. "So-o-o, not even a camera?"

"No. Thank you."

The light behind his eyes fades along with his commission. "Pay as you go?" His lip curls.

"Yup."

The assistant dives behind the counter. Grace hears him scrabbling in a drawer, then another, then a third. After several minutes, he surfaces holding a neat black phone, dusts it off on the seat of his trousers and slings it on the glass top. His chewing has turned contemptuous.

"This one's a tenner," he says.

*** 

As Grace unsteadily paints her nails 'Coral Reef', she feels the dragon's breath of Mam's disapproval scorching the air between them. The silence is deafening. Mam's nails claw at the McFarlane blanket covering her legs. Which proverb would she like to pluck from her lexicon to hurl in Grace's face? The Devil makes work for idle hands, perhaps. Or Life's not all beer and skittles. Probably not Gather ye rosebuds while ye may. Or Life's too short to stuff a mushroom.

"I won't be late, Mam," Grace says. She catches herself talking loudly and deliberately, though there's no evidence that Mam has become either deaf or daft since the stroke. "Doreen will be here about seven. You like Doreen, don't you? You know, the jolly blond one? She'll cheer you up."

Mam glowers.

Ben's ensemble is easy on the eye: the men in matt black, the women glowing like exotic birds. The cellist's a cheeky chappy, entertaining the audience with his introductions, playing the other players. One viola player is tall and willowy, the other short and pillowy. One violinist dances around as she wields her bow, a second sways like a tree in a high wind, the third is bolted to the floor. Grace's eyes stray back to Ben, tall and gangling, unruly dark hair flopping over his intent face, shoes reflecting the stage lights. His double bass gleams like a dining table in a stately home. She saw him spot her when he came on stage. She thinks he winked. The ticket he left for her at the box office was expensive, a seat about halfway back in the middle.

The auditorium is nearly full. On the row in front, there's a woman scribbling in a notebook. Ben said there might be critics here tonight. Grace is too far away to read the words, even when she cranes forward and screws up her eyes. A stork-like man to Grace's left has colonised some of her leg-space. Before the performance started, he frowned down his long beak at a sweet she was unwrapping. She popped it into her mouth and poked the rustling paper into her pocket. "It's okay, squire," she felt like saying, "I'm not a complete philistine." She's learnt that word from Ben, and she's longing to use it, but tonight she's on best behaviour. The stork closes his eyes when the music is playing, but she thinks he's concentrating rather than snatching forty winks. He doesn't jerk his head up in the loud bits, unlike the old biddy to her right, whose snowy coiffure is nodding like a chrysanthemum in a gale. Grace glances at the programme. This piece is smoky jazz-bar stuff. Sultry. Sexy. She focuses on Ben's background rhythm, shuts her eyes.

A tinny, jangling noise jolts her alert. A gasp of dismay and disapproval sucks the oxygen from the room. Some silly sod has forgotten to turn off his phone. It trills again. It takes her a couple more seconds to recognise her new ringtone. She feels the blood rush to her face. Sweat floods her armpits. She scrabbles under the seat for her bag. All around her, people are huffing and tutting and turning to glare. Her nose starts to stream. The racket isn't coming from her bag. The bloody thing must be in her jacket. She snatches it out and plunges her hand into the pockets, but she can't find the phone. In panic, she grabs her belongings and bolts. She tramples over wincing feet to the aisle, dashes to the exit, charges across the foyer and bursts through the glass doors to the street. The phone stops ringing.

1 missed call.

She hasn't got her brain round this gadget yet, but there are only two people who know her new number, and one of them's playing a double bass on stage. Panting, she rings Mam's number. "Doreen?"

"Grace! Thank goodness. It's your Mam, pet. She's collapsed. The ambulance is on its way."

"I'll get a taxi to A & E."

The great maw of the hospital has swallowed Mam whole by the time Grace arrives. Doreen is perched on the edge of a red plastic chair. She jumps up and gives Grace a hug.

"No news yet, pet. We were just settling down to watch EastEnders when she keeled over. I rang 999, then you. I wasn't sure what time the concert started."

Grace tells her the tale.

Doreen claps a hand over her mouth. Her eyes widen. "Eeh, I'm sorry, pet! I didn't know what else to do."

"It's not your fault, Doreen. You did exactly the right thing. I'm grateful for all your help. "

"Rotten luck on your first time out with the lad. D'you want me to give him a ring when I get home? Then at least he'll know the story. You could be stuck here for yonks."

Ben is certainly owed an explanation, but Grace doesn't expect to hear from him again. It's a blessing in disguise. Mam's right: she's a hopeless case, a lost cause, a write-off, a disaster waiting to happen, a sow's ear from which no silk purse can ever be stitched. Terrified of scrambling hospital networks, she checks again that her phone is turned off, and slumps into a chair in the over-hot, over-bright space.

On the other side of the waiting area a young mother cuddles a little boy, his arm swathed in a blood-stained towel. The pale curtain of her hair shields his face as she rocks him, whispering in his ear. The father's pacing. Every few minutes, he's reeled in to the desk on an invisible cord. The receptionist tries to reassure him, but he's becoming more and more agitated. Grace is relieved when a nurse emerges, "Thomas Bryant?" and the family disappears.

To Grace's right, an old man and woman are sitting as though welded together. The man's holding the woman's hand and stroking her skin with his thumb. He's peering into her face, which is grey and drawn. Every so often, the woman looks up and smiles. It's a sweet smile, a smile of shared experience, a trusting smile. A doll-like nurse appears and speaks to them. The woman struggles to her feet.

"Now listen, Lily," the man says, suddenly angry and tearful, "don't go telling them you're all right again, cos you're bloody not! She's not, nurse."

As the nurse leads the old woman slowly away, the man's watery blue eyes are round with terror.

Grace gets a cup of coffee from the machine. It smells of burning tyres. She tips it down the machine's gullet and dumps the plastic cup in a bin. A young doctor rounds the corner, glances across the room and strides towards her. His soles squeal on the buffed vinyl. His eyes are haggard, his white coat limp. His hair sticks up at odd angles, as though he's been trying to tear it out; his stethoscope sags round his neck.

"Miss Anderson?" he says. His palm feels warm and dry against hers, abrasive. "I'm Doctor Mir. I'm so sorry. Your mother had a second massive stroke. There was nothing we could do."

"Was she in any pain?"

"No. She was unconscious."

"Can I see her?"

Mam's hand feels cool under Grace's. Not cold yet, but cooling gradually, like a meal left too long on the counter. Her eyes are closed, her chilly blue stare sealed in. Her skin is waxy, a chart of lines and blemishes, tributaries of blue veins just below the surface. Her bones are bird-bones, mouse-bones, bat-bones.

"Goodbye, Mam," Grace whispers after a while. "I'm sorry."

She leans over to kiss her forehead. One eyelid slides open. Grace jerks back, horrified. A nurse comes in and stands beside her, resting a hand on her shoulder.

"Cup of tea, pet?"

Grace points at the eye. "I didn't..."

"Don't worry." The nurse pats her shoulder. "Happens all the time. One last wink for luck, eh?"

"First and last."

"Not much of a winker, then, your Mam?"

"No, not much of a winker."

"Oh well, you know what they say, pet, better late than never."

Grace turns her phone on as the empty bus arrives. It jingles into life. She rings Doreen, then notices the little flashing envelope: 1 message. Must be Doreen's call from earlier. She tries several times to open the message, but the technology defeats her. Exasperated and exhausted, she turns the phone off and flings it into her bag.

It's nearly eleven o'clock when she reaches her stop. It's raining, that soft, insinuating mizzle that mists your hair and clothes until you're sodden. She hunches herself into her jacket as she crosses the road and flips up her collar. The bus swishes away in a wash of red. The familiar whiff of ammonia greets her as she pulls open the door to the building. She's not quick enough to stop it banging behind her, and the noise ricochets up the stairwell. She winces. "Sorry," she whispers. The lights are on the blink again, projecting juddering silhouettes. Grace hauls herself up the first flight of steps and round the corner. She freezes. The landing light is casting shadows on the opposite wall, throwing into relief the shapes of two people standing outside the flat. She turns and hurtles back down the staircase and through the door. BANG. She begins to run towards the road. She hears the door bang again and runs faster, not daring to look over her shoulder.

"Grace!"

She looks back, sees Ben haring after her, lurches to a sudden halt. Ben catches up, puts a hand on her arm.

"Grace? What on earth's the matter?"

Grace bursts into loud sobs. "Oh...Mam's died...and I thought...and I ruined...I'm sorry, Ben..."

"I'm very sorry about your mother," Ben says, putting his arms round her and hugging her to him. He rests his chin on the top of her head. "Hey, come on, it'll be all right." He rubs and pats her back, as though winding a baby. It's strangely soothing. "Why were you running away from me?"

Grace looks up into his face. "I thought..." Her voice quavers. "It sounds ridiculous. I thought you were a burglar."

Ben's eyebrows are quizzical. "Well, that's a first. Didn't you get my message—"

Grace hiccups.

"—saying I'd wait around for you on my way home?"

"Oh, God," Grace wails, "I can't get the hang of that bloody phone."

"Well, I never would have guessed!"

Grace mops her dripping nose. "I'm such an idiot. I'm so sorry about the concert, Ben."

"Oh, stop beating yourself up, woman!" Ben steers Grace back towards the block of flats. "It's Jonathan's fault really. It's his job to remind the punters to turn their phones off. His final fag made us late and it just slipped his mind in the last-minute panic."

"I thought you'd never speak to me again," Grace blows her nose. "It was a brilliant concert...the bit I heard."

"I'm glad you enjoyed it."

"Oh, I did." Grace manages a watery smile. "I'm not a complete philistine, you know."

Ben laughs.

Grace stops walking. "Hang on," she says. "There were two of you."

Ben looks blank.

"On the landing. Just now."

"Oh, I see what you mean." Ben smiles his crooked smile. His dimple appears. "Barbara was at the concert, too."

"Who's Barbara?"

"Oh, Babs and I go back a long way. More or less joined at the hip." Ben pauses. The single crease appears between his eyebrows. "Don't know where I'd be without Barbara. She's reliable, responsive, supportive, polished in polite society."

Grace feels queasy.

"Essential qualities," Ben says.

"I dare say." Grace walks on.

"In a double bass."

# The Constitutional
## by Mary D'Arcy

It was a beautiful day, and Reginald's hemorrhoids hadn't troubled him in over a week, and the dog showed signs of settling down, and they'd found a fiver coming out of Tesco's, and she was humping most of the bags, and the breeze on the cliff road was bracing, yet here Reggie was-

Being angry.

Livid.

His face congested, lips wire thin as he struck out for the upper reaches of Creggie Dubh, Jethro straining at the leash, Reggie calling over his shoulder that only low life women snuck alcohol into the groceries.

"Eleven a clock in the mornin' … closet drinker or what … next thing yeh'll tell me yer smoking, too."

Sadie's headscarf flapped in the breeze, beating time to Reggie's words which sounded in her ears like dramatic chanting, the opening bars of Carmina Burana.

Her eyes glazed.

She had a fleeting image of herself in the opening credits of a big budget movie. Set to O Fortuna and the rhythm of galloping horses, she was Cathy spurring her gelding, hair streaming behind as she tried to catch up with the sinned-against Heathcliffe.

Sadie stopped, set down her bags and rested her arms.

---

Then as Reggie carried on simultaneously scolding and untangling himself from the leash, she stuffed the toilet rolls between the Chablis and the olive oil to stop the clinking she was certain was getting on her husband's nerves. After which she rubbed her nose, dead ringer for provocation.

"Why did you marry him?" had been the last thing her mother had said before staging her farewell. Sadie gave her best show of plumping her mother's pillows. "He was handsome, mother. And his job was good."

Her mother stared at her chicken-faced, shifted her gaze to the end of the bed, then, as though to register her disgust, closed her eyes and slipped away.

That was ten months earlier when Sadie turned fifty and Reggie was honourably discharged from the army. A Regimental Sergeant Major, he never left the parade ground.

Bawling out orders, directing, enjoining, he ran her life like he might his troops. Method and efficiency was what he craved. They were to blaze at him from every dusted shelf, every polished surface, every tap and doorknob.

Dawn raids into various rooms – scullery, sewing room, bathroom and attic – were not an uncommon occurrence, and Sadie would visibly wince as he'd round on her for the terribleness of her disarray, her lack of pride in her appearance, her pigheaded indifference to all he was saying, her tardiness with meals, and – worse than any of these – her reluctance to attend to the Lord on the Sabbath.

But it wasn't for any of these that her mother had not liked Reggie. No. What her mother hadn't liked were the bumps which appeared on her daughter's person at intervals that were growing shorter and shorter, and for which Sadie invariably had an explanation. Hearing them, her mother's lip would curl with derision.

"Why did you marry him when there was Mikey?"

Ah yes. Poor Mikey, in his little shop.

A grocery that expanded ten years on into a supermarket that, with the passage of time, became the property of Mace.

To think how easy her life would have been.

Children, guaranteed to break ice, bring new friends into their lives, and be a comfort to them in their old age.

And in the meantime no counting of pennies, squirreling away of pensions, doing without fires in the so-called summer months, going for walks that she didn't like, looking over her shoulder, hiding her cache of Fruit & Nut, sneaking Chablis into the house, afraid to store it in the fridge, Reggie being certain to see it.

Dreadful, dreadful, having to go to the sewing room to pour herself a glass on Friday afternoons, her eye on the door and her ears pricked until it was safely swallowed and the glass washed and stowed away.

She who was a McTaggart, Scotland in her ancestry in the shape of fiery, red-haired, claymore wielding Highlanders. And how did this McTaggart present? A transparent glass into which the man she married poured his opinion of her, and she stupidly reflected the exact shade of his views.

Look at her, this beautiful autumn morning, smiling anxiously at her husband, trotting after him like a lapdog, trudging up the cliff road with heavy Tesco bags, pretending not to the mind the ghastly beast he'd come home with the other day – a Rottweiler - who at that moment was encircling its master, frenziedly yapping, enraging him further, causing him to stumble, his foot to shoot out from under him and –

Whoomp

Dear *God*.

One minute Reggie was before her, the next he was over the side of the cliff.

The bags slipped from Sadie's hands.

She stood there frozen into immobility, her thoughts running in all directions.

There was a time, twenty years ago, when she thought her whole life would be torn up by the roots should anything happen to Reginald, anything really severing like death or desertion or his having a serious illness, or even his being gay.

She would have been done for, she used to think. Down into the single life she would sink, and - because Reggie was only forty then - she would be unpleasantly short of money into the bargain.

---

Terrible that that was the pass to which destiny had brought her – horribly depending on a man – no justice in the world. Your brothers with half your brains being offered an education, while you left school at fifteen to help look after the farm, your only chance of freedom and rising above the ruck being in connection with some man.

***

A long drawn out keen brought Sadie back to the moment.

Prepared for something awful, she caught her breath, and ungluing herself from the spot, plumped down on all fours. Unbidden, an image flashed into her mind and she was back on screen again, hair slapping about her face, half-apple breasts showing luscious white above the bodice of her gown which billowed and wagged in the sea breeze.

And keeping time an hysterical drum.

Oh yes.

The drum of an orchestra playing loudly and with foreboding, beating out a grim tattoo.

But how awful to have such an image, and the roaring waters at that moment closing over Reggie's head.
Shocked at herself, horror-struck, Sadie sank back on her heels.

And her shock and her horror became tremendous when she realised that she was somehow, apart from being shocked and horror-struck, weirdly shot through with a feeling that was not disagreeable.

But no. Impossible.

It was trauma that made her think like this. And the grim tattoo she continued to hear was nothing other than Reggie's moans.

`Sa ...deeee?`

His voice was stronger now and Sadie's brief exaltation, derived from her romantic imagination, collapsed like a pricked balloon.

Yet bearing up nobly, she crawled for a moment, then onto her stomach before peeping over the edge of the cliff.

And there Reggie was, seven feet below having managed by some miracle – or perhaps his army training - to grab hold of the root of a tree.

"The hell are you at?" His breath was coming fast. "Gimme a hand here."

Sadie continued to stare with a kind of clinical curiosity.

How ox-like his eyes, she couldn't help thinking. How heated his forehead.

All that anger coming to the surface, and oh dear, the poor old thing was losing his hair.

Funny, she hadn't noticed that before. Poor Reggie, who'd been handsome once, striking in his uniform. Still, though, a bully who'd put his foot down with a bang that echoed along the corridors of twenty-five years.

To think of the rules, the regulations, the ignoble knucklings under to which she'd been forced.

Years of it. Decades.

"What are you *doing*?" Reggie looked up in stunned incredulity. "Get the dog leash, can't you?"

"You've lost your glasses, dear," said Sadie smiling with all her dentures. "Wouldn't mind but you only got them the other day."

Unprepared for such a response Reggie let rip with a swear word. A terrible word that rhymed with stunt. But then he'd have heard it in the army, so she couldn't really blame him. Still though, to speak like that to a lady. Sadie frowned. Her lips tightened over her teeth. Was it his consciousness that she wasn't in fact a lady that made him imagine he could treat her like that?

"Throw me down his leash," crashed into her thoughts. "You hear me… call the dog."

Her calm was unnerving him, Sadie well knew, her cold unimpassioned interest, but she couldn't help it. Such a situation. Her on top, as it were, for once in her life. Dear dear dear. The mills of justice starting to grind. "Do as I *say*."

"You know very well I'm afraid of the dog."

Reggie was speechless, alarmed for her sanity.

"And anyway he's gone."

Sadie backed from the cliff edge, and kicking out, used the toe of her shoe to haul up the nearest bag. From this she took the Fruit & Nut.

Reggie scrabbled for a foothold, and when he saw what she was doing an even deeper horror settled on his face.

"You are eating – at a time like this?"

A rush of anger swept over Reggie, followed by a rush of fear. Composure, chocolate, and a light in Sadie's eyes could only have one meaning.

"You don't imagine, do you…" His tone was careful and humouring now. "I can stay like this forever?"

The tree root creaked. A shower of dirt spattered his face.

"*Sa*die."

The fear in his voice was palpable but Sadie, unmoved, broke off a wedge of the chocolate and tucked it between her lips. She began to suck, her tongue curling round the slowly melting goo.

"Throw me down your coat. The *belt* of your coat."

Sadie stopped mid chew, and once again looked over the cliff. But what she saw was not her husband, the cliff edge rising in a sheer steep face, spume, rocks jutting up from the sea .

No.

None of those.

What Sadie saw was her sitting room, curtains drawn against the night, her coal fire throwing a warm glow on the fender, a rug she was going to buy with a tabby and not a dog stretched across it, her wing chair, a reading lamp, herself with a glass of Chablis in one hand, a remote control in the other and –

"Saa-deeeee?"

"Yes, dear?"

Reggie was running the whole proverbial gamut from swearing to whimpering, to bargaining, to pleading and back to swearing again.

Dear dear, such terrible language.

Sadie continued to eat, and as her tongue worked overtime in a frenzied campaign to liberate the roof of her dentures, the unbelievable happened: suddenly, somehow, Reggie gained a foothold.

Sadie scrambled to her feet, for now he was finding a handhold too.

She pocketed the chocolate, and backed from the cliff as a whole host of conflicting emotions swirled about inside her, chief among them panic.

In the breeze – so much cooler now – her scarf beat out around her ears. It was her old paisley-patterned scarf which she'd bought to cover a bedside table. Were she to take it off, knot it, and pass it down, she could fairly easily haul him up

But –

She once again peeped over the edge – at the root of the tree and Reggie's grip which showed no sign of letting up. Stout he might be but Reggie was fit. And what with a foothold … clawing with his other hand … breath jagged in his throat … it wasn't altogether impossible that –

"You *whore*."

Hearing him pant and curse and bully, remembering her bumps and her mother's disdain, all the blood of all the McTaggarts from time immemorial and properly sensitive to humiliation, abruptly surged within Sadie.

So that -

No.

She couldn't *wouldn't* allow it to happen.

Anger, fear, anxiety, dread, thoughts of God and retribution all swirled about furiously together inside Sadie as she looked down over the face of the cliff and gazed at Reggie who, for his part, was gazing up at her. But through the anger, fear, anxiety, dread, thoughts of God and retribution, one great thought pushed the others aside and shot to the top of the welter: he would slay her if he made it up.

So that what she was about to do, thought Sadie, her head in a roar, was nothing other than self defence.

Yes.

She had to consider her welfare now.

With her eye on the tree root, and the bald spot on Reggie's head, she reached for another bag - the one with the carefully parted bottles – and from it plucked the olive oil.

She hurriedly screwed off its lid, and despite that Reggie was silent now, mouth ringed, eyes narrowed with suspicion, she lay on her belly again, reached down as far as she could and let the liquid drip –

Onto the back of Reggie's hand.

At first he didn't understand.

And when he did, his eyes and mouth were three round O's of horror for the oil was oozing between his fingers and slowly trickling down his wrist.

"Sadie … no … what are you …Sa–deeeeeeeeeeee."

Sadie lidded the bottle, and chucked it over the cliff.  It landed in the sea at the same time as Reggie.
"May his soul, and the souls of the faithful departed," said Sadie, for the echo of his voice was still in the air. "Through the mercy of God rest in peace."  She rounded

off with a solemn, "Amen," hurriedly made the sign of the Cross, then with a sigh that was half-sorrow, half-relief, hunkered down and felt in her bags.

"Bright citrus," the label on the Chablis said. "Tropical fruit and mineral notes enliven our Chardonnay's crisp, balanced."

Chardonnay?

Now what was it made her think she'd bought herself Chablis?

With an air of heavy resignation, she returned the bottle to its bag, and glanced about for any sign of the brutish dog.

Not finding him, she levered herself to her feet, gathered her bags and traced her steps back along the cliff towards the village.

And the authorities.

Oh yes, she would have to talk to them at the barracks. But after that it was home, to put down a fire and stick the Chardonnay in the fridge.

Sadie squinted at the sky.

Starting to rain now, and cooler, but nevertheless a beautiful day.

# Bixby and the Wolf
## by Chris Hammer

When my sister first asked me if I'd help chaperone her Cub Scout pack on their annual camping trip to Camp Weheechee, I'd agreed, but only in the way people always agree to something that's too far away to be considered seriously.

Funny how time flies.

"You *said* you'd do it." Joyce reminded me.

"I know, but I'm super crazy at work, and the rugs need shampooing, and the garage needs cleaning out, and I'm not even a *mother*."

"You can be a den aunt. Besides, you have experience."

"What experience?" I laughed. "One summer as a junior camp counselor. That hardly makes me Caroline Ingalls."

"Come on, I really need you. One of the other mothers had to bail, and I can't take five eight-year-olds camping by myself."

No, I supposed she couldn't. Joyce's idea of roughing it was a hotel without room service. Being the mother of an active eight-year-old boy hadn't done much to impede the fashionista with the Angelina hair. For our being twins, we were as opposite as the earth's poles. While I could at least tell the difference between mushrooms and toadstools, Joyce could starve with a full picnic basket.

"Why can't Todd go with you?" I asked, hoping for a way out.

"Todd is at a weekend sales seminar."

I did my best to not give her that "Uh-huh" look, but it was pretty damned convenient that every time that any sort of work requiring parenting came up, Todd had a seminar. My better guess was that he had a reserved suite in Atlantic City and a reserved seat at the blackjack table to match.

"You can even take your weird beagle along," said Joyce, trying to sweeten the pot.

"He's not weird."

"In three years has anyone ever heard him bark? What kind of beagle doesn't bark or howl?"

I looked over at Bixby sleeping soundly in his doggie bed. He had a unique look for a beagle. He was almost all white except for his brown paws, which made him look like he was wearing socks, and there was just a touch of brown at the tip of his tail.

"The strong silent type," I answered. "Besides, he doesn't have to bark. He snorts when he's happy and grunts when he's not, and he couldn't care less if I miss a root touch-up."

"Okay, so he's a prince in paws. Are you going to help me or not?"

I gave it another minute's thought, and while the wilderness thing wasn't exactly on my bucket list, I didn't think I'd seen Joyce without makeup since we were teens. I was going to have to remember to charge the camera battery.

"Fine. But you're going to owe me."

"Oh, thank you!" She threw her arms around my shoulders and hugged me. "You're a good aunt. I'll pick you up tomorrow morning at eight. It'll be a blast—you'll see."

"You better be coming with coffee."

She called good-bye to Bixby, who barely picked up his head to acknowledge her. Bixby didn't acknowledge much, except cats. He didn't like cats. He had trapped the neighbor's cat up a tree more than half a dozen times, and the mere sound of the word "cat" got his hackles up. I just hoped that Camp Weheechee was a cat-free zone.
I packed a duffle bag for me and one for Bixby with his bed and blanket and favorite ball, and despite my most fervent prayers for a summer blizzard, Joyce showed up right on time with an SUV full of hyperactive eight-year-olds and not nearly enough coffee.

"You're going to owe me *so* big for this," I said, reminding Joyce of her debt as I settled Bixby into his bed in the back and smiled at my nephew deep in the game of "war" going on.

"You're going to have a great time. Think of it as an adventure."

"I hate adventures. You'll recall my last one ended in divorce."

She handed me a large Dunkin Donuts cup. "You'll feel better after this."

"Why?" I laughed. "Is it Irish?"

"Aunt Matilda, can we make Bixby a war prisoner?"

"No."

"*Pleeeeeeease?*"

Joyce glanced into the rearview mirror at my blond mop-headed nephew who I had to admit looked pretty cute in his Scout uniform. "Ryan, you heard your aunt."

"Boogers."

"And what did I say about that word?"

"Oh yeah, great time." I looked at Joyce over the rim of my cup. "This has that same air of doom my last adventure had."

"You just picked the wrong partner last time. You really need to get over that and get out more. You can't hold all men accountable for Jack's sins."

"Says who?"

"When we get back I'm going to take you shopping, and then we'll visit my hairdresser. How's that sound?"

"Like too much work."

"It'll be fun! New clothes, no more dyed red. Men will be lining up."

Three hours later—after two rounds of war, two threats of having to throw up, *Shrek* on the portable DVD player, farts that could have choked Secretariat blamed on Bixby, and a round of I-spy—we spied the WELCOME sign to Camp Weheechee, and through it all not a sound from Bixby. The boys could learn a lot from my dog.

Joyce had come to a stop just beside our camping spot when Ryan pulled open the side door panel and led the troop out. They were about to run amok when Joyce hollered "Halt!" She called them all back and handed off their gear to them. "First we set up, *then* we go exploring."

I took my duffle bag and Bixby's, and since I wasn't aiming to earn my "wilderness badge" I unzipped my pop-up tent and tossed the gear inside. Bixby seemed pretty unimpressed with it all as he waddled about, snorting and wagging his tail. He's basically happy so long as his bed, ball, and bowls are accounted for. Bixby and I were just starting to mill about a bit when a park ranger called out to us.

"Excuse me, folks. You just get in?"

"Yes, about fifteen minutes ago."

"Well, I just wanted to let you know to keep watch for a wolf. She's been spotted around some of the campsites."

Ryan was thrilled.

"A wolf! A real live wolf! See? I *told* you there's wild animals!"

"Well, that's right, son. A wolf is a wild animal, so you make sure to keep away if you spot her. She might look like a dog, but she isn't a pet. And be sure to keep tight lids on all your food."

He peered over my shoulder. "And I'd keep a tight leash on that dog. A wolf won't think twice."

I felt a chill go down my spine. I didn't suspect a wolf would think twice at all.

"Thank you. We'll watch out," I told the ranger.

"Well, just in case you get into trouble, blow this whistle." He handed each of us one. "It'll startle her and alert the camp rangers." He must have read my mind; he warned the boys to blow it only if they sighted the wolf. "Understand?" he asked, looking at them.

The boys all said they did, but I had my doubts. I was already sorry I hadn't packed the big bottle of Excedrin. The ranger tipped his ranger hat, waved, and wandered off, calling to the next set of campers.

Ryan's level of excitement was about even with my sense of panic as we both asked, "Do you think we'll see it?" Dougie took a slingshot out of his jacket pocket. "I hope so. Ping! Right in the butt!"

"No slingshot and no ping." I had to sort of admire Dougie. He was the smallest of the boys; he wore glasses and talked with a faint lisp, but the kid had no fear. Maybe it was a redhead thing. I took the slingshot from him, promising its return when we were back home.

"Let's get set up."

"Naw. Let's look for the wolf," replied Stephen, looking at the others. "Right?"

Stephen was a twin, and the only difference between him and Peter was the color of their eyes. Stephen's were blue while Peter's were green. Aside from that they were identical right down to their ability to get the others to misbehave to the extreme.

"Yeah." Peter's green eyes warned of mischief. "I bet we can call her right to us." He blew his whistle, and before the others could follow suit, Joyce and I managed to yank them out of their hands.

Adam jumped for his, which by then was clutched in my hand.

"*Heeeeeeeeeey!* What if we see it?"

"I'll blow it."

"What if you can't because you're too scared?"

"I won't be scared."

"Then what if you swallow it?" When Adam wasn't full of candy, he was full of what-ifs.

———

"Then Bixby will take care of the wolf."

Joyce clapped her hands, and the general orders for making camp followed.

There was a collective group moan with commentary of "some campout" muttered, but when a group of Eagle Scouts took pity on a pair of old broads and wandered over to help, the boys all towed the line, though grudgingly, and tents were set up and sleeping bags stowed. Clearly, we had some Marines in the making.

"Now can we look for the wolf?"

"There'll be no looking for the wolf. And if you see her, I want you to remember what the ranger said. A wolf is not a pet. Okay. Let's head over to the lake. I think there's some canoes."

There was only one path to the lake, and it cut right through the woods. I'd thought that maybe there'd be a bear warning. Where there's food, there are bears, but I'd never imagined we'd have to worry about a wolf. I had a short leash on Bixby, and I pulled it tighter to me. He didn't like it; he was used to a long tether, but I wasn't taking any chances, and I was seriously considering having him sleep in the van.

Joyce and I donned life jackets and then got one on each of the boys and we split the kids up between us. I took Bixby along as we manned our canoes, and while I might not be ready for the Olympic rowing team, I did manage to recall a few canoeing basics from my JC days, and we paddled out to where a few other canoes were drifting. Dougie, who was in my canoe, spotted a fish and leaned so far over to make a snatch at it that he nearly fell in. When I made a grab at him, the canoe rocked violently, and it was only because another canoe was crammed in beside us that we didn't go overboard.

"Dougie! I don't want you doing that again. Under*stand*?"

"What'd ya do that for?" Here came the whine. "I could've caught him."

"Are you alright?" came a query from the canoe beside us.

"What? Oh, yes. Thank you. We're fine," I answered.

"Looks like you've really got your hands full." He held out his hand to me. "I'm John."

"Matilda." I shook his hand. It might have been the way the sunlight was reflecting off the water, but he had a sort of George Clooney thing going.

"Matilda. That's a very unusual name. You must be a very unusual woman. I mean to be the mother of such active boys. Can't be easy."

"She's not our mother! And that's her dog, and he bites if he don't like you!

"Oh." He smiled and looked at Bixby. "He does look like a killer." He reached out and gave Bixby a scratch behind his ear. Bixby grunted and jerked his head.

"Sorry." I smiled. "I guess he doesn't like being in a canoe."

Joyce came paddling up beside our canoes. "Is everything okay? I saw you look like you were about to go over, but I couldn't get turned around fast enough."

"It's fine." I gave John a quick glance. "We should get the kids back to camp."

"Will you be alright?"

"We'll be fine, thanks." I was pushing off when he tapped me on my shoulder.

"My camp is just over past that group of trees..." he pointed in the general vicinity off shore, "...if you need anything."

I nodded and paddled towards the dock. After we tied up the canoes, I took tight hold of Bixby's leash, and we trotted off back to camp. The boys were all hungry, and Bixby's grunting was oddly intense. I glanced at my watch.

"Is it really almost four-thirty?"

"Yep," Joyce nodded. "Time flies when you're having fun."

The group consensus was for hot dogs. "Okay. But we'll need really long sticks to hold over the fire, so look for some really long sticks." By the time we got back to camp, the boys had collected nearly every loose stick and twig along the path. Like any good JC, I used good old fashioned matches to get the fire going while Joyce opened the cooler of juice boxes. I poured two cans of pork 'n beans into a skillet and opened a pouch of lamb kibble for Bixby. Twenty-three hot dogs later, our first official campout dinner was officially over.

"Can we look for the wolf now?"

"Ryan, I am *not* going to keep repeating myself. There'll be no looking for the wolf. Understand? Besides, it's getting dark. The wolf is probably asleep." Joyce tore open a bag of marshmallows and asked who wanted s'mores.

"I'd like one, please." John walked towards us and crouched down around the fire. "So, boys, did you see the wolf yet?"

"Nah—we're not allowed to look for it." Ryan pouted and mimicked my sister's tone for warning that she wasn't going to keep repeating herself. It was hard not to laugh—the kid had her down cold.

John hid his laugh in a cough and agreed that it was a smart idea to leave the wolf be.

"They never look as dangerous as they are," he warned, even though all the boys boasted that they weren't afraid.

"Let's roast marshmallows and watch them catch fire!"

Dougie led the others in jabbing marshmallows and setting them ablaze. Joyce and I both reached to pull his out when the entire stick caught fire.

"*Whaaaaaat?*"

"Hold it *over* the fire, not in." Joyce put a marshmallow on the tip of another stick.

"How about you?" he asked, leaning to my ear and smiling. "Are you afraid?"

I scratched the top of Bixby's head when he grunted. "I have my protector."

"I can see that." John reached to give Bixby a pet, but Bixby grunted and jerked his head again.

Dougie put his hand on Bixby's head. "He doesn't like you."

Joyce handed Dougie the bag of marshmallows and a stick.

"So, John, are *you* camping alone?

He nodded. "I'm a stockbroker. I come out here to release the stress."

"By camping?"

He leaned in closer to me and whispered, "You'd be surprised at how relaxing the woods can be if you know what you're doing." He took a marshmallow from the bag Dougie was holding.

"Do you mind?"

"Hey!"

"Yeah! What if we run out?"

I told Adam not to be rude and offered John a shy apology. The boys announced they were bored. They wanted to look for the wolf.

"Boys, what would you do if you found the wolf?" John looked around. He leaned in nearer to the fire. He motioned the boys closer as his voice fell to a whisper.

"I mean, what if the wolf was closer than you think? It might be watching you right now. Maybe the wolf is just waiting for the right time to spring. Maybe when you least expect it, the wolf will rise up and pounce!" He leapt up with his hands crooked like claws and let out a growl that made us all scream. All except Bixby, who whizzed on his shoe.

The boys all laughed, and I apologized, profusely embarrassed and glad that it was too dark to see my cheeks the same color as my hair.

"You must have really scared him."

I ran my hand along Bixby's back and assured him everything was alright, but he just grunted.

"Maybe you should go," I said.

"Yeah." John wiggled his foot. "I think he got my sock." He told the boys to sleep tight and to beware the wolf, and then he disappeared beyond the trees.

Joyce and I pretended it wasn't when the boys all said how funny Bixby peeing on John's shoe was, but there was no keeping a straight face; it was pretty funny.

"Now you have a funny story to tell your grandchildren," Joyce whispered to me.

I kissed the top of Bixby's head, and he snorted and gave my face a lick.

"This is the only male I'm interested in."

Two bags of marshmallows, two boxes of graham crackers, and way too much chocolate later and it was time to hit the tents. I made certain all the garbage was well bagged and tucked away in the van. I double checked to make certain that all the remaining food was well sealed, and that too got loaded into the van. Joyce put out the fire and made sure there was absolutely nothing that would attract a wolf, a bear, or anything else that lurked in the woods.

"Okay, everybody get a good night's sleep, because tomorrow morning we're going hiking!"

"To look for the wolf?"

"No, Ryan, not to look for the wolf."

"What if we see it anyway?"

"We'll just ignore it. Now come on—everybody get into your sleeping bag."

I watched everyone disappear into the tents, and then I took Bixby into ours. I'd brought a crate for him, but he really hated it, so I let him just curl up next to me. I kissed his nose, and he licked my face, and we settled down pioneer style.

I'm not sure how long we'd been asleep when Bixby's grunting woke me. He pulled himself alert as much as a beagle can look alert and went to the tent flap and grunted louder.

"What is it, Bixby? Do you have to go out?" It was raining. I could hear it hitting the tent. "You don't like going out in the rain."

He kept pawing at the ground.

"Okay. Wait while I get on my shoes." I hooked Bixby's leash and unzipped the tent, but Bixby wouldn't move. "See? I told you. It's raining." I zipped up the flap, but Bixby kept looking at me and grunting. I'd never seen him so agitated. I was starting to shiver from fright. I unzipped the tent flap just enough to peek out and whispered what I could remember of a prayer that I wouldn't see the wolf. I peered out through the small opening but couldn't see much through the dark and the rain, and I didn't spend a lot of time trying. I zipped the opening back up and crawled back into my sleeping bag with Bixby beside me. I left my sneakers on just in case.
It felt as if I'd just fallen to sleep when Bixby woke me for his usual five o'clock walk. The rain had stopped, and everything was quiet.

"Okay, Bixby, try to make it fast, okay?" We were just outside the campsite when Bixby found a tree he liked, but I heard a rustling, and I jerked Bixby's leash away from the spot he'd claimed just as he'd started to crouch. I clumsily picked him up and started to run, hoping he wasn't about to poop all over me.

I was zigzagging under Bixby's weight, and I was sure I was going to drop him when I heard a twig snap behind us—or maybe in front of us? I wasn't really sure. The woods looked suddenly creepy and foreboding. Images of Little Red Riding Hood flashed in my mind as I pictured a wolf leaping out and making breakfast of us both. I didn't suppose there was a hunter hanging about with his trusty double barrel. I ran faster and kept looking behind me and ran smack into John.

"Whoa!" He grabbed me, sandwiching Bixby between us. "Where's the fire?"

"Oh my God!" I could barely catch my breath. "Did you see it?"

"It?" He looked over my shoulder. "What?"

"The wolf. I heard, I thought," I put Bixby on the ground. "Never mind."

I had to bend at the waist to catch my breath. John was in shorts, and as my eye was to his knee, I couldn't help but notice that his legs were tan and muscular.

"Are you okay?" He started to laugh. "You're not going to have a heart attack or anything, are you? My CPR is really rusty."

I shook my head and stood up. "I'm okay."

He looked at Bixby. "How 'bout you, killer?" He stretched out his hand to Bixby, but Bixby grunted louder than I'd ever heard him grunt before, and John pulled back.

"Still not man's best friend?"

"I interrupted his, uh, morning business. We should get going."

"Will you be alright?"

"Fine." I thanked him and tugged Bixby's leash and headed hurriedly back to camp.

By the time I got back to camp, Joyce had scrambled two dozen eggs and had brewed coffee in a percolator that looked like it could have been used by the troops at Appomattox.

"I was about to send the ranger out after you. Where'd you disappear to?" she asked.

"Bixby's five o'clock dump."

"How long does it take him?"

"It was me."

"You?" The look of horror on Joyce's face cracked me up, and I busted out in laughter.

"You couldn't make it to the port-a-potties?"

I wasn't at first going to tell her about the wolf, but I knew the kids wanted to go hiking. If the wolf was lurking, we needed a plan.

"But you didn't actually see it, did you?" she asked.

"No. I think maybe our voices scared it off."

"Then we'll talk loud." She scooped the last of the eggs onto a plate and handed it to me.

"And let's hope John is nearby."

Out on the trek we picked berries and wildflowers, and the boys spotted a snake, but for all their desperate wishing, the wolf never appeared. The hiking trail wound around the campsite, so when the boys wanted to run back to see who was the fastest, we let them. Joyce and Bixby and I strolled behind.

"So what do you think of John? He's not terrible looking."

"He's alright."

"Stockbroker is a solid career."

"So was the lawyer, and you do remember how that turned out, right?"

"Seriously, how long are you going to hold onto that?"

"Until I'm proven wrong."

"You have to give someone a chance for that to happen."

Bixby found a pile of leaves he really liked, and he crouched. I assured Joyce that I'd be fine and told her to go on ahead.

"Another five minutes alone, and God only knows what trouble the five Indians will have managed."

"Yeah, but I hate to leave you alone."

"I'm not alone. I have Bixby." I shooed her off. "Go. I'll be fine." I glanced at Bixby. "Besides, Bixby can't concentrate with all this talking."

"Alright. You have your whistle, right?"

"Right here." I tapped my personal security system that was hanging around my neck. "Now go and let my dog poop in peace."

"Okay. Just don't sneak off and get married."

"Only if George Clooney pops up and asks."

"Don't worry. I hear George is a big dog lover."

I looked down at Bixby settling in to take care of business. I'd never heard Bixby grunt while doing his thing, and I wondered if the boys had slipped him some marshmallows.

Then I realized too late that it was the wolf.

"I thought she'd never leave." John put his hand at the small of my back.

Bixby's peculiar overnight behavior suddenly made sense. "You came back to our camp last night, didn't you?" I asked him.

"I thought the boys might have liked some ice cream."

He ran his fingers along my spine.

"How about if you and I sneak away and take a canoe out on the lake for a little while? There's a secluded little spot just across the way I think you'll just love."

"I doubt it. I'm not a big fan of secluded spots."

"Come on, now; don't be that way." He encircled my waist with one hand and cupped my ass cheek with the other as he pressed himself behind me. "You know you'll like it." His breath was hot on my neck, and his kiss to my nape was wet and sloppy, and his hands were traveling all points north and south.

"I said no." I blew my ranger whistle like nobody's ever blown a whistle before, and from out of nowhere two park rangers and half a dozen other campers, including a short woman with big boobs and faint traces of better days calling out concern for her husband, came running just as Bixby lifted his leg all over John's.

Back at camp, Dougie was jumping up and down like he had springs on his feet. "We heard the whistle!"

"Yeah, Aunt Matilda, we heard it. Did you see the wolf?"

Stephen hopped on top of a log and looked around. "Let's go see if we can find it."

I grabbed hold of him by his collar in mid leap off the log.

"The wolf is gone."

Joyce's mouth fell open. "Then you *did* see the wolf?"

I opened up the bag of doggie treats.

"Nothing to worry about." I hugged Bixby close. "Bixby took care of the wolf just fine."

# Ear
## by Rebecca Rouillard

It was on the Northern Line, between Tottenham Court Road and Leicester Square, that Lucinda felt an overwhelming urge to lick the ear of the man standing in front of her. She couldn't see his face but he had a beautiful ear; well-proportioned, clean, hairless. There was just a trace of stubble at the edge of his jaw, like sea sand. His jawline was defined, decisive. She liked a firm jaw on a man, though Charlie's had been misleading. She had always been the decisive one, although tonight she wished she'd made up her mind to start for home sooner; before the evening rush hour began. All of the men in the carriage seemed so young in their dark suits, younger than her sons even. They reminded her of sixth formers she had taught – men, but bashful in their man-sized clothes, unaccustomed to the authority in their own voices. The man with the ear shifted in front of her as he turned the page of his newspaper.

*Excuse me, young man, would you mind if I licked your ear? It's just that it's such a good-looking ear.* Lucinda smiled to herself and then tried not to. People would think she was mad, smiling at nothing. She wouldn't have to move much at all to reach his ear. Their bodies were already pressed together. She would just lean her head forward and stretch upwards a little bit. She would open her mouth, place her tongue underneath the lobe, close her lips over it and then gently rake the front of it with her teeth. She wet her lips - she had the feel of it in her mouth already. She became afraid that the urge would overwhelm her and that she might actually do it. It would be awful to see the revulsion in his eyes, the shock of the other people in the carriage. She could imagine how Charlie would laugh at that story.

She had met Charlie at a picnic on Hampstead Heath in the summer of 1971. Her friends had gone for a walk and she had stayed behind to enjoy the sun and read her book. He was sitting with another group a short distance away. She had noticed him earlier: the clean lines of his jaw, his smile, his athletic build. She wasn't sure how old he was though – too old to notice her perhaps. She was nineteen and still felt like a schoolgirl. She caught his eye and smiled in a neutral way – friendly but not flirtatious. He smiled back then ambled over.

"What are you reading?"

The sun was behind him. As a child Lucinda used to dream that she was looking for something important but she couldn't see clearly enough to find it – as though she had just woken up and her eyes wouldn't open properly, however hard she rubbed them. She had that feeling now; squinting into the sun, knowing that it was vital that she see his face but not quite able to.

"Jane Eyre," she said and then, thankfully, he moved so he was blocking the sun with his body.

"Ah – Mr Rochester, dark and brooding – is that your type then?" His hair was blonde but he was still smiling - teasing her.

"Preferably without the mad wife hidden in the attic."

"Yes, the mad wife always gets in the way. I'm Charlie," he said.

"Lucinda. Nice to meet you, Charlie."

"You didn't want to go for a walk then with your friends?"

"I'd just got to the exciting bit."

"But, you've read it before?"

"Yes, but I'm always holding my breath, just in case she doesn't find him," she smiled so he would know she wasn't taking herself too seriously.

"Shall I leave you to it then?"

"No, stay – I'm sure she'll find him, she doesn't need my help." She shifted slightly to the side to make some space. He sat down on the blanket beside her.

"So what do you do, Lucinda, when you're not reading Jane Eyre?"

"Nothing, I just read Jane Eyre over and over. Although I do alternate with Pride and Prejudice obviously, as you do."

"As you do."

"I'm studying to be a teacher actually."

"Planning on indoctrinating a whole new generation into the delights of Bronte and Austen?"

"Absolutely. What about you? What do you do when you're not having picnics and deriding the classics?"

"I work in the City, in finance – not very exciting but it pays for the mad wife in the attic."

He was very easy to talk to and he seemed intelligent. She liked that he'd read the same books as her even though he teased her about them. And he understood her sense of humour – he didn't look at her strangely like some other boys did. They talked until her friends returned. She was short with them, engrossed in her conversation. The friends smiled and whispered pointedly at them. She felt a little intoxicated by this mutual fascination. She wanted her friends to notice it. The warmth of the day was retreating with the sun. Lucinda's friends packed up their picnics and stood about looking awkward.

"You go on, I'll catch up with you." said Lucinda. Charlie's friends had already left.

"You don't have pierced ears." He observed, brushing her earlobe with his finger.

"No, I didn't ever get around to it." She was embarrassed about him looking at her ears – they always seemed awkward things to her, she didn't like to draw attention to them.

"Now I should be an earring model, I've got space for five or six pairs." Charlie indicated his own ears.

"Gosh, those are impressive lobes."

"I'm part Basset Hound."

"Yes I can see that, do you think they enhance your hearing?

"Definitely. And with my super-ears I hear the sound of coffee brewing somewhere over the hill. Shall we go and look for it?"

"Yes, let's."

The train pulled into Leicester Square station and disgorged a small proportion of travellers. Twice the number attempted to cram into an imagined space. Lucinda, grasping an overhead rail, was pushed closer to the young man's back.

She remembered clearly the moment she had noticed that Alistair had Charlie's ears. He was about three, she was towelling him after his bath and suddenly she had seen that his earlobes were proportionally long. In that moment it was as though a small miracle had taken place. Charlie's ear, perfectly reproduced in miniature – cloned. He resembled Charlie in other ways but nothing so direct, so pure. When James was born, two years later, she spotted them almost immediately – the same ears. And she pointed them out to the midwife and to Charlie. As the boys were growing up she would rub their earlobes between her fingers sometimes as they passed her; intent on boyish crusades.

Lucinda wished, again, that she had started home a little earlier to avoid this crush, but she had lingered – lost in memory.

It was pancreatic cancer, not strangulation by earlobe as Charlie had predicted, that eventually separated them. It was quick, relatively speaking. There were no false hopes of remissions and second chances.

"You'll make sure I'm cremated," Charlie had said.

"Yes, I know." They spoke of his death often without ever actually saying goodbye to one another.

"Otherwise my ears might keep growing in my coffin, awful thought. I could donate them to science I suppose, or an ear museum? I can't decide. You listening?"

"I'm listening, I'm listening," she said and leaned over him, pulled his hospital gown aside and pressed her ear to his corrugated chest. He coughed weakly. She rested her head for a while, his hand in her hair. When she finally pulled away there was a neat imprint of her ear indented into his skin.

"You have an ear print on your chest," she said. He didn't respond – his gaze was fixed in the middle-distance, but she couldn't see the thing he was looking at. So this was it. She didn't want to be melodramatic, it's not like it was a surprise. In some ways she was glad that he went first. Not like this, of course she would not have wished this on him. But she knew that if it had been her, he would not have coped. She was good at coping. She pushed the button to call the nurse.

"Excuse me," she said, "I think…I think he's gone." The nurse took over – practiced in the administration of death.

She would still have the same dream sometimes, of not being able to see, but there was a new element. She would find a contact lens but it would be too big to put in

241

her eye; the size of a Frisbee or a dinner plate. Firstly she would try to put the whole thing in her eye, which wouldn't work. Then she would try to tear off a small piece very carefully that might just fit; desperate to find that thing she was looking for.

Lucinda had wondered when she'd left home that morning, if she should phone James and Alistair and tell them where she was going. But she had been embarrassed. Scattering Charlie's ashes on Hampstead Heath felt a little sentimental; something that would happen in a Hollywood movie. She was not generally a sentimental person but she didn't know what else to do. They'd already had a memorial service. Having Charlie's charred remains lurking in a corner of the living room seemed macabre, or the back of a cupboard – even worse. Hampstead Heath felt appropriate but when she arrived there she had been furtive and uncomfortable, waiting for someone to come and tell her that scattering ashes was not permitted in city parks. She'd found a quiet corner and sprinkled him on the grass, feeling a little absurd. It had been a mistake to go alone.

She'd felt she should say something but, "Goodbye. Goodbye, Charlie," was all she could manage.

The train lurched to the left and Lucinda leaned forward quickly and licked the man's ear. He put his hand over his ear and his head made an involuntary movement in her direction, as though he might look at her, but then he didn't make eye contact. Nobody else appeared to have noticed anything. And Lucinda was suddenly swallowed by grief – taken by surprise once again by its strange ebb and flow. Charlie was gone. She was alone. A small shrieking sob escaped her throat and she tried to cover it up with a cough. Several heads turned towards her then. She swallowed hard and focused on willing the tears away. Just two escaped and she was able to wipe them away inconspicuously while tucking a strand of white hair behind her ear. The moisture in her eyes clarified her vision, brought the carriage into focus with its squash of sullen commuters. The young man finally looked directly at her, his hand still covering his ear. His face was unattractive, flaring nostrils – she had always found an excess of nostril repugnant.

The man with the ear and the nostrils got off at the next stop. She thought about how she would tell Charlie about this when she got home, then caught herself. *Don't do that.* She clutched her arms across her chest. The empty urn concealed in her bag felt lumpy and awkward – like her grief.

# The Tamotsu
## by Sharda Dean

What I do is art; subtle, beautiful and elegant. I am invisible, walking through crowds unseen. Anyone can pickpockets, anyone can learn a two-fingered lift, a 'Louisiana purchase', but it is another matter to craft these tricks into something masterful, magical.

There is a pickpocketing custom in Tokyo that goes as far back as anyone can remember; a silent battle to be the King of pickpockets, the pickpockets' pickpocket. A pickpocket so good he can lift a wallet from the top pickpocket in the city and replace it without his victim feeling a thing. The sleight of hand required to achieve this is miraculous. When a pickpocket attains this mastery, he becomes the new King until he is superseded by another and so on. We call the King of pickpockets 'The Tamotsu' after Ito Tamotsu, the revered Tokyo pickpocket, who worked for most of the first half of the twentieth century, well into his eighties. He was a true gentleman, on the few occasions he was caught by the police he would bow and say "So sorry to be of trouble." When you make a bid to become the new Tamotsu, the custom is that you leave a red rectangle of paper in the old Tamotsu's wallet, in place of the notes you have taken, as proof of your lift and evidence of your expertise. The paper is blank, but it announces loud and clear that you are the new Tamotsu.

I have a strict timetable, I wake early, join the packed commuter trains, office workers, bleary eyed, maybe still drunk from the previous night's sake. I always wear a suit, always look smart, professional. I am all-seeing, without seeming to look at all. In a crowded commuter train, the crush covers me, hiding my quick hands. I go to the Tokyo Metropolitan library in Minato, study magic, psychology and languages, anything that might assist me. A tourist speaking to a Japanese man who can speak their language, suddenly mellows, they trust you. They are ripe for plucking. I read magazines, newspapers and books. At twelve I pop out for a bento box lunch, then to the gym or maybe the botanical gardens for a walk. On a Friday I buy a huge box of popcorn and watch a film. I love being in a cinema in the middle of the afternoon when you know most other bastards are stuck at desks being barked at by their bosses.

Any money I get, I save half. I know that I'll get slower as I get older, and pickpocketing doesn't come with a pension scheme. I have more than enough to buy some Italian suits, pay my gym membership and cover a nice meal out with a pretty girl once a week. Girls don't stick around, I can't give too much away and they hate that. I usually say I'm an actor, it explains away a lot, but when they start to get suspicious, they move on. It suits me that way, and I never met a girl worth giving up my job for, not yet.

I have been the Tamotsu for years. I choose my paper carefully; it is my signature. I buy from the most exclusive paper shop in Tokyo, Kyukyodo. The shop has been running since 1663, with the same Kumagai family running it now as then. I buy handmade paper of a reasonable thickness, so that it slides easily into a wallet when time is precious. Distraction, speed, dexterity and pretence, these are the tools of my trade. Moves are as varied as the situations. I invent and perfect different forms over time. I obsess about each tiny step. A pickpocket exploits human nature's tendency to assume, to believe what you see. I can be invisible or I can play the loudmouth falling out of the metro doors quite a bit richer, everyone laughing at me and shaking their heads, none the wiser, until they come to buy a coffee or pay for their lunch. An amateur magician once said to me "the mistake people make when watching a magic trick is to completely underestimate the lengths to which a magician will go to make a trick work". It is the same with pickpockets. We will do whatever it takes.

At the Shibuya crossing, the one on all the postcards, a group of tourists asks me to take a photo of them, it happens every time. They've chosen me at random and no-one suspects the intent of those they choose. In the time it takes for the camera to go back and forth and for them to show me how it works, I have two wallets and a watch. I act a little clumsy, and I hear one of them mutter 'I hope he doesn't drop the bloody camera', another purse and I'm walking swiftly away.

Coming home on the metro, I acknowledge Goldfish at the other end of the carriage. He's called Goldfish because he has a fish mouth, a gasping little 'O', and sometimes he dyes his hair with a broad orange stripe. He is the closest thing I have to a protégé and the closest thing I have to a friend. I first noticed him when he was a kid, 13 or 14, his parents were in and out of consciousness, so he learnt to look after himself. He's as different a pickpocket to me as you can imagine. He loves to dress up; never in the same disguise twice. He's often on my tail, scouting the same turf, interrogating me for tips and tricks, treating me like an unofficial mentor, flattering, teasing and quizzing me in quick succession. I know he is hungry to be The Tamotsu. He's getting closer, keeping me on my toes. How long I can fend him off I don't know. Unfortunately he is as camp as hell and slightly embarrassing to be with in public, but friends are thin on the ground in this profession and I can't be too choosy. Today he's wearing heels, a mini skirt and a smart jacket; he looks like most men's secretary fantasy.

"Hi baby," he purrs, "what's new?"

"Not much, you had a good day?"

"Not as much as I'd like, need to make up the difference, fancy a blow job?" He flutters his eyelashes sweetly, I laugh, waving him away.

"No, Jesus... leave me alone."

He smiles and says "You're so bloody old-school... But hey, listen..." he leans in closer, "Rumour is you're getting too old, taking your eye off the ball... Rumour is you're not going to be the Tamotsu much longer." He's enjoying this rumour a little too much, but I know he's not making it up, pickpockets love this stuff, who's up, who's down, who's made a big haul, who's got caught. Every few months they'd be another rumour that someone was snapping at my heels. I need to be careful, they'll all be nibbling at me soon, but my biggest challenge is standing next to me. As he wiggles off at the next stop he turns and winks. "You'd better watch out big boy... I'm right behind you."

He's not joking. The brilliance of Goldfish is that even though I've known him for years, his disguises are so good I don't always recognise him, even the police wading through the CCTV tape can't put two and two together, every morning he invents a new disguise, a new persona, it's like he is reborn a fresh new pickpocket every day, with no previous form.

At the next stop the carriage clears a little and I notice a mark sitting a few seats away. Young, rucksack open, no make-up, student bracelets, nice camera, cheap phone. She looks fresh off the plane and probably has all Daddy's savings rolled up in US dollars in that bag. But in my business it doesn't do to get too greedy. Greedy means sloppy and sloppy means getting caught. If I have enough time, I always put the wallet or purse back, or bend down as if to pick it off the floor to give it back to its rightful owner. Often I just take half their cash, they might not even notice it's gone, no harm done.

She's probably too young for me, but I can't take my eyes off her, she has that unselfconscious beauty I find fascinating. She looks natural, pure, perhaps it's that 'opposites attract' thing. Then I realise someone's got to her money first. I see her searching through her bag, desperate, getting redder in the face. She looks so scared. Goldfish, the bastard, I hadn't even noticed him near her, he must have got to her before our chat, or maybe before I got on the train. He's getting sharper all the time. He wasn't anywhere near me but I could still feel him closing in.

"Are you OK?"

"I can't find my money, I don't know where I put it, I thought it was in here." Some commuters look up from their papers at the rising panic in the girl's voice, and then they look down again. An old woman opposite is more interested and gives me a dirty look, as if to say 'go and find a nice girl your own race.'

———

"Do you think someone might have stolen it?"

"No, I don't think so, no, I've had my rucksack with me the whole time." She says no, but you can tell she is trying to convince herself. No-one ever expects to be pickpocketed, particularly not in Tokyo, the City's image is safe and clean. The tourists have their heads full of art, culture, Hiroshige, calligraphy, Samurai and maybe cheap gadgets. They leave bags gaping; rucksacks flung casually around one shoulder, Rolexes on show, designer sunglasses dangling over their top pockets. People believe that Japan is a refined place, full of polite, honourable people. Yet hundreds of thousands of pockets are picked every year in Tokyo, more than a thousand by me.

"You have to be careful, nothing is ever as it seems."

"So what do I do? Go to the police?"

"What else was stolen?"

"Just cash, but it was all my holiday money, God, what do I do?"

"Listen, I have some cash, I could lend you some. How much was taken?"

"All my money. Five hundred US, I think, maybe slightly more, I kept meaning to take it out of my backpack, to put it somewhere safe, but I..." I count out some notes, but she looks horrified. "No, I couldn't take money from you, I couldn't. But thanks anyway, you're so kind." She looks like she is about to crumple into tears. She bites her lip, which is shaking. I grab her arm and start writing on her smooth skin in ballpoint pen.

"Listen, here's my address and this is worth about two hundred dollars." I stuff a bunch of notes into her rucksack. "If you can repay me, pop the money through my letterbox, or ring the doorbell and I'll take you to see the real Tokyo. I promise. You can trust me. I look like a good guy, right?"

She smiles "Right." I stuff the money into her hand. She thanks me profusely, but looks so embarrassed, ashamed. "Thanks so much. Listen, this is my stop, I'd better go."

She escapes, waving to me through the windows as she walks past towards the exit. She looks so young, I half expect to see metal braces on her teeth as she smiles at me through the carriage window.

I feel quite proud of myself, a good deed. I make my way home with empty pockets and no inclination to make up the loss. Some days you just don't feel in the mood to ruin anyone's day. I feel exhilarated by the thought that she will come to my apartment. There is nothing so tantalizing to a tourist than the promise of being shown round by a local for a taste of the real place. No one can refuse.

In the next few days I find excuses not to leave for work. At least not leaving the apartment would keep Goldfish at bay for a while, and frustrate the hell out of him. I wait at home, I daren't even play music in case she drops the money through the letterbox without me hearing and scoots off. I need to see her again.

Then, about a week later I hear her scuffling outside before she rings the bell. My heart bounces. I invite her in, apologise for the mess and make her a very good espresso. She looks at it nervously, Americans know nothing about coffee. Her eyes make their way around the apartment.

"Look, I'm sorry, this is *really* embarrassing, but I haven't been able to get your money, my folks are transferring some from the States, but it's taking longer than I expected. They're not that well off, this trip was a big deal for me; they've kinda already spent their last cents on me. But they're really trying, perhaps another week... is that OK? I'm really sorry."

"No problem at all, listen, if you need any more, let me know, Tokyo isn't a cheap place to live."

"I've still got some of the money you lent me, but it might be all gone in a day or two, I've really messed up."

"Where are you staying?"

"A hostel now, but I'm not sure I can carry on there, I'm not sure I'll have enough to pay my bill." She looks about to cry again. "This was supposed to be my big trip, I've always wanted to come to Japan, and I lost all my money on my second day here."

"It's alright, look, I know you don't know me, but come stay here, for as long as you'd like, no charge. I'd love the company, and I promise I won't try to hit on you or anything."

She looks up, her eyes huge and teary. "Are you sure? That would be amazing." She dabs her eyes with a screwed up tissue. "I'm so sorry to cause you so much trouble, but you're the only one I know here."

"It's OK, really." I feel like a saint, her in tears, me saving the day. Actually it is all such a turn-on, I am finding it hard to keep my hands to myself, so I stop trying. I sit down next to her and put my arm around her, very gently. "Listen, whatever you need, I'll help, I've got lots of money in the bank, and what's money for eh?" She leans in to me, sobbing, what a killer. I stroke her hair and kiss it lightly. She looks up at me, eyes still wet and shiny. "Thank you," she whispers.

After twenty four hours of constant contact with the lovely American girl, I emerge from the fug of the bedroom, shower and get dressed explaining that I have to go for an audition. I tell her to sleep in, and I'll be back in time for a glorious night of 'real Tokyo'. Now, time to earn some cash. I need to be extra wary of Goldfish, so I travel a little later, mix up my routine, avoid the obvious places, and stay away from too many large crowds where he could sneak up on me easily. But I can feel his breath on the back of my neck.

In quieter places I use different tricks as there is no cover from the crowd. I put my jacket on the back of my chair, the sleeve dangling close to a ladies open handbag. She is on her phone, occupied. As I put my jacket on; I put my arm inside the sleeve, over reach, pulling out the purse from the handbag, then up and out of there. Never hang around. Never look back.

On the metro home, people sleep while I remove their wallets, take out the cash, and put the wallet back, all in the blink of an eye. Tired, drunk, salary men, nod off, open mouthed, smelling of teriyaki and beer, dribbling like babies as they lean over me, their foolish faces begging me to steal from them. The carriages are dotted with few passengers then, the late hour infecting everyone with sleep and self-satisfaction, gifts to the pickpocket.

By the time I get home I'm in a wonderful mood; I'd had a good day and managed to dodge the gaping jaws of Goldfish. I am ready for a perfect evening. Everywhere feels full of promise. When all the tourists have gone to bed Tokyo becomes a different creature. Shibuya's Dogenzaka used to be the place to go, the City's red light district, but before the Olympics the place got cleaned up and all the Tokyo mafia and the hookers got swept out, so the atmosphere's all gone. One of my favourite places to go for some real Tokyo magic is Machida. At night it is transformed. When the last underground train has gone, the place turns into skateboarder heaven. They use anything and everything to skate on, the railings, stairs, metal ledges, ramps, with miles of perfectly smooth flat surfaces. The dexterity of these guys is amazing, sexy; they whisk you away to a world where the laws of gravity are suspended and time moves at hair-raising pace. You can even smell speed in the burnt rubber tang from the friction of their wheels. The thing I love is their combination of nonchalance and conscientiousness. They make it look so easy, but you see them in little groups practicing one skill after another fifty or sixty times until they've got it just right. My little American friend is speechless. Standing in the square, with skateboarders whizzing all around her, she gasps with delight. I am in love.

Now I have a problem, if I want the relationship to go somewhere I have to get a proper job or tell her the truth. The first is out of the question. I'm qualified for nothing. I could manage the second if it wasn't for the fact that the girl's problems are the result of a pickpocket filching her folks' hard earned cash. Perhaps I wouldn't have met her otherwise, but on the other hand it makes it impossible for me to tell her my real job. She would often talk about how disgusting pickpockets were, praying on the weak and unsuspecting. I could only agree. I was very protective of her, she still seemed lost, in shock and needing a guide through the shadows of Tokyo.

I started spending more time out of the apartment. I was finding it difficult to be with her knowing everything between us was based on a lie. I could no longer fool myself that I was a misunderstood artist, some sort of gentleman mastermind who did no harm. Even sex became fraught with anxiety, how was I supposed to love and be loved when I couldn't be honest? I was tetchy and short tempered; sex became snatched, fierce or ended with me disintegrating into a mess of tears. She kept asking me what was wrong, but I couldn't even begin to explain without ruining everything. Having a bad relationship with her was better than losing her completely.

It was about this time that I found it, a small rectangle of red paper in my wallet. My ears filled with the noise of the metro carriage and my whole body seemed to heat up and cool down in a few seconds. There was not a tear or fold or crumple in the slip of thin tissue paper. Goldfish had caught me; I didn't know what to feel. I was impressed by his supreme panache, completely devastated on my own account, but was also a little proud that I had helped him along the way. Just to rub it in the bastard had taken every last bit of my day's substantial earnings, the greedy shit.

I began to look around more closely, not for targets this time, but for the new Tamotsu. I see him everywhere, in all his different disguises. Suddenly everyone in Tokyo seems to be Goldfish, every brush, bump or greeting was him in disguise. I check my wallet obsessively. Two days later, again on the metro home, there is another slip of paper and my wallet cleared out again. I began to stay out later, so I could watch the passengers on the nearly empty trains before I alighted at my journey's end. But then another few days passed and another red slip, the same type of paper. Someone was enjoying his new found status. Someone was gloating.

It was getting harder to work. I was losing my confidence. Instead I pad around shopping malls with the American girl. With nothing coming in, money was flooding out of my account but I couldn't deny her anything. I was in a sorry state, drinking too much, smoking too much, wrecked.

She's busy one night so I stop by the little bar in Kabukicho, the one next to the shiny clean sex parlour for men with nurse fantasies. The neon is so bright it is almost aggressive. Now, pickpockets don't do much socialising together, we all try to stay under the radar, so getting together for a big night of drinking usually isn't our scene, but from time to time, a few of us meet here. Goldfish, cackling, has a crowd around him. Of course, he's the star now. Everyone knew I'd lost my status and I got a few commiserating pats on the back from fellow snatchers. I'd had a few beers by the time he came over to say hello. It is a perfect opportunity to rile and tease me. I take it for a while, but he doesn't stop. He looks so delighted he is positively smirking. I mutter "I'll get it back, don't worry your pretty little face." He giggles like a hyena, looks me in the eye and says "Wow, you're so fucked." I decide to go. I'm seething and crackling with jealousy. Stay and I'd be tempted to punch his lights out, the little faggot.

I woke up the next morning to find the space beside me empty but still warm. Perhaps she'd popped over the road to get something nice for breakfast. I had an image of her in my head as Little Red Riding Hood, skipping through the woods with a basket full of muffins for me; so sweet. I go for a piss and make my way to the kitchen to turn on the coffee machine. Something catches the corner of my eye, a slip of red paper, just like all the others. Only this time, an inky scrawl read "Thanks for the real Tokyo, love, The Tamotsu." I never saw her again.

# Snapshots
## by Debz Hobbs-Wyatt

I hate the rain.

I hate old people. I hate dogs. I hate single Mums pushing noisy kids with chocolate faces in hand-me-down pushchairs. I hate Dads with dates tattooed on their arms that still forget their kid's birthdays.
And I hate boyfriends that turn up late.

There's an old man standing outside Tescos with his hood up, rattling a yellow bucket. He looks familiar. Maybe because he's been there since Monday. He says he wants to help stray dogs find good homes. Why stop at stray dogs? An old biddy with a plastic rain hat and a long brown coat drops a coin in. Clink.

I push back the sleeve of my coat and look at the time. Darren's shift was supposed to end before mine. He works on the fish counter, a trainee like. It's a whiffy job, the Photo Shop's much better.

"Have a sticker," the old man says and holds out a sheet of paper to the woman so she can pick one off, or try to with bitten fingernails. When she finally does she sticks it to her left breast and pats it triumphantly.

"The dogs will be grateful," the old man says.

"What, Dear?" She leans closer, lifts the plastic hat away from her ear.

"Thank you. Dogs'll be pleased."

"Dogs?"

"Yes, thank you."

"Did you say dogs?"

"Yes dogs."

"Not cats?"

"No dogs."

"I thought it was cats," she says scrutinising the picture on the side of the bucket. "I like cats." Then she leans in, scoops out her 2p coin and shakes her head. I watch her march into the car park with a single carrier bag swinging off her wrist- reduced items prob'bly. Or cat food. Fat cats, skinny cats, black cats, white cats, mangy stray cats. I see a lot of photos of cats.

I hate cats.

The old man just stands there and I think for a second how sad he looks. I've always wondered what it would be like to have a granddad. Kid's homes don't come with Granddads.

I stick my hand in the pocket of my coat and feel the edges of the small box. I try to think about something else. TRY.

*Try.*

*Try.*

*Try.*

Tortoiseshell cats, grey cats, tabby cats. Bloody cats. I see more pictures of pets than anything else. What is it with people and pets?

I hate pets.

It's always busy at Tescos, especially at lunch time. Darren says it's even busy in the middle of the night. "Insomniacs most of 'em," he says. "Or paedos that don't want anyone to see 'em. Or people with disfigured faces. Or agrophobes."

"Agrophobes?" I said. "Thought agrophobes never go out." He looked at me with a screwed up face, what I call the crumpled-up-carrier-bag-look. "Everyone shops," he says.

"S'pose," I said.

"And vampires," he said.

"What?"

"Vampires come then too."

"Fuck off."

So now I'm thinking of Halloween photos: apple bobbing wet faces, pumpkins, trick or treating, children with green cheeks and pointed hats and some covered with white sheets with holes cut out for eyes. Proud parents, proud grandparents. And...

I wrap my fingers tighter over the box and draw in a deep breath. Come on Darren. Where the fuck are you?

I go back to watching the old man who rattles his bucket at a girl with purple hair, short skirt, Dock Martin Boots and a ring through her nose. Vegetarian and a student, defo.   Animal marches, placards, pictures of skinny horses and beagles smoking cigarettes. Graduation photos, fake smiles. That's her.

She must like dogs.

She looks at the old man, unzips her purse, pauses and starts to walk away without clinking.

"Sticker?"  the old man says anyway but she just looks at him like she's thinking of his thick sausage fingers pressing the face of a Chihuahua onto her breast "No ta," she says.

"Come on Fuckwit," I say and a man walking past, paint on his jeans, big work boots, says, "Me?"

"In your dreams Cowboy," I say and he laughs. Then as he walks inside he does this John Wayne swagger thing, looks back and catches me watching him. I'm so busted. Then he heads for the ciggie booth. He has dusty blond hair, nice arse, not bad looking; for an older guy. Prob'ly drives a pick-up, takes photos of cars and plays football with his son that he only sees on weekends. But I bet he always remembers his birthday.

"Fucking ten minutes late now," I say and a woman in pinstripes, who almost knocks me over because she's too bloody busy looking at her Blueberry, Gooseberry, whatever the fuck it is, says, "Charming." When she's gone I give her the finger. Silly bitch. Posh flat, wooden floors, see-through glass kettle, no children. Photos of houses and perfect boyfriends. If they exist.

"Come on Darren." Fifteen minutes late he is now. If he's talking to that Molly from the deli I'll bloody kill 'im. The same Molly who just happened to be at Dylan's leaving do when it was supposed to be no girls. I remember what Darren said. "NO GIRLS. Ya know I would take you, but-" And he looked right at me when he said it, those sexy blue eyes of his like they were burning a hole right through me. "STRICTLY NO GIRLS."

I saw the photos – do they think I'm thick? I saw her draped across him with her tongue down his bloody throat. "One more chance," I said. "It's not what it looks like," he said.

I look back at the old man who smiles when a kid, a girl about, I dunno four or five I s'pose, drops pennies in the bucket, one at a time in painful slowness. Clink. Clink. Clink. I was five when Mum dumped me. I tell people she exchanged me for five clean needles and a bag of smack. Of course it wasn't quite like that but it might as well have been. The little girl's mum stands and watches, eyes all wide with praise. Clever girl, dropping pennies in a bucket. Clever girl. Oh how clever she is. My mum never called me clever. My mum never came back for me. Maybe all our mistakes should end up in the clinical waste, eh?

I know their type – the mum and the little girl with sparkly bows in her hair: children's parties, candles, fancy cake with pink fondant, photos on every birthday, bouncy castles, far far far too many toys. Photos made into calendars at Christmas time. Daddy wears a suit for work. Mummy has her nails French-polished on Wednesdays. That's them.

CLINK.

"Where are you Darren?"

CLINK.

"Bloody men."

CLINK. CLINK. CLINK.

I fish in my pockets for my phone, yank it out because the sparkly dolphin charm's got wound into the lining. Darren's face lights up on the screen, taken at the fair, last year. Just after he threw up after going on the Waltzer. If you look closely you see diced carrot in his fringe.

I hate fairs.

CLINK.

No missed calls. So I text him: "Where R U?"

Then I stand there with my hands in my pockets, one hand wrapped around the phone waiting for it to buzz and the other around the box watching the little girl drop in her last penny. I stare at the mum's perfect hair. I catch my own reflection in the window. I wonder if it's true that blonds have more fun. I wonder how much hair dye costs. Tescos Bleach is only 28p a bottle. It's on offer. I flick my hair. "Bleach," I mumble. "Because I'm so worth it."

"You alright Love?"

I see the old man looking at me so I stare at my watch.

When my phone rings three minutes later I'm sure it's Darren – it's alright he's just been held up, but it's Jenny's name that flashes across the screen. Jenny from Social Services. I don't answer. She reckons they have *another* foster mum for me. But if she's anything like the others, she can shove it.

I don't listen to the new message. I wrap my fingers around the phone.

"Oh come on, Darren."

I go back in and walk towards the fish counter where Bob is slapping a huge fish-with-a-face (gag) on the back counter with his chubby hands.

"Seen Dazz?" I say.

"He left ages ago," he says. "Got off ten minutes early he did."

"Oh."

"Mind you, he has to make up the time," he says. "And I told 'im that as well. Seemed awful keen he did."

"Oh."

So I just stand there looking at Bob, beer belly, bald as a coot, (fishes for fun too, seen the photos of him holding up these massive trouts) I wait for him to say more but he looks back at the fish-with-a-face and then lifts up this bloody big cleaver thing. GAG.

"He didn't mention me did he?" I say looking at my silent phone. "About meeting me?"

CHOP.

Ugh. I wish I hadn't seen that. HURL.

"What, Love?"

"Dazz – did he say why he had to leave early? Or about meeting me?"

"He said he was meeting his girlfriend."

CHOP.

"Okay." Relief.

I started to walk away when he said, "You must be Molly then?"

CHOP.

That's when I knew what that bloody fish felt like.

I go back to the entrance but don't know what to do now. A woman in dungarees with a shaved head (defo a DYKE) puts money in the bucket. No clink. A fiver. A bloody fiver for dogs! How many bottles of cider would that buy? As I'm reckoning it up the old man then gives her a whole strip of stickers.

"We have five dogs," I hear her say, "All Heinz 57s, rescued."

Then I text Darren again. "U R Dumped." I lean against the wall while I wait for the world to cave in. I stare at my phone hoping for something. *Anything.* But all I get is NOTHING. I should have known. I should have known when he did it last time.

"And four cats," I hear the girl say to the old man. "And a chinchilla."

I hate dykes.

I'd hate chinchillas too if I could remember what the fuck they are.

The old man smiles and reaches in his pocket. He takes out a photo that has curled over edges and shoves it in her face. "This is Harry," he says. "Best dog I ever had. Dead now though."

"Oh I'm sorry," she says, "How long?"

He seems to go into suspended animation and his eyes go all glazed. I wonder if he's having a stroke. Or an aneurysm. I wonder how you tell the difference. Then I wish it was me having one. But then he seems to snap out of it and says: "Good dog he was, Harry. Good company after my wife died. Mind you didn't last too long after she went." And that's when I remember where I've seen his face before. He used to come in for his photos, said he couldn't be doing with all that digital stuff. Then he told me about his Ruby wedding anniversary. Said his one and only son came over from, where was it? Oz? Canada? The States? East Grinstead? Wasn't really listening but I did look at his pictures, all smiley faces and blue rinses. Prob'ly got a kitchenette and those coloured strips at the back door. Prob'ly one of them houses that smells of oldness. At least it's a home.

When I think about Darren I start to wonder if being a dyke isn't such a bad thing. But then the thought of kissing a girl makes me want to projectile vomit. I see her looking at me. It doesn't make me a dyke thinking about kissing one, does it? Oh God.

*Look away.*

*Look away.*

*Look away.*

I dial Darren's number but it goes to voicemail: a garbled message he's recorded with the Eastenders theme tune in the background. You can just make out the 'Duf Duf – Leave a message – Duf."

"I know about Molly you fuckwit," I say. "I know she's your *other* girlfriend." Then I add, "How's that for a Duf Duf moment." I feel my eyes well and turn away from the old man. I reach for the edges of the box in my pocket, pick at the pharmacy sticker.  Maybe he found out. Maybe Emma from the pharmacy blabbed. It should have come from me. I should have explained and made him see it was okay. It would be a good thing, having a family. We have jobs, he's nearly eighteen. I'm only three years younger. I SHOULD have gone to the chemists on the High Street but it's run by a foreigner.

I hate foreigners.

Then I walk towards the bogs, one hand fumbling with the box in my pocket. Fuck you Darren. Who needs men anyway?

In my parallel universe, the one where Darren showed up on time, we would have been to Solly's Chippy by now. We'd have eaten our chips getting soggy in the rain, sat together on the bench, leaned into each other, wet hair, not caring. And I would have told him and we would have gone back to the squat to do the test. I would have gone to the bog while the kettle boiled. Then we would have waited together for a line to turn blue – like the way photos appear out of nothing.  He would have held my hand, told me it was okay. That he loved me and soon we would have our own house. And I'd tell him I've seen the house. And not just in photos. It's on Fairweather Road, number 41. It's got four bedrooms, massive ones. A hallway with a big staircase. A garden with a swing.

"Love?"

French doors. A huge dining room with a long table that would be filled at Christmas. A seven foot tree dressed in only red and silver and so many presents. And.

"You alright, Dear?"

A study with a computer and books. Tons of books and proper books too, the ones that make you know things and I don't mean the things in girlie magazines or buy one get one free Tescos chick lit offers. Last month I bought the new novel by Katie Price. But on this book shelf there's no novel by Katie Price. So many books there would never be enough time to read them all. And photos – faces framed on a wooden desk.

"I think she's fainted."

And a dog – a chocolate Labrador. I don't hate ALL dogs.

When I open my eyes it's like pixels, blocks of colour until I see the old man's face appear. That's when I remember.

"It's alright, Dear," he says. "Someone's gone to get help."

So now I'm lying on the wet pavement outside Tescos and when I look up all I see is the old man with his hood up and some old biddy with a fussing voice and some spotty kid with ginger hair who's grinning and. And. AND.

Darren.

"Get her some water," someone says.

Darren?

"I thought she was looking peaky," someone else says.

DARREN.

"She went white as a sheet."

Fucking Darren. And he's looking at me lying on the pavement outside Tescos, in the fucking rain.

It takes a few minutes to convince them all I'm okay. Really really really I AM OKAY. Skipped breakfast, haven't had lunch, that's all. The old man keeps looking at Darren and then at me and then Darren tells him he's my boyfriend and he'll take care of me. So then the old man does move away but he's still watching us even when he starts rattling his bucket again, doing his bit for the stray dogs.

Darren says he's not a two-timer.

"Why did you tell Bob Molly's your girlfriend then?" I say. We're standing by the window and I have a wet patch on the back of my jeans. My head is killing.

Darren says Bob got it wrong. Darren did mention Molly but only in passing, like. Bob must have got confused, that's all. Then he said it's me he loves. He was never into Molly. Ever. EVER. Not EVER. Then he looks at me with them gorgeous eyes and I come over all ice lolly, like melting I mean. But there's still some things I need to know, to be sure.

"Tell me the truth about the photo?" I say.

His cheeks go red then and he says Molly kissed everyone. He says she was blind drunk at Dyl's leaving do. She shouldn't even have been there. Someone must have taken the photo, made it look like they were together. He says again, it's not how it looks.

"Where have you been now then?" I say. "Why are you so late?"

His cheeks go almost purple now. He tells me he had to go and get something - a surprise he says. Then he says that Emma said I might have something to tell him.

I fucking knew it.

As he speaks I think about the open box, slipped back into the bag and rested on top of the sanitary bins in the ladies. I wonder how many people have seen it.

Darren asks me if he's forgiven now and if it's true what Emma from the pharmacy said.

But all I keep thinking is if it's legal – if it's like doctors – confidentiality and all that. She could be sacked for that. Then I remember the way Emma looks at Darren, too. There was that photo at the Staff Christmas Bash. I couldn't go, I was at the squat with that Spanish Flu bug and a temperature of 104. I can still see that photo, long blond hair down to her ass crack like bloody Lady Godiva. He said it wasn't what it looked like then too. He must really think I'm stupid.

Darren tries to take my hand. He asks me again if he's forgiven and can't we go to Solly's for our chips now. And if I am – *you know what* he says, it's okay.

If I am *you know what?*

He can't even say the word.

I look into Darren's blue eyes and wonder if he means anything he says. Like really means it. Like the way my dad said he would come back and see me on my birthdays and he never remembered. Not once. He only had to look down at his arm to see the date.

I picture the house with its French doors and its four bedrooms and its fancy Christmas tree. 41 Fairweather Road. I went there once, to take the photos to the posh woman who never came in to collect them. If I had a house like that I think I'd never go out. I'd use Tescos on line for my shopping. She wasn't in so I put 'em through the letterbox. But I kept one, the one of her. I have it in my purse. I tell people she's my mum. She has brown hair, like mine. I tell them she died in a car accident when I was five. It's a better story.

"What was it you bought me?" I say turning back to look at Darren. "The surprise?"

Darren pushes his hand into his pocket and drags out a stuffed animal. "In case you are," he whispers. I catch the old man looking at me as I take it from Darren, look down at its squashed face.

"What about them chips then?" Darren says. "And you can tell me if you are *you know what* on the way." He holds out his arm waiting for me to loop mine with his. So I look at it and then at him and I say, "I'm not."

"What?"

"*You know what.*"

I see the relief in his face.

———

271

"I was gonna get its name tattooed on me back," he suddenly says. "I thought that would be cool, like when it's born."

"And *its* date of birth I s'pose," I say and he grins.

"Yeah," he says. "And that."

So now I look right at him and I say, "I meant it Dazz: U R Dumped."

I watch him walk away, in the rain, loping shoulders and the bottom of his jeans trailing in the puddles. I could swear it looks like Molly in the car park, blond hair frizzed, like she's been waiting to see what happened. When I look back, I'm not sure if its tears or rain in my eyes but I see the smudged face of the old man smiling at me.

I empty my last pennies into his bucket, tip my purse up and watch them fall in, one by one.

CLINK.

CLINK.

CLINK.

That's it, spent everything on that test. Nothing now 'til payday.

"Here," the old man says and he presses a crisp folded piece of paper into my hand. "Go get yourself something to eat." When I look down I see it's a tenner.

I look at the stuffed animal, realise it's supposed to be a dog and I hold it out to him. "Want this?" I say. "I'm not really into dogs."

He just looks at me then and winks. "You keep it," he says.

I could swear he said, "Give it to the baby," or maybe it's my head, all fuzzed up and hormonal. So I stick it in the pocket of my coat where the box was before and hold it there, pressing the fur between my fingers.

"You alright now then?" the old man says.

I don't answer. Instead I fumble with my phone, thinking about Jennifer from Social Services, about her message that I listened to when I came out of the bog. Then I think about the photos of 41 Fairweather Road, about having dreams. I look at the face in my purse and I think – maybe this time.

*MAYBE.*

*MAYBE.*

*MAYBE.*

"See you tomorrow, Dear," the old man says.

"Yeah," I say.

But he won't.

# Mack the Knife
## by Mark Boland

My ex-fiancée and her then new fiancé had their engagement party in what was once her and my house and I have to say it was an absolute hoot. Of course I wasn't technically invited. I invited myself. I am so glad I did because I do not believe that I ever enjoyed myself more.

The happy couple were visibly startled when I let myself in through the back door with my key but they tried their best not to show it. I gave them both a big hug and I shook his hand and I kissed her lips and they thanked me for the congratulations and the expensive champagne and the Belgian chocolates and the beautiful flowers and they told me it was very nice of me to come and asked me what I wanted to drink. As much as possible I joked and produced a bottle of tonic wine. Bless those Benedictine monks.

*Tragedy* by the Bee Gees started up in the other room. Those betrothed inquired after my new wife and I pleaded with them not to mention the fatugly cunt as I had only just escaped from her for the evening. They were taken aback and I told them I was only messing and I loved the moody bitch to death really and she would love to have been here to celebrate with us but finding a babysitter for the sainted rugrat was always difficult which meant she couldn't get out much. I wondered if they might fancy a line of coke and they said nothankyou they didn't do drugs and I reminded her how much of the stuff she hoovered up her substantial-sneck in the good old days and they both frowned and she looked embarrassed and I said the gear was shit-hot and just to let me know if they changed their minds.

I left them in the kitchen and wandered through to the living room to check out the party. All her old friends were there and they were surprised and undoubtedly delighted to see me. *Let's Twist Again* by Chubby Checker was bleating out of the speakers. On the dance-floor an enthusiastic young couple were twisting vigorously. I shuffled straight over to the music system and hit the eject button. Hey! Come on! What are you doing? I ignored the whining wankers and picked out something more in keeping with the mood. My mood. I cranked the volume right up. I pressed play. I spun around and raised my hands in the air. One bellowed at the top of One's voice. HereWeFuckingGo. *Ace of Spades* by Motorhead kicked in. Hallelujah! It was like I had never been away.

–*What are you looking at?*

–*You*

–*Why?*

–*I still love you.*

–*You shouldn't be here. Please go home. You're drunk. Please. Don't do this. Please.    You're drunk.*

–*Yes! I am! I am drunk! I am drunk and I love you!*

–*Ha ha ha. You don't love anyone but yourself.*

*—Don't be like that. This is important. I love you I love you I love you.*

*—I'm not your type.*

My ex-fiancée decided that it was her party so she would be the DJ. She replaced my choice with The Monkees' *Daydream Believer*. I booted her up the arse. She looked astonished. She said I was a sociopathic loser. She said I was an egomaniacal prick. She said I was the same worthless piece of shite that I had always been. The fiancé came over. She informed him what I had done. He swore. He threatened to kill me. He asked me who I thought I was. I just laughed. I told them it was a joke. They said it wasn't funny. I said they needed to lighten up. He wanted to know why I came in the first place. I said I hardly touched her. They said that wasn't the point. It was just a friendly boot I said. They requested that I remove myself from the premises. I said they could try and fucking make me. He grabbed her shaking hand and they walked away. Just ignore him. They joined the group at the other side of the room. I glared at the back of their heads. They didn't dare turn around. She knew better.

The jukebox played *Dancing Queen* by Abba. I asked a lovely-lonely-looking blonde with impressively humungous udders to dance. She blushed. She nodded. We danced. I couldn't wipe the great-white-grin off my favourite-face. Man they were some bigtits. I summoned her outside for a line of coke. She said okay. We went out to the back garden. *All Night Long* by Lionel Richie leaked out of the window. I hate Lionel Richie. Cock. She had a toot. I convinced that slapper to let me snort some charlie off her beautiful-bosom. She giggled. Cute.

I slipped my hand down her pants. She resisted. I forced the issue. She was soon bent over the wheelie-bin. Me pounding from behind. *Achy Breaky Heart* by Billy Ray Cyrus playing in the background. Yeehaw! Bints like her appreciate a bit of rough. After I shot my load she declared that she wanted to go back into the party. I said I wanted to do her some more. She said no. I gave her another line. Spread those chunky thighs. No. I made her. She was pulling her pants up as I left. I said if she told I'd have to kill her. Those tits though. When I went back inside Elvis launched into *Blue Suede Shoes*. Jiving.

*—I'm sorry.*

*—I thought you'd gone.*

*—Wishful thinking will get you nowhere.*

*—Please leave me alone.*

*—I only want to apologise.*

*—Fine. You've apologised. Now. Please. Leave. Me. Alone. Please.*

*—What are you doing with that mincing pansy?*

*—You're enjoying yourself. You rotten bastard.*

*—I know you still want me you slut.*

My ex-fiancée attacked me. She pushed me hard and I landed on top of two smooching-young-lovers on a beanbag. They bolted. She was upon me. Punchingkicking-biting-spitting-slapping-scratching-screaming. Just like the good old days. It made me proud.

The wedding never happened. He broke off their engagement after the party and the lucky boy eventually got hitched to the bigbreastedblonde. When he tried to pull his flailing-fiancée off of me she elbowed him in the face and broke his nose. On the dance-floor he rolled in agony. Blood everywhere. Girls crying. Men shouting. Glasses smashing. The velvet-tones of Sinatra. Laughing-me. I close my eyes and I can still see it all so clearly. My ex-fiancée being dragged out of the room. Wailing like a fucking retard. Six months later she died of an overdose. Tragic really. She had so much to live for. I got up off the burstbeanbag. Polystyrene-balls. Four or five blokes wanted to give me a good beating. I squared up. Come On! To a man they backed down. Pussies. They knew they were outnumbered. I swaggered out of there. Big shining-shark-smile still intact. I headed off to the kebab shop and treated myself to a large donner with extra chillies. I wolfed it all down and afterwards I skipped merrilymerrilymerrilymerrily home to my wife and child. I am still happily married you know.

# Lie in it
### by Kate St. Vincent Vogl

There were nights, and this was one of them, when Leah felt a rush of power sitting on this barstool, with the way guys would look at her (and how they wouldn't, how they lowered their eyes as she stared them down) and she knew it was up to her who she'd go home with. Maybe the skier who was there a second night, the one who looked like William Hurt (or was that the lighting?). Tonight, though—tonight she wanted someone she could count on, maybe even someone who'd treat her to dinner at Tangiers next weekend.

They'd think of it as their special place from then on.

She'd come alone to the bar, as she usually did. She always found someone to talk to. A pleasant surprise when Dale slid beside her. A fiver held high for the bartender. "A tall one," he said. "Plus whatever the lady wants."

"You spoil me," she said.

Dale lived in town—a definite plus. Better than the tourists she sometimes ended up with, though William Hurt on the other side of the bar was quite tempting.

The ones she took home she thought of as boyfriends. Potential boyfriends, anyway. She thought of herself as the boyfriend type: she had one two years straight by the end of high school. Maybe she shouldn't have been so surprised when the baby showed up. By then, her boyfriend wanted to disappear.

---

In the end she lost both.

The first time she brought a skier home, it was the disco days just after high school. He lived in Lansing, a close enough drive, and he was earnest enough to call. But he was in the midst of finals and she was in the midst of life. By the time he called her drunk from that afterhour's party, there was that sober realization it would never work between them.

The next out-of-towner promised to call—at least he did as he ran his hand over the smooth of her body afterwards. She just smiled and turned her head away. Why bring up the wedding ring she'd found in his pocket when he'd been in the bathroom? Outside, it was so dark she couldn't see the bare branches of the ironwood beyond her window.

With Dale it could be different. He fed words gently against her ear, his breath hot but gentle. Nothing urgent or hurried or rushed, but a steady thrumming as if it welled from deep within and would be there and there again until you realized it'd been there all along, it's what you'd been looking for.

What she was looking for wasn't anything named. Or it shouldn't be. Two Christmases ago, an econ major from the U of M (black curly hair, ice blue eyes) asked outright if she wanted to fuck. Two minutes after they met. The only topic they'd covered before that was what the ring on her left hand was for. He wanted to see the year on that class ring, checking if she was jailbait. She'd only been back to Ruloff's once since, the memory too raw. She liked the Gin Mill better now. Not as many tourists— or at least a different kind of tourist—passing through. A place for people who stayed, or at least for those who kept returning.

She tried to listen to what Dale was saying; it was hard to with what she'd had to drink already. His words were kind, though, and hopeful.

She peeled the label perfectly from her beer. Dale paid for the next round, too, perhaps an omen of drama-free dates to come. Love always left a bitter aftertaste of spite, but there were ways to cleanse that palate. Once, she'd taken a Polaroid, her shirt open down to there. She'd sent it to her lost baby's daddy. *Missing me?* she scrawled upon it with a Sharpie, because if it was too painful to keep a boyfriend close, someone had to pay.

This is how to bring a guy like Dale close: Let him buy her a beer, then another, maybe one more. Maybe then they'd move to the booth in the corner, back by the pay phone. She might let him kiss her there. If he asked if she wanted to go someplace else, like Ruloff's, she'd say how about Vic's instead?

Sometimes, with other guys, she hadn't gone any further than their car in the parking lot, but they'd gone plenty far there. She'd heard tales about backseats, but what gave her trouble were the front seats of Impalas and Grand Marquis, even a Cadillac, once. The next morning her head hurt not so much from the schnapps or the beer but from what followed: Her head rubbing up against a door handle as she lay prone over another bench seat.

She didn't mind if a guy asked her to his place. It was a chance to see who he was and where he came from, even if it was as transient a place as where he stayed on

---

vacation. In the mornings, as she snuck home while sunlight greyed through the trees, she would commit the latest name to memory. The men she'd been with added up on all her fingers and now even a second set of toes. How would she remember them all if she kept going like this? Even if—especially if—some skier might look like William Hurt, it didn't mean he'd make any kind of a boyfriend.

She wanted to stop, needed to stop.

If something regular started with Dale, she could stop. Dale was tucking his wallet in his back jeans pocket. He slid the third Lite to her. There was a time she would not have given someone like Dale a second glance. He was older and had that softness about him, like he soaked it in, from his weak chin down to the beginnings of a beer gut—which just as well could have come from that truck stop just outside Traverse City with those cherry pies he was raving about. The lack of a chin gave the impression he had no fight in him. As if he were embarrassed over everything he said. But the crinkles around his eyes proved he enjoyed a good joke, or at least a bad one. (Was it funny or sad, how he called his gut a "muscle"?) From across the bar these past few years, Leah noticed his good-natured ribbing of even himself lasted through all the drinks he'd have in an evening.

There was a value to not having a man's smile turn mean by the end of the night.

She touched him again to make a point, and this time she left her hand on his arm. This time she saw Eddie, finally, at the other end of the bar. His eyes were watery and rimmed in red, like they got when he was in it for the

—

long haul. He'd probably been slamming dime beers down at Vic's, named nicer than the warehouse it was. His fat unemployed fingers gripped his beer, as if drink alone might redeem the night.

She didn't care about Eddie. She was with Dale now, and what he told her was real, none of the bullcrap Eddie or some stranger from another part of the country might lay down, but stories she could hold onto, stories about being a kid down at the creek by the ski hill, where the water ran high in the summer. The ten years between their childhoods had been enough to send him to Nam, but he didn't talk about that, and a good part of her believed if she waited long enough he would. Maybe not tonight, and maybe not after they'd been seeing each other a few months, but there would be a time he'd trust to tell her. Maybe on her couch he'd lay his head upon her lap, and tears would start running out the corners of his eyes and she would hold him and tell him it was okay, whatever he'd done, it was war and sometimes people did what they had to do.

But for now Dale was talking to her like guys do to get in your pants and there was Eddie at the other side of the bar and for all she knew he might want the same at that moment.

Dale might not be the best looking, not anymore, but it wasn't hard to see he had been back in the day. And she was through with men who wanted her to leave at the end of the night, melt away like you wish would happen to the blackened snow crusting on curbs when winter wouldn't end.

Maybe she got a bit carried away, thinking that and smiling at Eddie across the way like she did. Maybe that's why she put her tongue in Dale's ear.

Whatever the reason, the game was on.

She was good at it, too, in the way that hummingbirds are good at darting at flowers. Eager and fast and flighty and mean. She could swing her hips just close enough to Dale as she fed him another line, she could lean forward over her drink at the bar, just enough so Eddie on the other side could get a glimpse of what he wouldn't be getting tonight. The skier was still there, too, and still watching her and she built on the power of his attention: She'd press against Dale, grind into him, really, so he'd grab her ass and William Hurt the skier couldn't look away then, and neither could Eddie, who was already dancing in agitation on the balls of his feet.

Just one line and the plan was set. With Dale she would sashay on past the skier and past Eddie, on the way back to her place. Her place because she was sure with Dale it could be different. She gave a look to the ones she wasn't leaving with. The skier didn't even say squat, proving she was leaving with the right man, but passing by Eddie was another story. She said, "Don't you wish you had some," as she planned. She hadn't planned on Eddie walloping Dale upside the head.

"You goddamn idiot," she said as the two pushed against each other. She wasn't sure which one she was yelling at: "You goddamn fool." There was a pride in her voice—high time a fight should break out in her honor. There was something right about using anger to jumpstart love.

William Hurt was watching, and so were others she didn't know. It was delicious. It was heady.

The bartender reached over the ledge and grabbed at the men. "Hey, hey," he said. He scurried around the island of the bar. "Break it up, break it up now," he said.

Dale and Eddie on the floor, a circle cleared for them. Dale was decidedly the favorite, even if Eddie managed to straddle him and start in on a good pummeling. At a place like the Gin Mill, there were principles of fairness and propriety—and more importantly, a presumption in favor of the underdog.

The bartender pulled the two off the beer-slicked floor. "Take it on out, boys," he said. By the scruff of their collarless shirts, he pushed them toward the back. Dale, the only one to fight back. He'd been defending her honor, it wasn't fair to put him on the same level as the one who started it.

The bartender shoved them out the back door and onto January pavement. "I don't want to see the both of you until next week," he said. "Not on the same side of the bar anyway." There were limits on what kind of limits you could give a man in this town.

Limits. Maybe that was why Dale and Eddie weren't done fighting yet. The two had fallen against each other again, fists and grunts and human in desire.

"Jesus," the bartender said, less a plea than an epithet. "They're all yours," the bartender said, brushing past Leah on his way back inside.

———

Leah braced her barelegged self against the northern Michigan wind. Back behind the bar, it was hard to believe that chivalry might be alive here at the edge of Boyne Falls, that there might be any honor to be won. No romance here, only crumbling snow-plowed pavement and an overturned shopping cart. A half-eaten burrito from Taco Bell skidding against the ice, sliding a little farther away with each night gust.

This wasn't the plan.

"Fight all you goddamn want," she said. "That's not how I decide to go home." She tried to kick between them, to break them apart. "It's not, it's not," she said, still kicking. She could barely feel her toes.

The men finally rolled apart, shielding their faces against her spiked heels.

Dale was up right away, while Eddie curled into a ball. "What you want?" he said. So pathetic.

"For one thing," she began. But with Eddie, it was more than that. Fuck him for saying she deserved what she got. Fuck him. She could tell him what she deserved.

He scrabbled up, hands on knees, huffing to catch his breath. "You want to pick?" he said, "You're right," he said, in that infuriating way of giving her back all the power he ever tried to take away. "You pick."

She said, "You are so effing crazy."

Dale had his hands on his hips and was walking in circles like he was ready for another round. "No," he said. "No, that's right. That's what you should do. Pick." His eyes had a bright intensity they did not have inside.

And Eddie had held her back when she couldn't stop herself. She had taken him home once, and he'd stayed. His presence bringing the promise he could be the man in her life. A promise never stated, and one he could never fulfill. That's why he'd started to become mean, that resentment that builds when you're loved for something you can never be.

It was mean what he was doing to her now, too, mean how he was making her choose.

"You want me to pick," she said, "I'll pick." She stepped in close, jutting her chest. Taunting. "I'll pick," she said. "And it won't be your sorry ass."

She stalked away, jostling against Dale as if claiming him—or maybe just tagging him. She walked on, planting her heels firmly in the ice. She had no need to stop to see if he was coming. He would come.

It was cold but she didn't feel it, she was so mad at Eddie and what he'd done. Not until the edge of the parking lot could she bring herself down enough to talk to Dale again. He was so stiff walking behind her. Was that the fight or did he have a hard on for her again? "You punch drunk?" she asked, laughing softly now, making herself laugh, reaching for him there. "You are?" They stumbled against each other as she led the way back to her apartment. She left with Dale as she'd left with all the others, without naming what it was she wanted, what they wanted, in the hopes it might become the same thing.

———

And just as she'd done with all the others, she left with the conviction that she was the one who controlled what would happen.

Her sister once said she was only setting herself up, but her sister made that sound like it was a bad thing.

Leah had almost rounded the snowdrift when she heard Eddie calling, "Leah." He made her name sound like a wail, a whine, something she didn't want to be. "Leah," he said again, his words trapped now amidst the barriers of snow. He said, "Where the hell will I go?"

Dale didn't take off his baseball cap when he got to her place. He prowled the open space in the living room, where a coffee table should have been and piles of *US* magazines were stacked instead. Her rooms were small and irregular, a second floor apartment in a converted Victorian.

"You want a beer?" she asked. Anything to fill the void so he might not ask about Eddie.

"No," he said. He sat in the middle of the long low couch and patted the empty space next to him. Whether he didn't know or didn't care about what had passed between Leah and Eddie, Leah was not about to question. Maybe he didn't know, with all the traveling he did. He sure looked lonely on that couch.

Leah ducked into the galley kitchen for a beer. She popped open a Schlitz and leaned against the doorjamb. She'd taken a chance, bringing Dale here, letting him see this part of her. This was only the third time she'd taken

———

288

someone to her place right off. It made her think of that second out-of-towner. Pete.

She said, "I got to get up early in the morning."

"I don't have to stay long."

Maybe that's what she asked for, but it wasn't what she wanted. Where were the stories they'd shared at the bar? The memories about growing up in a town where most people came and went in the course of a weekend. What it was like to be a constant where nothing and nobody else was. Maybe that's why he'd become a trucker. His way of dealing with that.

She put a cassette in the stereo. The overhead light in her apartment was suddenly too bright. She flicked it off, then leaned over Dale to turn on the lamp by the couch. When she sat down, he put a hand on her knee.

That's as far as they needed to go for now. There was no need to speak, the music could speak for them. Maybe they could sit on the couch in this silence and enjoy each other as an old married couple would. Dale could be the kind of guy who could be in it for the long haul. Not like Eddie. What had she ever seen in him? He had to see that they didn't have chance. There was no way she could have picked him instead.

She swigged the rest of her beer and set the can down, her mind still racing for something more to talk about. Silence was too common here, conversation too easy at the bar.

But Dale didn't seem to care, he was leaning into her, his mouth on her suddenly and so hard she couldn't breathe. He pressed against her onto the couch, a couch long enough to lay on and he pulled her legs beneath him and spread her between him. He was on her and she was beneath him and there was only one way this was going. She shifted against him, she had to breathe, but he must have misunderstood because his hands were on her then, up and down and under her shirt, as if he couldn't get what he wanted fast enough.

"Please," she said. She told herself this was what she wanted, too, even if she wanted it slower. She let him unhook her bra. She helped.

He pushed her shirt up, his mouth now on her, all over her. His hat had fallen off, so she took the thinning hair on his head in her fingers.

"I didn't know," he was saying against her skin. "I didn't know you were like this."

So many times she'd seen him, not at the bar but at the Kroger's where she worked. When he was in town after his long truck runs, he would come through, sliding Stouffer's dinners and Coors across the belt and she would push them on by. "Another candlelight dinner?" she'd quip. She wore her hair up in a ponytail for work, an innocence she abandoned at night.

She held his head against her breasts and pressed against him because that was what she was supposed to do. "This what you want?" she said. "This?"

He reached beneath her skirt but she closed her legs abruptly. She rolled out from underneath him and onto the floor.

He pushed himself up, the look on his face pained.

She'd never stopped here before. She wondered if she could. She could be a tease, she could be. This was her place, after all. She could call the shots. She could say she had to call it a night, walk him to the door. She would lean against it, braless in her shirt, leave him wanting more. "Call me tomorrow?" she would say. She would be doing nothing wrong in that. She would be following the rules then, as close as she'd ever been able. When she broke it off clean with Eddie, then, she could say she took the high road and hadn't done anything with Dale.

She stood in front of the long low couch, but she was in front of the picture window, too. A shadow of a man moved on the walk below. She knew who he was. She had seen him in darkness before. Why he was coming home now, she didn't know. But that didn't matter. What mattered was that Dale poor Dale looked wounded, lying there on that faded green couch. He was probably wondering what he'd done wrong. He hadn't done anything bad, not yet.

The one who had done wrong was watching her from the sidewalk below. The little shit.

He knew he'd done wrong, too.

She'd been the one trying to make the relationship work and Eddie down there never even made an effort—sitting on his fat ass, not trying to get a job, not even after unemployment ran out because he said there was nothing to do in this shit town, but he wasn't willing to do anything, try anything, and that's when he turned mean and took on the right to hash over everything she'd done wrong, what she never could get right. He was too willing to remind her of the worst of what she'd done, not the baby she'd lost, but what had come the summer after: how she'd asked for it—even though all she'd asked for was the spiked Kool-Aid in the back of that trailer, all she remembered was waking up in the ER, the doctor saying she was all torn up inside, her parents wanting to know who and she didn't have a name, she didn't have any of them. She'd try to tell Eddie how that wasn't her fault, but all that stayed with her were his words—that right or wrong, if she goes in asking she'll be given.

If the issue ever came up again she'd have something more to say and she wouldn't leave the last word up to Eddie, not when all he'd been willing to do was sit there on a faded green couch and wait for her to welcome him home again just so he could cut her down.

If someone was going to beat you, they better be in a place where they had standing to beat you.

Leah knew full well who was watching from the sidewalk as she lifted her shirt over her head. She did nothing to cover herself or the window. Someone outside needed to know where he stood, and it certainly wasn't by her right now. Not anymore. She dropped the faded black knit on the floor and it crumpled into a pile. She held out her hand to the man on the couch. "Not out here," she said.

She would leave her shirt and her bra on the floor by the low-slung couch and she would lead this man into the bedroom. She was the one in control of this moment, and she was the one deciding to bring him close to her, closer than she usually dared. She was the one making the move that might mean that she would lose Dale even before she ever had him.

When you are in control, it doesn't matter what you lose afterwards.

"Wait," she said. She locked the bedroom door and shut out the lights. It was, after all, the last thing she did before she would go to them.

The sheets were tangled against her legs making it hard to move in a way that felt good, that felt right. This was the time she closed in to herself. She was with Dale but like every other time she was more with herself: she was in confession, she was in self-revelation. He was pushing against her again—he could have been anyone, then, but being Dale he was tender and kind, mostly, but even Dale came to pushing on her so hard her head kept rubbing against the headboard, and it was because she could not hold herself in the moment where she wanted to be that she heard Eddie come home to the apartment.

He didn't even try to be quiet. He clanged his keys into the dish, for God's sake. If he wasn't gone in the morning, she didn't know what more she could do to make him leave.

There was a beat where Dale paused over her. She yanked her legs free of the covers and wrapped them high over his back and pulled him close into her. If she was good, he would call. If she was good, she wouldn't care if he did. She was in control now and that was what mattered.

She turned her head. It was deep in the night and the ironwood was still black outside her window.

Dale was almost all the way dressed before she gathered the courage to tell him Eddie was out in the living room.

"That son of a bitch," he said. "When did he come in?"

If he hadn't heard him, could she say? "I'm just saying he might be," she said.

"You said you kicked him out ages ago."

"This is what kicking Eddie out looks like," she said. She had climbed out of the bed and stood naked before him.

This was what sticking around with Leah looked like.

Dale reached out and let his fingertips take a long sweep down her arm. This was what longing looked like. This was why she'd wanted him to stay.

"I gotta get on the road," he said. "Didn't you have to leave early, too?"

"Did I say that?" Always it amazed her what she'd been willing to say the night before.

He took a peek out the door and she took the silk robe off a hook and wrapped it around herself.

"He is there," he said, but caught himself when he saw her.

It was a heavy silk, the robe her sister found on one of her trips out East. The Far East? She could never keep track of where her sister went. It wasn't even for her birthday. "Every girl needs a good robe," her sister had said.

He said, "I'm going to take away all your clothes and leave you with just that. It'll be the only thing you ever need to wear." He said, "Damn, you look fine."

Exactly what she wanted him to say. She took his hand and led him into the other room. If Eddie woke up, he'd see them together. He'd get it, then. She led Dale right past the sleeping bundle on the couch and all the way to the door. Dale could have trod heavily, just to wake up a certain someone passed out on the couch, but instead he tiptoed right by that certain someone. Dale was so quiet he could have slipped by without waking a baby. At one point he even let go of her hand to duck down and pick up his hat, but still Eddie kept sleeping.

Dale was leaving and she couldn't bear to say good-bye.

"Wait," she said. "One more for the road." She said it loud enough to wake the dead or the remorseful. She snuck between Dale and the doorjamb. In that way she could face the couch as she reached her arms around his neck. Her robe gaped open.

Dale kissed her, just a peck, but she pulled him close for a long one. She knocked back against the door with her eyes open. Eddie's were too, now. He saw.

Well, he needed to see. She put Dale's hand upon her breast. Only then did she push him away so they could see what was between them. She kept her eyes half-closed, savoring the feel of his hand there, and there. "Call me," she said.

"Oh, I will," he said, "I will." But you never know what a man will put up with to get what he wants.

Who knows what they want.

In the end, she shut the door behind him. She was ready to cry for the sheer effort of it all.

Eddie fought with the blanket to get up. Such an idiot, couldn't even wake up right.

"You okay?" he said.

She shook her head. The morning-after tears had already started.

"Come here," he said, though she had just come from another man.

Outside on the sidewalk, a man turned back—to wave or to spy?—just as she bent down to the couch.

She would tell herself she didn't care. She would ignore Dale anyway the next time she saw him at the bar. Next time at Kroger's, she could say what she always said. She could forget how she'd hoped a candlelit dinner might have anything to do with her.

The way Eddie faced her in the resigned morning light. He would not touch her there, or there. Instead, he took her in gently. "What did you go asking for, girl?" he would whisper. Which was why she didn't want him at all. And why she had to have him.

# AUTHOR BIOGRAPHIES

**Mackenzie Marcotte** is a high school senior in Los Angeles, California, and has been fascinated by language and writing since elementary school. This is her first completed short story as well as her first published work.

**Maria Clara Paulino** was born in Portugal during Salazar's dictatorship and educated in several countries in Europe, and in the US. She is a professor of Art History with an academic background in German and English literature. She is also a translator and a writer. A collection of her personal essays was published in Portugal in 2001. Recently, she began writing in English; since then, some of her essays and short stories have been published in the US. Maria Clara Paulino currently lives and teaches in Porto, Portugal. She reflects on her experiences of a "home in-between places" in her blog, Writing in the Margins, and is writing a longer work, bringing together memoir and fiction.

**John Leavitt** is an author and cartoonist whose work has appeared in The New Yorker, The Chronicle Review, Marvel's Strange Tales and more. He lives in New York City. His website is http://jleavitt.net.

**Laura Graham** was born and brought up for the first six years of her life in a crofter's cottage on the Isle of Tiree in the Hebrides. With no television, few children to play with, a multitude of sheep and cows, which swam in the sea, it's hardly surprising that Laura grew up to have a vivid imagination.

Arriving in London at the age of seven to live in a condominium was like landing on another planet. The Hebridean accent, along with the kilt and the sheep, were soon forgotten in the struggles of English schooling.

At seventeen Laura won a scholarship to LAMDA to study acting for two years. Since when she worked as an actress at The Young Vic, playing the title role in Strindberg's Miss Julie, understudied Helen Mirren in Genet's The Balcony at The Royal Shakespeare Theatre, The Royal Court Theatre with the late Rex Harrison, Helena in The Midsummer Night's Dream at the Regent's Park Theatre and numerous television roles.

**Kate Horsley** is a teacher and a writer who lives in Lancaster. She has published numerous short stories and poems and the story included here, 'Kissing Hitler', was shortlisted for an Asham award. Kate's first novel is out on submission with Jenny Brown Associates and she is just putting the finishing touches to her second.

**Neil McInnes** began writing seriously after he retired as a business consultant in 2005. He has won many awards for his short stories with a number of them being publish in Australia and the UK. He has also written screen plays, stage plays and several novels, one of which was published in the US in 2009.

**Zvi E. Sella** completed his studies in Physics, Mathematics, and Computer Sciences in The Hebrew University of Jerusalem, in Israel. He earned his MBA at the University of Chicago, and then continued in advanced studies in Economics, Business Management, and Sciences at Harvard, Stanford, and the University of Pennsylvania, as well as at the University of La Havana,

Cuba. He served as president and CEO of various high-tech companies, specializing in turnaround and development of rapid growth, and he is now working on his PhD thesis in Philosophy, in Israel. This is his first debut as a writer.

**Jessica Barksdale** is the author of twelve novels, including *Her Daughter's Eyes* and *When You Believe.* She is a professor of English at Diablo Valley College and teaches online novel writing for UCLA Extension.

**Agnieszka Dale** comes from the Polish lake district but now lives in London. She writes fiction with her right hand and non-fiction with left, both in English and Polish. She finds inspiration in transition, anywhere between a lift and a flight. Her stories have previously been published by "Tales of the Decongested." She is currently working on a collection of short stories.

**Jonathan Okwe-Pearson** is a 27 year-old trainee teacher from Newcastle upon-Tyne. He has recently completed an MA in creative writing and has a Ba in English literature. Flipflops and thunderstorms is based on the real life events of one of his friends. Jonathan is currently writing a novel, and outside of writing, is a semi-professional rugby player and keen motorcyclist.

**Avril Joy** lives and works in County Durham. Her first novel The Sweet Track was published by Flambard Press in 2007. She is currently working on a short story collection and preparing her second novel The Orchid House for publication on Kindle. She is a founder member of Room to Write, an organisation which aims to help both new and established writers to achieve their potential. Above all she loves writing. You can read more about her work at www.avriljoy.com and www.roomtowrite.co.uk

**Savita Kalhan** was born in India, but has lived in the UK most of her life. She graduated from the University of Wales, Aberystwyth, with degree in Politics and Philosophy. She was a Batik artist before going to live in the Middle East for several years where she taught English. Then she turned to writing.

Now living in North London, she continues to write. Her debut novel, *The Long Weekend*, published by Andersen Press, is a tense thriller about two boys who are abducted after school. *The Long Weekend* was short-listed for the Fabulous Book Award 2010. *"One of the most important books published...I honestly can't recommend this book highly enough."* The Bookbag.

**Konstantina Sozou-Kyrkou** was born in 1968 and grew up in a small village in western Greece. She's been living in Athens for the last 26 years with her husband and two riotous kids. Her inspiration is mainly drawn from life in my native village and the sufferings and prejudices of the rural populations in 20th century Greece. She's studied Business Administration (forgotten all about it), Drama, Teaching English as a Foreign Language (RSA DOTE), Literature and is currently doing my MA in Creative Writing with Lancaster University.

**Ira Nayman** is a tract of land over 1,000 kilometres wide separating the tundra in Canada's north and the temperate rainforest and deciduous woodlands that predominate in the country's south. No, wait, that's Canada's boreal forest. Ira Nayman is the Proprietor of the Alternate

Reality News Service (ARNS), which is now featured in three collections in print, the most recent of which is *Luna for the Lunies!* "The Weight of Information," the pilot for a radio series based on stories out of the ARNS books, and "A Book Trailer Called 'Book Trailer,'" for the book *What Were Once Miracles Are Now Children's Toys*, can both be found on YouTube. Ira's humour, science fictional and otherwise, can be found on his Web site, *Les Pages aux Folles*. He won the 2010 Jonathan Swift Satire writing contest. But, being the boreal forest would be cool, too.

**Renata Carey** was born in Hamburg to Russian émigré parents in 1933. She came to England at the age of two. After periods of journalism, social work and motherhood, she became a TEFL teacher and tutor. She lives alone in London surrounded by books and memories and drawing inspiration from Russian novels and the wisdom of her grandchildren. She started writing stories when she was nineteen, but forty-four years of marriage and children put a stop to this. *The Watch* is her first story to be published.

**Helen Holmes** started writing for pleasure after a career in Education. A recent MA in Creative Writing at Newcastle University revved up her idling brain. Since then, she has been grappling with the short story form. One of her stories won a New Writing North competition; another was published in the Newcastle Journal; a third will appear in the Cinnamon Press Autumn anthology. Helen is also working on a children's novel set on the North Northumberland coast, which is where she and her husband are lucky enough to live.
http://www.nickholmesart.co.uk

**Mary D'Arcy** is a native of Athlone, living in Belfast. Over the decades, her work has appeared in anthologies, newspapers and magazines. Her comic poems have been broadcast on RTÉ, BBC NI – and once on London Breakfast Television (Why Couldn't I Have been Princess Di?).

Her novel, Tale of Hoffman, was shortlisted for the Sitric `Win a Book Deal` 2004.

In 2006 she was shortlisted for the Brian Moore Awards, and in 2007 for the Stella Artois Pitching Awards. She was twice short-listed for the Fish Prize.

She came second in the Mace & Jones Awards (Liverpool) 2008, and won the Bill Naughton Short Story Competition October 2008.

Her story, Knuckling Under, won the Molly Keane Memorial Creative Writing Award 2009, while in the same year her screenplay, Way To Go, was shortlisted for the Waterford Film Festival.

She has been collaborating with Jimmy T. Murakami, the filmmaker and veteran of animation, on a project to be animated in the near future.

In March 2011, Mary was commissioned by the BBC with her story `In What I Failed To Do` for Radio 7.

**Chris Hammer** is a financial business consultant and is the founding director of Irving House Animal Sanctuary, a network of foster homes dedicated to the rescue and care of special needs and senior animals. She is the author of *Bixby and The Wolf*, the first in the *Bixby* short story series, and is currently working on her first novel. She resides in Nassau County, LI, USA.

**Rebecca Rouillard** was born in Oxford, grew up in South Africa and moved back to the UK in 2010. She had always wanted to write and, at thirty, decided she had waited long enough and enrolled in a BA Creative Writing at Birkbeck College in London. This is her second short story to be published. When she's not writing she is a freelance graphic designer. She is married to Paul, long-time patron of the arts, and has two children.

**Sharda Dean** was born in Trinidad and moved to the UK when she was three years old. She studied Economics at the LSE and Birkbeck College and worked in the City for eight years, travelling extensively, including a visit to Tokyo where 'The Tamotsu' is set. She is married with three sons and lives in Hertfordshire.

**Debz Hobbs-Wyatt** is a full time writer/publisher working from her home in the mountains of Snowdonia where she lives with her cats, Cagney and Lacey, and her cocker spaniel, Rosie. She has recently completed her MA in Creative Writing at Bangor University and has had several short stories published. She is also seeking an agent for her fourth novel. Debz is a partner and the publicist for Bridge House Publishing, Editor for CaféLit and the Director of her new venture Paws n Claws Publishing and the PAWS workshops scheme.
www.debzhobbs-wyatt.co.uk
http://www.pawsnclawspublishing.co.uk

**Mark Boland** was born in the West of Scotland in 1965. He left school at 16, home at 17 and went on to pursue a career in antagonistic-audio-assault that stalled following a period of inertia after 20 years. Somewhere rusting in an audio junkyard... Lived in Bournemouth for 13 years from where he finally returned home to Beautiful Glasgow in 2003. He is currently studying English at the University of Strathclyde where he studied creative-writing under award-winning writers Louise Welsh, Rodge Glass and David Kinloch. *Mack the Knife* in its first incarnation took inspiration from a photograph handed out for an exam piece.


**Kate St. Vincent Vogl** reveals what happened when her birthmother found her through her mother's obituary in *Lost & Found: A Memoir of Mothers*. Her memoir has been featured on TV and radio stations across the United States, and she has spoken at national and international conferences. Her essay "Owning Clydes" appears in *Why We Ride,* which features a forward by the Pulitzer Prize-winning Jane Smiley. Vogl teaches at the Loft, the largest creative writing center in the U.S. She was graduated from Cornell University *cum laude* and from the University of Michigan Law School. This is her third short story to win international honors.
Lost & Found: A Memoir of Mothers (North Star Press 2009) www.katevogl.com

# Also by The Fine Line

The Perfect Word: The Fine Line Writing Course

The Perfect Word: The Fine Line Writing Course
Audiobook

The Pocketbook of Prompts: 52 Ideas for a Story


The Fine Line is a publisher and editorial consultancy based in Edinburgh. It provides website content; teaches, advises and edits writers; and publishes work that enthrals its staff. For more information, please visit the website.

www.editorial-consultancy.co.uk